SKIM

SKIM

A
NOVEL OF
INTERNATIONAL
INTRIGUE

A.F. GILLOTTI

ACADEMY CHICAGO PUBLISHERS

Published by
Academy Chicago Publishers
363 West Erie Street
Chicago, Illinois 60654

Second printing 2010

© 1984, 2010 by A.F. Gillotti

Printed and bound in the U.S.A.

Library of Congress Cataloging-in-Publication Data
on file with the publisher.

PREFACE

At the beginning of deregulation in the early 1980s, commercial banks looked for ways in which they could duplicate the success of the investment banks, which seemed to keep very few loans on their books and make enormous sums from fees and commissions. Commercial banks continued for a time to make loans, especially to second- and even third-tier countries—first world countries, with rare exceptions, did not need this kind of loan—taking large risks because that was the only way they could increase the spread over the London interbank offered rate (Libor) that they received. That ultimately turned out to be a bad idea.

They then tried the leveraged buyout game, which was more successful in terms of spreads, but still left a large amount of risk on their books, some of which turned around and bit them.

In all of this feverish activity, the point was to avoid risk, rather than to have sound risk, which would involve credit risk managers and a lot of questions that very few people could answer. They didn't have a solution until they turned to their trading rooms.

With help from their traders, therefore—because these guys seemed to have the keys to the kingdom, and were assuming more and more power in the banks—they began to reduce the amount of loans on their books by selling the risk to third parties, and to increase exponentially the amount of business for which they received fees and commissions. And they began to call themselves investment banks.

At first, derivatives were simply transactions that protected against interest rate or currency exposure. It was somewhat later that derivatives became Hydra-headed monsters so complicated that they could never be properly explained, nor their risks understood. Many of the risk managers went along, either because they became converted, or because they couldn't understand the risks themselves and could not let anyone know, or because they were just trying to keep their jobs. There was a hardy species, however, that resisted the Siren calls: in mild cases, they got no bonuses; the truly obstreperous were downsized. We now know where that led.

And it all began around the time of *Skim*.

MANHATTAN BANKING CORPORATION N.A.

Chairman   Miles Vanderpane
President   Benjamin F. Kincaid
Balance Sheet as of December 31, 1979
  Loans $5.6 billion
  Deposits $8.5 billion
  Assets $18 billion
  Capital and Surplus $340 million
Year ended December 31, 1979
  Net Income $22 million
  Earnings per share $2.82
  Dividends per share $1.25
  Employees   9,300

Skim: What the lead manager or managers of a syndicated loan take off the top of the underwriting and management fees before sharing them with the other participants in the loan. The skim is an accepted method of compensating the major lenders in a syndicated credit.
—From *Banking Terms*, page 259

—The best lack all conviction,
While the worst are full of passionate intensity.

W.B. Yeats, "The Second Coming"

Precisely at seven o'clock, small, slight Tony Gould, department head of international banking at the Manhattan Banking Corporation, eyebrows bristling above his clear-rimmed glasses, mouth set in a tense line that turned down slightly at the corners, said good morning to the doorman, went through the doorway out onto the corner of Ninety-first Street and Fifth Avenue, and, hefting two thick black briefcases, stepped into the waiting taxi.

He went to the bank every day at seven o'clock. It did not matter whether he was in New York, or in Tokyo, or in Jakarta or Cairo. He used the early hours to clear his mind, think strategic thoughts, maintain his image, impress senior management. He went to the office early because it enabled him to avoid all distracting encounters with his wife and their two children. And he went early because, for a very long time, he had been impotent.

It caused him one or two moments of anguish every morning

while he was shaving and vulnerable to fragments of thought catching him unawares; but he was no longer obsessed by it. For a time he had thought about almost nothing else, and it had begun to interfere with his work. He read the manuals, studied the books of technique and of sexual malfunction. Nothing had helped.

He had wondered vaguely why Maureen hadn't complained; in fact had hardly seemed to notice, except once or twice to suggest, in that curious disinterested way she had, that he see a doctor. Tony had entertained—briefly—the idea that she might have been having affairs, with the kids in school all day and nothing to do but shopping, or the occasional tennis match with a girl friend or swimming in the club pool, and bridge in the winter.

But there was no longer any question in his mind that Maureen simply wasn't interested, might in fact be frigid, and very probably was the cause of his own incapacity; he had no need to see a doctor. He had yet to put his theory to a test, but at least he had come to terms with the problem. It was his total dedication to his career that had finally taken him out of his funk. Maureen couldn't—and wouldn't—complain. He had always been on the fast track and he was only one place from the top.

The cab was going east on Eighty-sixth Street, but Tony Gould, slumped deeply into the broken springs, his arms caressing his briefcases, staring straight ahead at the scratched Lucite taxi divider—Tony Gould did not notice. His mind was now completely occupied with the Manhattan Banking Corporation. Miles Vanderpane, the chairman of the board and chief executive officer, was a benign nonentity who everyone thought would be taking early retirement in one or two years, sooner if forced. The president, Ben Kincaid, was in Tony's way, but not for long; Kincaid was nobody's fool, but he was a farmer. He didn't have the right image for Manhattan Banking. And Gould had been cultivating directors.

Vanderpane had to be briefed that morning in preparation for his lunch with the Finance Minister of Maraka. Tony knew that the Minister was going to ask Manhattan Banking to syndicate a jumbo credit for the Republic, if Vanderpane could be kept from, say, starting to tell a joke about blacks. Such a credit for Maraka, done under Tony Gould's firm guidance, would put Manhattan Banking into the top tier of American world-class banks, on the same level of importance if not in assets, as Morgan and Chemical and Bankers Trust and Continental Illinois. And incidentally, it would likely make Tony Gould the chief executive officer of Manhattan Banking in one or two years.

Maraka was a West African country of twenty-five million, a former British colony, rich in copper, diamonds, uranium, cobalt, tin, sissal, cacao, almost everything, in fact, but oil: huge potential and an insatiable need for funds to develop it. Manhattan Banking couldn't lose.

It was a dry, chilly spring morning, but Tony Gould didn't see. His pale gray eyes shielded behind his glasses stared into the gloom, and he listened to his breath in his ears and the rattle of the cab jolting down Park Avenue, and they sounded far away, as if they had nothing at all to do with him.

Miles Vanderpane woke easily, as usual, but he woke disquieted, which was not at all usual. He swung his legs over the edge of the bed and put his feet into soft slippers. He pulled on a dressing gown over his pajamas and shuffled through the dressing room into his large bathroom.

Having passed comatose through his shower, the sense of unease growing stronger and stronger, Vanderpane remembered the source of his distress while he was shaving. He was entertaining visitors at lunch today and the visitors were African. Miles never felt comfortable with Africans; he knew that some were black and some were white and some were in between, and he hardly ever remembered which was which; nor did he believe that it mattered. He could not recall ever having heard Africa mentioned at school.

He carefully scraped his pink cheeks, swept back the thin gray-brown hair with a brush, put on a little understated cologne, and looked approvingly at the result through clear blue eyes.

Dressed in a quiet medium-weight Oxford-gray chalk-striped suit, he went to the breakfast room, where his wife Samantha was studying the *Financial Times* amid the debris of her breakfast. As always, he said, "Good morning, Sam," and received with pleasure her somewhat distracted smile; and kissed her upturned cheek.

Samantha Vanderpane was a handsome woman, dark hair pulled back into a severe bun, eyes almost black (and that could make one extremely uncomfortable when she stared at one too long), skin taut, high cheekbones, sculpted jaw, flawless teeth. She wore no makeup. She was dressed in a lavender silk blouse and a dark skirt and wore a single strand of pearls, her trademark.

She made a marginal note on the newspaper with a black nylon-tipped pen while Miles addressed his breakfast.

"The egg, um, is overdone again, dear. Could you—"

"For heaven's sake, Miles," she said, making an effort to control her impatience. "Yes, of course I'll talk to Mrs. Wilkes again." She reached across the table and touched his hand, which made him feel a little better.

"But can we talk about something besides our breakfast now?" she purred.

He was immediately on his guard. Whenever Sam cooed, it was a sign that she wanted to talk about something unpleasant. Sometimes it was about money, when she wanted to discuss the latest changes she'd made in their portfolio; usually, however, it was about business.

"You're seeing the Finance Minister of Maraka today."

On rare occasions—and this was one of them—Miles wished Sam had never worked in a bank. Samantha had been one of the brightest postwar trainees Manhattan Banking had had—alert, keen, good-looking, a twenty-year-old economics major just out of Vassar. She had been hired despite a general lack of interest in women on the part of the banking community; but as a woman in a New York bank in the fifties, it was unlikely that she was going to get much beyond platform assistant or assistant cashier for a long time.

In 1952 Miles Vanderpane was a thirty-two-year-old assistant vice-president whose star was rising fast, due partly to his in-offensive nature, but largely to the happy accident that his father was on the board and his uncle was chairman. It was then that he met Samantha, with whom he fell in love, and they were married within the year. Of course she could not continue to work at the bank. First, Miles wouldn't allow it; second, the bank wouldn't allow it. Now she did what other wives did: museum boards, hospital boards, bridge, tennis, running the household.

It was lovely in a way that she knew the bank and could understand the context in which he found himself on a daily basis. But deep within, Miles rather regretted that Sam knew so much about banking.

"You're seeing the Finance Minister of Maraka today."

It was a statement, not a question. On the other hand, he was grateful to her for reminding him whom it was he was giving lunch. They must be black, coming from a country with a name like that.

"Yes."

"You should be careful, Miles. Maraka is running a whopping great current account deficit, and they have enormous debt ser-vice requirements. They're going to want more money. Their development is not nearly what it should be, given the funds that have been poured into the country, and the price of oil has nothing to do with the problem. Maraka is rich in resources, Miles, but their greatest talent is for mismanagement and their biggest service industry is corruption. I don't like the smell of it, Miles. Don't let yourself be pushed into doing something you shouldn't do. The bank's exposure is big enough."

"Now, dear, we have balances to protect."

"I know. I've read the briefing memo you had in your attaché case. It's back. But I want you to read the article I've put in by the Marakan correspondent of the *FT*, someone named Ashton-Brooke, who calls a spade a spade."

Miles chuckled appreciatively. He couldn't wait to use that one at the bank.

"Please pay attention, Miles. You can't afford a mistake. You

5

have directors who are not impressed with the bank's performance, and that little shit Tony Gould is after your job."

"Everyone is after the chairman's job, my dear," he said philosophically.

"But not everyone cultivates disgruntled directors."

"Ah." His day had not begun well, and was not improving: African visitors, an egg that was practically hard-boiled, Tony Gould, troublemaking directors. "Who told you, Sam?"

"Charles."

Miles only nodded slightly and remained with his eyes unfocused as if he were deep in thought. He was trying to get around the memory that Charlie Houston, one of his best friends from Princeton, and a director of Manhattan Banking, had been his wife's lover. One of his wife's lovers. Samantha said, "I hope you'll remember what we've talked about, Miles," and returned to the *Financial Times*. Vanderpane mused over his coffee until he heard the car crunch on the gravel drive in front of the house.

"I think I'll be home about a quarter past six, dear. Will you be home for dinner?"

"Yes, Miles. I have lunch with Maggie at the Bird and Bottle, and a meeting at Storm King Art Center this afternoon."

"Good," Vanderpane said, kissing her lightly. "That's lovely. Well, good-bye then." And left, picking up his attaché case in the front hall.

"Good morning, Tommy," Miles said to the man in a brown blazer who was holding open the rear door of a beige Imperial.

"Morning, Mr. Vanderpane," Tommy responded in a Brooklyn accent. With a practiced motion, he relieved Miles of the attaché case, handed him the *Daily News*, saw him into the car, and closed the door. Tommy got into the driver's seat and the car started down the drive.

Vanderpane turned immediately to the Jumble word game, as he did every morning, but either it was more difficult than usual or else he was distracted. He couldn't take his mind off the blacks or Tony Gould or Charlie Houston. He stared out of the window at the light spring foliage, gold in the morning sun. The more he thought about his conversation with Sam the more mixed up it all became; but in the warm car, and with the whisper of the tires on the Palisades Parkway lulling him, he fell into a light and restorative sleep.

Samantha finished reading the *Financial Times* and marked on the front the page numbers of four articles that she thought Miles ought to read. And while she was pleased to do it for him with the papers he brought home every night, she knew he had neither the will nor—well yes—the capacity to appreciate half of what she had indicated. Vicarious banking was as fundamentally unsatisfying as anything that was vicarious: better perhaps than nothing at all, but for Samantha Vanderpane, who had early developed a taste for the management of men and money, the volunteer boards on which she served were a mere shadow of what the real thing could be like. It was like reading a description of someone else's orgasm.

She used occasionally to wonder whether she ought to have given up her career, but she had become convinced that in the forties and fifties for a woman to have reached the top of a bank would have exhausted all her energy without having given her any of the satisfaction. But the gnawing emptiness remained.

Samantha rose from the table, tall, slim, strong, passionate, unsatisfied. For Miles she felt an affection she had never felt for any of her lovers; but neither Miles nor any other of her lovers had been adequate, at least for very long. She had never known anyone who had satisfied her, either physically or intellectually.

In the corridor on the second floor on the way to her bedroom, she encountered her maid.

"Good morning, Fiona. How are you today?"

"Very well, ma'am, thank you," Fiona answered with a soft Scottish burr. Fiona was the picture of youth and health. Her light brown hair was shining clean, her color was high, and her eyes were blue. Her figure, which ran to lushness, was complimented by her pale blue uniform, and the calves of her legs were strong without having been overdeveloped running through the heather. Had Fiona not been an employee, Samantha Vander-

7

pane would not have hesitated to take her to bed to plunge herself into Fiona's freshness and innocence.

Samantha realized that she was staring and that Fiona was to some degree staring back. "You're very attractive, Fiona," she said.

"Thank you, Mrs. Vanderpane," she replied, flushing slightly and smiling demurely.

Samantha smiled and nodded and passed down the hall to her bedroom, entered, and closed the door.

She had been skating on thin ice indeed, and took several deep breaths to calm herself. She had recognized suddenly that Fiona had been responding to her and that simply would not do at all.

"If you keep doing that, I'm going to be late for work." Chris Webb was lying on his back trying to breathe normally. The glow on the ceiling, sunlight reflected through the spring leaves of the trees outside their bedroom window, seemed subaqueous.

"So will I, chauvinist pig," Catherine said into his ear.

"Why don't you say MCP?"

"The M is redundant," she said huskily.

"What I mean is that I have to go to a meeting it would not be diplomatic to be late for."

Catherine stopped caressing him. "What's it about?"

"At nine-thirty, Tony Gould, Max Fougere, John Howe, and I are briefing Miles Vanderpane on the Republic of Maraka and the relations of Manhattan Banking therewith."

"Who's John Howe?"

"He's the head of syndications in London. The well-beloved Max is head of the Africa division."

"I know. I know who the others are."

"By God, she listens to her old husband."

"Brief me about Maraka."

"You mean, have a dry run? Goddammit, Catherine, that hurt. What do you know about Maraka?"

"West Africa. Biggest population after Nigeria. Very rich."

"It's a cesspool situated between Nigeria and Cameroon. Rotten climate, a population that is hideously poor and disease-ridden, a crumbling capital with open sewers and traffic jams that make New York look like Two Gun, Arizona, on Sunday morning. A rapacious elite with German cars, French cigarette lighters, British suits, mistresses every color of the rainbow, and Swiss bank accounts stuffed to overflowing."

She propped herself on her left elbow, leaning her head on her hand, and fixed him with sapphire eyes. Looked at the brown hair going gray, the lines in his forehead, the profound tiredness around his eyes and mouth.

"Is that what you're going to tell Miles Vanderpane?"

"Not in so many words. Differently. With numbers. But in the most delicate possible way, yes."

"Why does the bank deal with them?"

"You have lovely breasts, Catherine."

She flopped back onto the bed and turned her back to him.

"I'm sorry, Catherine. Really. You were making it difficult for me to concentrate on Maraka."

"You think of me as nothing but a sex object," she whimpered, so that he knew she wasn't serious.

"No, no. I think of *myself* as a sex object, not you." He rubbed the point of her shoulder.

"Why do you deal with Maraka?" she said, turning back under his hand.

"Does any of you edit anything but children's books? We deal with Maraka because we make lots of money doing it. And because all our big multinational customers do too, and expect us to provide the finance, and take the risk, for the business they do there. Lots of people are getting rich dealing with Maraka, including a certain group of Marakans who take what they call with a straight face a commission on every deal that's done, whether it's building an airport or importing a shipment of Indian bicycles. And more and more people are looking for a piece of the action."

"I think it's disgusting," Catherine said.

"But as Tony Gould says, 'In business, we are not our brother's keeper.'"

9

"Tony's just a teddy bear." She was holding his hand now.

"I think the end is in sight for Maraka, though. The party's nearly over. Things are coming crashing down." He looked at the shifting pattern of light on the ceiling. "'The centre cannot hold/Mere anarchy is loosed upon the world/The blood-dimmed tide is loosed, and everywhere/The ceremony of innocence is drowned.'"

"Brave one," Catherine said, without irony.

"What the hell," Webb said, turning on his side and holding her tightly.

"You're going to be late for your meeting," she said, a little breathlessly.

"Mmmm," he answered.

For a short time after he opened his eyes, Nick Stewart watched the lizard on the ceiling. The room was shuttered against the midday heat and was stifling. The air conditioning had broken down again and the ceiling fan moved the air listlessly. Neither the lizard nor Stewart paid any attention to the fan, both of them having got used to it by now. The lizard was definitely watching Stewart.

With a practiced motion, Nick turned on his side, reached over the edge of the bed, and shook out his slippers. Nothing. He swung his legs over the side of the bed and put his feet into the slippers. He was naked otherwise.

He had after all to return to the office. Okubu's visit had not begun yet, so there would be no results, but New York might call him prior to the lunch. He sat on the bed and sweated and watched a large spider crossing the wall between the door to the hallway and the loo. In addition to which, Hilary might be wanting another lesson in Third World realities.

On the way to the bathroom, he swatted the spider with a slipper. The resulting stain joined the others that he had accumulated over the past sixteen months like graffiti.

He urinated and pulled the chain. Nothing happened. He stood on the toilet seat and looked into the cistern, which was empty save for a scorpion that had been discomfited by the scrape of the chain and was scurrying back and forth. Stewart wondered how the scorpion had gotten trapped in the cistern, running mindlessly back and forth until the Ministry of Public Works found the problem and turned the water back on and drowned it.

Nick looked closely into the mirror. No obvious signs of further change and decay. The hair was no thinner, the pale face no more drawn, the bones in no more sharper relief, the chest hair no grayer, than usual. He removed the foil and the plastic cap from a fresh bottle of Evian that he took from the case that stood on top of four other cases in the loo, sloshed some water over a toothbrush, and brushed his teeth, rinsing with Evian as well. He poured a glassful and took a malaria tablet. The water cost Manhattan Banking an arm and a leg, but it was a choice between bottled water and amoebic dysentery, cholera, or typhoid fever. No ice in the drinks unless it was made with bottled water, no salads, no raw vegetables. Holy shit. The ancestors who had been shipped by Her Majesty's Government to Botany Bay four generations before would not think the family had improved itself much.

He brushed his hair, put on more deodorant, and dressed: pants, suit trousers, long-sleeved shirt, tie. He took along a suit coat to wear in the office or anywhere else the air conditioning might be working.

He walked into the hallway, slipping links into his cuffs. At the head of the stairs, he pulled out his keys, opened the padlock and raised the steel grill that might impede marauders from gaining the second floor of the house, and descended the stairs. At the bottom, he found the seemingly eternally optimistic Ahmed. Ahmed was a Moslem Marakan, black as the ace of spades; couldn't do enough for you; a first-class human being, old Ahmed; and, of course, when the revolution came, what good would it have done old Ahmed? In his cups, Stewart could weep when he thought about it; therefore, he avoided thinking about it.

"Will you be home for dinner, sah?" said Ahmed brightly.

"Probably not, Ahmed," Stewart replied, "but I'm not certain. Leave something for me in the fridge."

11

"Very good, sah!"

Stewart waved his driver, Paul, away as he walked through the courtyard. It was faster at that time of day to go to the office on foot, and there was no one he had to impress. He nodded to the two guards with submachine guns who opened the gate of the compound for him and closed it after he left.

By the time he reached the street, his shirt was soaked with sweat, back and front. The air was fetid with the smell of feces.

It took him twenty minutes to walk slowly the half mile along Victoria Road to the office, and in those twenty minutes the line of cars he paralleled moved once, for thirty feet. Stewart was grateful for the smell of the auto exhaust, which tended to mask the other stinks of Maraka City on a hot afternoon.

His secretary, Miss Temba, another excellent human being, had kept a record of all the calls he had received during his lunchtime nap. Most she had taken care of herself; those she couldn't she noted for his attention. Miss Temba was a light-skinned, attractive black woman, about thirty-five, who, Stewart was certain, got a good deal of fun out of life with the French and Italian mining engineers who were always ringing her up or appearing in the office around quitting time; for which he was eternally grateful. Otherwise, he might have felt called upon to service her himself, and, at his age, he was not inclined to take on more than one job at a time. Had he been ten years younger and in another country . . .

One of the calls that needed his attention had come from Colin Mackintosh of the United Bank of Maraka. Mr. Mackintosh was another worthy: he had come out twenty years before with the Chartered Bank, had married a Marakan woman and had children by her, and had decided to stay when independence was granted. Mr. Mackintosh was a realist: he knew how warm would have been his welcome back in Surrey with a black wife and black children.

His request was very simple and straightforward: that Manhattan Banking increase its line of credit for letters of credit, advances, and acceptances from five million to seven and a half million dollars.

Stewart rang him back.

"I see no problem at all, Mr. Mackintosh. You understand our acceptance availability is restricted, however, and refinancing will more likely be by means of advances? Lovely. Is seven million five enough?"

"Yes, indeed. Thank you, Mr. Stewart. We have always appreciated your bank's understanding of our needs. I shall try to let you have as many CCC credits as I can."

"Thank you, Mr. Mackintosh. You should have a formal letter in a few days."

Technically, Stewart needed approval for such an increase from his division head, Max Fougere, and from Central Credit Group. But he anticipated no difficulty with approval for a trade line for the best-managed bank in Maraka, which was used to finance the import of farm machinery and small machine tools and the like, and getting CCC credits—U.S. government guaranteed finance for the import of grain—was simply gravy. Fougere—who in any event was extremely skillful at avoiding the assumption of responsibility for anything—would be no problem, nor would Chris Webb, the CCG man responsible for Africa.

The next call had come from Okubu's office. Jimmy Moshu, whom Stewart had met once but couldn't remember, invited him for a drink at the Intercontinental. Accepted with pleasure. Stewart was glad he had brought his coat. The bar at the Intercontinental was the coldest place in town.

The pressure about the jumbo credit was starting to build. It had been rumored in the market for weeks. It was thought that three or four banks were going to get a crack at it, but that Manhattan Banking was going to be the first.

The third and last call had been from Hilary. He rang her at the *Financial Times* office.

"I miss you," she said. "Have you anything you need to do after work?"

"A man from the Finance Ministry, for a drink at the Intercontinental. At six. Want to come?"

"Absolutely."

"It may be confidential. He may ask you to leave."

"I understand."

Stewart felt a little shiver in his bowels, which he recognized as the kind of thing he used to experience in Korea just before another bloody assault on another bloody hill.

"Hilary, darling, do you think you're being truly as careful as you might?"

"As I might, Nick," she said. "One can be careful to the point of incoherence. And I don't want to be incoherent. Let's talk later. Phone, you know."

He knew. Occasionally the phone went dead. Came back within forty-five seconds. The story among the expatriates was that it gave the secret police time enough to put on a new tape. Stewart didn't know a single seasoned expat who didn't think the story absolutely true.

He left his office to meet Jimmy Moshu at the bar of the Intercontinental at about the same time, given the six-hour time difference, that Thomas Okubu, the Finance Minister of Maraka, was arriving at the Manhattan Banking Corporation to lunch with Miles Vanderpane.

C hris Webb arrived a few minutes late for the meeting in Vanderpane's comfortable, softly lit office on the twelfth floor. As he had anticipated, Miles hardly noticed. Gould looked annoyed, and John Howe from Syndications nodded cautiously. Max Fougere, head of the Africa Division, turned a blandly benevolent face toward him as he came into the office and continued talking. Webb took the chair next to Howe.

In his slight, indefinable accent (that some people said was French and others, upper-class Lebanese; he was known to have hinted at both backgrounds, and indeed had an olive complexion and spoke French well), Fougere had begun his recitation: the long list of natural resources, the enormous potential for development, the interest of the multinational corporations, many of which were Manhattan Banking's customers, in doing business with Maraka, their expectation that the bank would support them in their efforts, the importance of the multinational corporations to the bank, the importance of Maraka to the bank.

"What do they keep in balances, Max?" Vanderpane said.

Fougere was looking particularly relaxed that morning. He sat—or rather half reclined, half sat—on the chair to Vanderpane's left, which meant that he was sitting a little higher than Gould, who was on the sofa to the chairman's right. His bulk filled the chair and his legs were crossed comfortably, and he was speaking almost languidly, eyes hooded, gesturing occasionally with the Davidoff cigar in his right hand. It was a style that Webb had watched Fougere refine over the years, one that was meant to mesmerize, like the sway of a cobra. It was meant also to annoy Tony Gould, who liked people to give the appearance of energetic effort.

"Forty million average demand balances through March."

"I thought there were more than that."

"You're quite correct, Miles. There used to be. But we'll come to that in a moment. The deposit breakdown is about twenty million from the Central Bank of Maraka and the rest from the four commercial banks. The investment bank keeps a nominal account. The banks are all government owned."

Gould began to drum silently with his fingers on the arm of the sofa.

"And what is our exposure?"

"A total of sixty-five million dollars. Twenty million maturing in 1986 to Air Maraka. Thirty million that was our final take as a lead manager in the Bank of Illinois syndication to the Republic. That matures in 1988. Five million in support of a joint venture for Childs Construction and Engineering." Max paused to relight his cigar. It seemed to take a long time.

Chris Webb waited what he thought was a respectful amount of time, but Vanderpane didn't appear to have been keeping his sums, or else he wasn't particularly concerned about the other ten million. Chris started to speak, but Gould interrupted him quickly.

"The last ten million was for a deal for the Investment Bank of Maraka, with the guarantee of the Republic. They were going to

16

purchase some secondhand vessels for the Shipping Corporation of Maraka, but that project never got off the ground. The funds were diverted to infrastructure development. Max, the loan matures in 1984, right?"

"Almost, Tony. 1985."

Gould looked at Fougere to see if he was being sarcastic. "As you know, Tony, I never felt that particular project was well conceived."

Gould started to speak, but decided against it. Vanderpane was staring out of the window, and a hush fell over the room. It lasted nearly long enough for Chris to wonder whether the chairman had fallen asleep with his eyes open, when suddenly Miles turned. "What about the corruption?"

Fougere was clearly taken aback and did not respond immediately. Chris was momentarily impressed with Vanderpane, until he realized that someone must have prompted him.

"Sure there's corruption," Gould said. Light flashed off his glasses. "There is in every Third World country. But that has nothing to do with Manhattan Banking. We lend funds for the development that the country needs to realize its potential, as Max has indicated."

Score one for Tony Gould. He was not going to let Fougere put distance between himself and the bank's involvement in Maraka. Fifteen all.

Chris watched Vanderpane with detached curiosity. Miles was sitting in his favorite wing chair, legs crossed, arms folded. Gould was making him nervous.

"I also want to remind you, Miles, that we are not riding as high as we used to in Maraka. Our balances are slipping, as you mentioned, and Nick Stewart has detected some coolness on the part of the Treasury and the Central Bank." And in response to the glaze in Vanderpane's eyes, Gould added, "Stewart is our representative in Maraka."

"The Australian fellow?"

"Yes, that's right, Miles. Very good man."

"Then what's caused the coolness?"

"Lack of responsiveness to Maraka's needs. Not in the field. In

New York." Gould looked significantly at Chris Webb. "I firmly believe we are going to have to step up the next time they ask us, Miles, or we're going to be out of the picture in Maraka. And being out of the picture in Maraka means being out of one of the biggest success stories in Africa."

"What are they going to ask us for?"

"They're going to offer us lead management of a billion-dollar syndication. Obviously they think John Howe and his band of merry men can put it together. But it's also a test, Miles, of how committed Manhattan Banking is to helping the development of Maraka.

"And you know better than I, Miles, what a deal like this will do for Manhattan Banking, not only in Maraka, but around the world."

Vanderpane nodded thoughtfully. "No question of that, Tony. What terms are we going to propose?"

"John?" Gould nodded to John Howe and sat back.

Howe cleared his throat. He was a thin Englishman, with long, straight blond hair and glasses with thin tortoise-shell frames that sat on an aquiline nose. He was wearing a blue suit with a vivid pinstripe and a light purple shirt with a white collar and cuffs, and handsome gold links.

"I think the tenor should be ten years," he began in a public school accent, "with a five-year grace period before repayment of principal begins. The margin I judge will settle at three-quarters over London interbank offered rate throughout, although I think we should start out at three-quarters for the first five years and seven-eighths for the rest. Commitment commission of one-half percent on the undrawn portion of the loan from the date of signing of the loan agreement, although I think we can agree to fall back to three-eighths if they really argue. The banks should have a prime rate option also, at three-eighths over, or a rate inversion—that is, when the cost of funds goes over prime—of three-quarters over our reserve adjusted cost of funds, whichever is higher, at the bank's option. The agency fee will be the usual twenty-five thousand per annum. Lastly, a management fee of one-quarter percent flat, on which we skim a sixteenth; we'll underwrite a hundred million and sell down to, say, seventy-five."

"John, you think the whole thing will be underwritten before it goes to general syndication?" Chris asked.

"No question. The lead managers will jump at a three-sixteenths fee." His voice dropped.

"I'm sorry, John, I didn't hear the end of your sentence."

Howe was annoyed that he had to repeat himself. "I said, 'and if nothing untoward happens.'"

"And if something untoward does happen?"

"Then the deal will be richer," Gould snapped, "because the spread and the fees will be higher." Chris could feel the chill in the air from across the room.

Miles Vanderpane folded his hands together and looked pensive. "Net net, John, what do the fees represent in terms of revenue for the bank?"

"Ceding an eighth on the selldown, although I think that's pretty generous, I should say a little over eight hundred and five thousand dollars."

For a few moments, Vanderpane sat with his eyes closed and his lips moving slightly. When he opened his eyes again, he said, to no one in particular, "That's seven cents a share after tax."

He looked at Chris Webb and said, in a mildly patronizing way, "Let's hear what Central Credit Group has to say."

"We are concerned about the situation in Maraka, economically, socially, and politically." Chris had considered his response to the inevitable question carefully. He did not want to piss off either the present or the future chairman of the board. On the other hand, a loan of a billion dollars to a country with the problems Maraka had was so patently absurd that he felt he had to try his best. And *au fond,* he never knew what pissed off Tony Gould anyway. "The economic data we can get on Maraka are rather spotty at best, but they do indicate a couple of things very clearly. For the past couple of years, the debt service ratio—that is, debt service divided by exports—has increased dramatically—"

"Two years do not constitute a trend," Gould said.

19

"Now, Tony," Vanderpane said benignly, "let Chris have his say."

"The increase in the debt service ratio is due both to a rapid increase in debt and a decrease in the rate of export growth. And while the balance of trade is still in surplus, the surplus has been declining for the past three years, and the current account deficit is enormous, due entirely to the item called invisibles. If this is the corruption you were referring to, Miles, it's on a grand scale."

"But as you said before, Chris," Tony said, "the figures are kind of spotty."

"Indeed they are. Nonetheless, the numbers show the balance of payments is in deficit overall, and Marakan reserves are declining. This might be at least part of the reason why our balances have declined."

The room was very quiet, and Webb knew he was getting nowhere. But he pressed ahead.

"Lastly, the economic gap between the well-educated Marakan elite, which is a relatively small group, and the rest of the population, which is ignorant, underfed, underemployed, and poorly paid when employed, is huge. It is an exploitable situation, and the situation is being exploited by a number of guerrilla organizations, some leftist, some not. In my judgment, there is going to be a revolution in Maraka within the next two years."

"Thank you, Chris," Gould said quickly. "I think it's useful to air these matters, and I think they're worth consideration—part of the due diligence, let's say, for the offering memo—but they're largely either a misunderstanding of the situation or else irrelevant. One, the loans perforce come before development takes place, so of course the debt service ratio is going to go up. And just as logically it will come down, when they've got a better distribution system in place, when their new mines and plants come on stream and they start producing and selling. It's simply that now there's a lag. Two, our own economics department supports this view. Three, about the corruption. I can repeat only that this has nothing to do with the bank, and when we get better figures on the economy—they have some economic consultants in there now, haven't they, Max?—these gaps will no longer exist. And fourth, that there might be a revolution. That may be the most irrelevant comment of all. Nigeria had a civil war and Nigeria is booming. Governments come and go. Loans are always honored. Countries don't go broke, Miles. They can't repudiate their debt because if they did, they'd never get another dime from a world-class bank."

"But how about the opportunity cost of rescheduled debt and the drop in liquidity?" Chris asked, but no one paid attention. He knew that Max Fougere had heard him, but Max said nothing.

"We need to protect our position, Miles," Gould said, "and we're going to be offered the opportunity to do that and to make a hell of a lot of money at the same time. And I guarantee you this: if we don't do it, some other bank will, and it's going to be a very, very fat deal."

Vanderpane leaned forward in his chair, brightening visibly. "I can see, Tony, that you call a spade a spade."

Howe studied the floor, Fougere forced a chuckle, Gould looked appalled, and Chris Webb laughed. Gould looked at him angrily.

"Well I do thank you fellows," Vanderpane said rising, signaling the end of the briefing. "I'm looking forward to the lunch. What is the chap's name again?"

"Thomas Okubu."

"And he's Minister of Finance?"

Gould nodded.

"And he'll be with someone named Kalama? Robert Kalama? I've met him before."

"Yes, Miles. At our IMF dinner two years ago. He's Governor of the Central Bank."

Webb knew that Vanderpane was sold on the deal as soon as he'd heard the amount of the fees, if not before, and there was nothing that could be done about it. He could not point out that none of the substantive issues he had raised had been addressed. He could not argue out questions of judgment and policy with the head of international banking in front of the chairman; it was the wrong forum. Indeed, it was difficult to know what was the right forum to disagree with someone like Tony Gould, whose opinions were formed very quickly and were thereafter irrevocable.

"You smug bastards in CCG have forgotten what it's like to be out in the pits getting your hands dirty," Gould said while they were waiting for the elevator. When the door opened, Gould got in first, followed by Howe, Webb, and Fougere.

"When are you rejoining international banking, Webb?" Gould asked lightly.

"Are you making an offer, Tony?"

Gould stared at him with opaque eyes. The elevator stopped at the eleventh floor. Howe and Fougere preceded Gould, who said, "Don't call us, Webb, we'll call you and so forth," and stepped nimbly off the elevator.

Not for nothing was he known among the cognoscenti as Tony Ghoul.

3

Hilary Ashton-Brooke was pretty in a fresh-faced English sort of way, although the climate in Maraka was doing her complexion no good at all; she often looked flushed and there were shadows beneath her eyes. Stewart did not think she was as young as she looked with her short brown hair and wide blue eyes—he thought she might be in her early thirties. And although she had a quick intelligence, there were still things she was not careful enough about—telling someone you'd just met at a drinks party your dismal opinion of the Marakan Minister of Public Works was not, after all, like discussing the new vicar in Middle Wallop—and Stewart kept reminding himself to talk to her about things like that and kept forgetting. Whenever they were together, they had other things on their minds.

She smiled at him now as he approached her across the vast, warmly lit lobby of the Intercontinental, and he thought of all the smiles across all the lobbies, rooms, halls he had seen in the past quarter century, and wondered briefly whether it meant anything; but only briefly. Contemplating with delectation his undiminished sexual appetite over that same period, he returned Hilary's smile and waved.

She kissed him on the lips and said, "Is this dinner too or just drinks?"

"Man said drinks."

"Who is it?"

"Man named Jimmy Moshu from the Finance Ministry."

They were walking up the broad staircase to the mezzanine to the American bar.

"He's Deputy Finance Minister, Nick. It must be important."

"They're looking for some money."

"Why else would he want to drink with a banker?"

"Why do you?" he said and slapped a well-rounded buttock.

"Lout," she said.

The bar was full as usual at cocktail hour, except for a semicircle of empty tables to the left, beyond which, in the vee of a corner, sat a very dark man, with a white-coated waiter standing at his shoulder. Stewart recognized Jimmy Moshu, and guided Hilary in his direction. It was even colder in the bar than it had been in the lobby, and he helped her slip a white cardigan across the shoulders of her blue dress, and put on his own jacket. All the empty tables had reserved signs.

As they approached, the waiter started to open a bottle of champagne with a good deal more flourish than the matter required. Jimmy Moshu stood and offered his hand. He was about Stewart's height, but much broader, particularly in the face and shoulders. Even in the sense-dulling, heavy air conditioning, Stewart could smell the expensive French cologne. Probably had cases of it at home. Didn't brush his teeth with it though, he bet.

"I'm Jimmy Moshu, Mr. Stewart," he said with the thinnest patina of West African lilt overlaying his educated British accent.

"I'm very pleased to see you, Mr. Moshu. Jimmy then. Thank you. I'm called Nick. I think we met once before, albeit briefly."

"The reception for the opening of the Dai Ichi Kangyo Bank?"

"Right you are. Bang on, Jimmy."

24

Jimmy Moshu seemed genuinely pleased.

"I hope you will not mind my friend Miss Ashton-Brooke joining us. We had a long-standing engagement for this evening. But she's a grown-up girl and will go away quietly at a word."

"Not at all. Please do join us, Miss Ashton-Brooke. I'm delighted to meet the person who has written those perceptive articles on Maraka in the *FT*. Please," he said, indicating their glasses. "Cheers."

They all drank.

"I regard your presence, Miss Ashton-Brooke, as yet one more benefit in our relationship with the Manhattan Banking Corporation."

"Thank you, Mr. Moshu," Hilary said. "You find my articles perceptive?"

"I do indeed. You know, when one is so heavily involved with one's work, one sometimes cannot see the forest for the trees. A couple of things you've written have caused me to rethink what I've been doing. You will ask for an example. You did an article last month concerning the percentage of funds available going into agricultural development as opposed to what we are putting into exploitation of our mineral resources. Mind you, I'm not saying I agree with you; but I am saying you made me test my ideas, question my assumptions. I'm happy to say I could award myself a first."

"Can I ask a frank question, Mr. Moshu?" Hilary said.

Moshu was gesturing for another bottle of champagne and said, "Of course," as if he hadn't quite heard what she was asking, but before she could begin, he fixed her with eyes that looked black in the dim light in the bar and added, "But only as Mr. Stewart's companion, and not as a reporter for the *FT*."

Nick Stewart had developed over many years a particular acumen for detecting all forms of subtle hint, and this one was not particularly subtle; but he knew as well as he knew he was going to enjoy his third glass of champagne that Hilary would not have noticed, or if she had she would ignore it.

"Oh, absolutely. But what I wanted to know was if you had any observations about my piece suggesting that there was a fair amount of . . . of under the counter dealing going on in Maraka?"

"My dear Miss Ashton-Brooke, you mean bribery?" Moshu chuckled. "You are very bright and if I may say so very attractive, but you are young and have some way to go to gain experience. My dear, believe me you are not the first person to have discovered bribery and corruption, nor will you be the last. The anticorruption squad of our CID is at least as interested as you. I'll be the first to admit that there are a few too many loose arrangements around the country. But we are living in an entrepreneurial environment here—and make no mistake about it, this is exactly the way we want it to be—and such things do happen. Fortunately or unfortunately, it's in the nature of the beast. The entrepreneur accepts no givens, no limits. That's his great value. He says if we can't do it this way, we'll do it that way, but we'll do it. And sometimes it's his drawback. But you asked me for any observations. This is my observation: with respect to bribery, corruption, et cetera, you have exaggerated both its extent and its importance."

Stewart heard the full stop clearly; Hilary had heard only a semicolon.

"But surely you'll agree, Mr. Moshu, that there is a vast amount of corruption in Maraka, so vast in fact—"

Stewart was staggered by the man's ability to control himself. He simply raised his left hand for her to stop, and with his right poured another round of champagne. Putting the bottle back into the ice bucket, and smiling benignly, he said, "Let me turn a question back on you. What right have you to judge the means by which Marakans create a better life for themselves? If the choice is between some ideal of honesty and starvation and disease, or corruption and health and food for the people, who would not choose corruption, except someone who does not know what starvation is and does?

"But enough of these upsetting matters. I had no idea that H. Ashton-Brooke was a young woman. I quite pictured someone like a cross between my old tutor Duncan Moore at Balliol and one of those scruffy reporters one sees in American films. You are a graduate, Miss Ashton-Brooke?"

"Yes. London School of Economics."

"Well, I must say, if you're an example of current economics graduates, then it cannot be a dismal science after all."

Very gallantly put, thought Stewart, and very nicely done. But old Jimmy Moshu was no fool. He would remember this conversation.

Moshu leaned forward and made a tent of his long brown fingers. His dark tropical worsted was certainly British; Hermès tie; Gucci shoes. Except for the color of his skin, Jimmy Moshu could have occupied an office in any merchant bank in the City of London.

"Now, Nick, we know that about now my Minister is discussing with your chairman the possibility of Manhattan Banking's putting together for us a new credit of one billion dollars." He was speaking more slowly than he had been before, and gave every indication that it was with great deliberation. "I shall not mince words, Nick. This credit is very important to us, and I want you to do all you can to see that your people in New York go along. Because this credit's very important for Manhattan Banking also. We want to see who our friends are. And it's a testimony to the work you've done here that we've come to you first."

Nick demurred but Moshu waved it away with a slight sign of impatience. "Let's be frank. Right now Maraka needs Manhattan Banking. And a lot of other international banks. You don't need us. But Nick, do you know what Maraka is going to be like in five years' time? Booming! More so even than now. And that's when you'll all want *us* as customers, and those of you who didn't go along will be kicking yourselves, because you won't be able to get us back on your books. We'll remember our friends. And we'll remember the others too."

I bet you will, thought Stewart.

"Now here, Miss Ashton-Brooke, I must enjoin you to secrecy for a week. Just a week because the final report isn't in yet, but

27

we've been told the conclusions preliminarily. Can I have your word as an Englishman, Miss Ashton-Brooke? Everyone knows the worth of an Englishman's word."

Stewart thought he was laying it on a little heavily. Poor Hilary had done herself a good deal of damage, and she was going to have to work hard to repair it.

"You have my word, Mr. Moshu."

He looked at each of them in turn and said quietly, "We've found oil. How does that billion-dollar credit look now? Ah, Nick, I know what you're going to say. All those years of fruitless searching, all those dry holes. But our new consultants—they're really a drilling company with M.B.A.'s—have come up with something real now. Six miles offshore, and every indication is that it's in commercially exploitable quantities."

"It's staggering news, Jimmy. Wonderful news for Maraka."

"That's why we had the champagne. I don't want you, particularly Miss Ashton-Brooke, to think I drink it all the time." And he winked, to put her at her ease. Moshu looked at his watch. "I'm sorry. I must be going. It's been extremely pleasant." They all stood. "Nick, can I count on your support with your chairman?"

"You can rely on me, Jimmy."

A strong pat on the shoulder and a squeeze. "And can I count on your help to assist me in aiding Hilary—may I call you that? thank you—in aiding Hilary to get rid of some of her crackpot ideas?" His hand was warm when he took hers but the grip was a little too tight.

They both laughed, and with a little wave Jimmy Moshu started out of the bar. Immediately two men in suits took a place walking in front of him, and two followed closely behind. In a few seconds they were through the door, accompanied in their passage by the briefest pause in the general noise of conversation in the bar.

Hilary was staring at the table and put her hand over her glass when Stewart tried to pour the last of the champagne.

"Hungry?" he said.

"Hardly."

"Good. I am too. Positively famished. How about Chinese?"

She knew that Nick must have a reason why he responded as if he hadn't heard her.

"Lovely," she said.

Y. S. Lee, of Lee's Chinese Garden, was taciturn and morose, but served a good cheap meal in the privacy that obtains in a constantly crowded restaurant. Marakans never went there; not that Y. S. would not have served them, but Lee's simply wasn't upmarket enough for the emerging Marakan rich, and the rest couldn't afford it. As a result, the restaurant was always full of expats: journalists, minor diplomats, and spies—Stewart was sure of that—mining and dredging engineers, heavy machinery specialists, airline crews, traders of all kinds, bankers, money brokers, miscellaneous hustlers looking for a quick turn.

The place was garishly lit and seemed decorated entirely in cheap plastic, no doubt highly flammable and toxic, Stewart thought. Lee nodded when they entered, an acknowledgment of their prior frequent custom. He spoke little English, and very little of anything else but his native tongue, so interchange in any event was limited. He always looked as if he had just lost someone very near and dear, or suffered a financial cataclysm; unless, thought Nick Stewart, one looked closely at his dark, close-set eyes and saw the Swiss francs dancing there.

Nick waved to Carlo Sanguineto, representative of the Banca Commerciale Italiana, as they entered. They were taken to a table in the center of the room by a young man in a short-sleeved khaki shirt, khaki trousers, and blue rubber thongs. The table was covered in torn red oilcloth. He handed them stained menus and went to get some tea. The noise level—both from the dripping air-conditioners and the crowd around them—was comfortably high.

"I think you rather pissed off Jimmy Moshu, sweetheart."

"Thanks for the comforting words, Nick."

The waiter returned with the tea. He poured cups for each of them, slopping some onto the oilcloth, and tugged a notepad from his shirt pocket.

"You order?"

"Chicken with ground nuts, pork with hot pepper, snow peas and Chinese cabbage, boiled rice, three-ingredient soup, two Cheetahs."

Nick waited until the waiter left. "You wanted me to tell you that it was all right, there, there, Hilary, let me help you get your foot out of your mouth?"

"No. No, Nick, you're absolutely right. I got so angry watching that self-satisfied turd sitting back in comfort and smacking his lips at the champagne. He probably kicks the cripples out of the way when he goes into the Intercontinental."

"A few home truths, my dear. Take them from one whom the years have made more cautious. *Primo*, if you want to be any kind of reporter doing a decent job of work in this or any hellhole, keep the crybaby shit out of your stories. I'm not saying you can't hold opinions, but keep them to yourself or you're going to get into big trouble."

Hilary looked at the table and sipped tea.

"*Secondo*, I think Moshu is willing to forgive, but don't let it go to your head. He won't forget; they never do that. And a little note is going to be added to your dossier. He gave you a warning tonight. He was telling you that he doesn't want you writing about certain subjects. Take heed, Hilary."

Stewart sat back as the food was delivered all at once. He poured their beers and began to eat rapidly with chopsticks. Hilary pushed the food around on her plate.

"What's the point if one can't be honest?"

"Hilary, you and I are too old to be having this conversation. You know damned well you can be honest. But you have to be discreet as well. Just avoid certain subjects. For Christ's sake, you know that. You don't mention bribery to a man who's so obviously on the take himself."

"That's why I brought it up."

"You're like a little kid playing with matches." Stewart gestured impatiently with his chopsticks. "I do wish you'd eat something. Do you have an open airline ticket?"

"No. I . . . actually I haven't thought about it since you first mentioned getting one."

"Tomorrow morning you'll get one first thing, promise? And if you don't pay attention to old Nick, I'll not be responsible." He ordered two more beers and returned to his food.

She smiled sheepishly in the way that always affected Stewart in his groin, and began to eat. He had more or less finished, confining himself to picking the occasional bit off one of the serving plates, sipping his Cheetah, and watching her while she ate: her lips, her breasts, her lips.

"You're making me self-conscious, Nick."

"Hilary, that's utter bullshit. You haven't been self-conscious since you got your first period."

Her blue eyes were limpid. "Take me home, Nick. Take me to bed."

"With pleasure." At the counter, while the woman they all assumed was Mrs. Lee totaled their bill with an abacus, Stewart rang for his car, which arrived in a few minutes.

As they left Lee's to get into the white Volvo sedan, they waved and smiled, as they customarily did, to the Marakan plainclothes policemen across the road who photographed everyone who entered and left the restaurant. There was no pretence about what they were doing; it was much easier to take the pictures if the cameras were not hidden in the bushes. In addition, the presence of the police made Lee's a safe place to go at night in Maraka City.

Stewart's chauffeur Paul was another of his faithful Marakans, but he was a Christian. Paul was from the west, near the Nigerian border, and regarded the shorter, broader, Moslem people of the southern tribes, in a most un-Christian way, with contempt.

Stewart and Hilary rode in silence, holding hands, to the expat compound in which she had a flat. They had to leave the car at the gate to have their papers checked by an armed guard, who waved them through.

Hilary's flat was in the part of the compound farthest from the gate, on the second floor along a brightly lit open gallery. The rear windows of the flat overlooked a scrubby patch of back

31

garden, a twelve-foot chain link fence topped with a thick tangle of barbed wire, and a heavy copse beyond.

Stewart, walking behind Hilary, put his hand on her shoulder and brought her to a halt.

"Did you leave your door ajar, darling?"

"Good heavens, no."

"Wait here."

Nick pushed the door wide open and standing to one side reached around the door post and felt for the light switch. No one was in the entrance hall and a quick glance suggested everything was in place. He signaled to her to come ahead, and while she waited in the sitting room, he looked into the tiny kitchen, the bedroom, and the bathroom. He was soaked in sweat, but only then did he turn on the air conditioning and close the front door.

"No harm done then. How about a drink?" He took off his jacket.

Hilary remained standing in the center of the sitting room, where he had left her. He thought she was watching the large moth circling and circling the round lamp in the middle of the ceiling.

"Someone has been here, Nick."

"How can you tell?"

"Everything is a little out of place. This table, that book, the glass. They've all been moved."

Stewart put his arm around her shoulder. "If that's the case, honey, then I think you were meant to notice. I think Jimmy Moshu is underlining his warning in case we missed the point. You're going to have to keep your nose clean. The place is bugged now, I'm sure, not just the phone. Well, old girl, let's give them something to listen to."

She began to shiver beneath his arm. He made her sit on the sofa and got her a large measure of whisky from the drinks tray. It was a moment before she unwrapped her arms from around her shoulders and accepted the glass. She took a large sip.

"It'll be okay, Hilary. They've warned you and you've accepted it, right? Don't nod, say it."

"Yes," she choked.

"Yes what?"

"Yes, I've accepted the warning."

"And you're going to be a good girl from now on, right?"

"Yes," she said and coughed. "I'm sorry." She rose and went into the kitchen coughing. When she returned she had a notepad on which she had scribbled, "Should I get out?"

"Hilary, do be a love and get me a whisky and soda," he said, simultaneously taking the pen and notepad from her and writing beneath her question, "No, don't think any need, besides I want you around."

Thomas Okubu, Minister of Finance of Maraka, was short and round, with sparse white crinkly hair close to his scalp, and a benign look like the principal of a happy secondary school. But Webb felt that the power he emanated was nearly palpable, an aura that filled the beige and green dining room on the fourteenth floor.

Okubu was at Vanderpane's right at the round table, and Robert Kalama, the head of the Central Bank, was at his left. Tony Gould and Max Fougere came next, and John Howe and Chris Webb were at the bottom of the table opposite Vanderpane.

The conversation throughout the meal was superficial, touching on the prospects for development of Maraka's resources, including the rather interesting news that they seemed to have found oil in commercially exploitable quantities. Okubu did not make much of this at the time, mentioning it almost *en passant*. They talked about what Okubu called border incursions by vari-

34

ous rebel groups operating from remote areas in the northwest. The Finance Minister described them as occasional mosquito bites, obviously Marxist inspired, Soviet supplied, and Cuban trained, calling forth in a single sentence nearly all the late twentieth-century bogeymen (Webb thought surely Libya could have been worked in as well). Although there was no doubt that some of the groups were Communist, Webb judged that others were anti-authoritarian or nationalist, and the makeup of all of them was rather more complicated than Okubu indicated.

The Finance Minister carried most of the conversation, punctuated from time to time by emphatic nods from Kalama, who kept his eyes on his chief and took his lead from what he said. Okubu ate little, which Webb deduced was a matter of habit rather than a comment on the inoffensive food that was served in the chairman's dining room.

After Okubu had been brought a pot of hot water with which to weaken his tea, he touched Vanderpane's forearm lightly and said, "Mr. Chairman, we have always regarded Manhattan Banking as a great friend of Maraka. We have had a few minor differences in the past, but they signify little. We are an emerging nation of great resources and great vitality, one of the leaders of the Third World, with a strong and willing populace, ready to go forth into the future with steady hearts."

Chris wondered that Miles Vanderpane could keep his handkerchief in his breast pocket. Tony Gould was as unreadable as ever, and Fougere's lips were trembling slightly, as if he were suppressing a guffaw.

Okubu was warming up. "But the days are long past when people could build a great nation on a shoestring—with a lick and a promise as the Americans say. What we require is money, a lot of money. We are looking for one billion dollars in the Euromarket—none of the prime-based business if you please; prime is not market-sensitive—and we are looking to Manhattan Banking to form the group that will provide it. Of course, we will talk to other banks; but we want Manhattan Banking to lead the deal, and I am prepared, if the terms are right—and if you would be so kind as to provide a secretary—to give Manhattan Banking a mandate before I leave this afternoon.

"What is the money for? For development of potentially the richest country after Nigeria in all of Africa. And I should like an answer from our friends at Manhattan Banking very quickly. Are you prepared to discuss terms now, or shall we wait for one or two days?"

Vanderpane waited an appropriate few seconds before replying. "We have spent some time, my colleagues and I, discussing this very matter, Your Excellency. As I'm sure you know, we value highly the relationship of many years standing we have had with the Republic of Maraka—since its independence, in fact— and I believe we are prepared to offer Maraka a facility on the very finest terms. John, please outline the terms we have discussed for His Excellency and Mr. Kalama."

Vanderpane rarely became involved with details, and when he did, he rarely remembered them. He never saw the point of his getting involved. There would always be someone around who knew them better than he to whom he could turn when necessary. He nodded encouragingly to John Howe.

Howe was clearly very pleased with the visibility this sort of arrangement gave him. "Thank you, Miles," he said, smiling quickly, then becoming serious. There was no nonsense about John Howe, thought Chris; no untoward levity. "The amount will be one billion dollars. Tenor ten years, with a five-year grace period, and repayment in eleven equal semiannual installments thereafter. Spread three-quarters over London interbank for five years . . ."

Webb watched Okubu during Howe's recitation. He seemed to be looking at his cuticles and deciding that they were in need of attention. Webb thought that Manhattan Banking Corporation was in for a surprise.

". . . seven-eighths for the last five years. Commitment commission of a half percent per annum on the undrawn portion from the date of signing. Management fee one-quarter percent flat. I think the agency fee will be twenty-five thousand dollars per annum. Legal and out-of-pocket expenses, as usual, for the account of the borrower."

Silence fell at the table. Okubu's cuticles definitely needed attention. Robert Kalama seemed to have turned gray.

Okubu leaned forward, his elbows on the table, his left hand folded inside his right, and his chin on his right hand. He looked at each of them in turn, reserving his last and longest gaze for Miles Vanderpane. It was not a penetrating gaze. It was more a look of unblinking bewilderment, and it made Vanderpane uncomfortable.

At last Okubu sat back and began tapping lightly on the table with an index finger.

"You have perhaps mistaken us for Malawi, Mr. Chairman? Are you trying to achieve your entire growth plan this year with a syndicated loan to the Republic of Maraka? No. I'm sorry, that is a bit harsh. Putting it simply then: the terms are unacceptable."

Silence fell again. Okubu used it to sip his tepid tea. He replaced the cup carefully, suggesting by his action that the situation was at least as fragile as the cup, and looked around the table again, raising his eyebrows interrogatively.

"As you don't seem to have an immediate response, let me suggest the terms. I ask you to keep in mind, gentlemen, that Maraka is about to become an oil producer. Now. Six years grace period, with a spread of one-half percent for six years and five-eighths for four. A commitment commission of one-quarter percent, to begin one month *after* the signing of the loan agreement. Management fee one million dollars. We will not pay any legal fees in excess of twenty-five thousand dollars."

Howe was obviously not used to being brushed off. He had turned quite red, which Chris Webb guessed was a mixture of embarrassment and rage. Vanderpane smiled, as if it all had nothing to do with him. Max Fougere looked at Tony Gould, who took up the gauntlet.

"We'll look carefully at your proposal, Your Excellency," he said. "You have reminded us that Maraka is about to become an oil producer, about which I assure you we are all very pleased for the people of Maraka. It is not an oil producer yet, and will not be for a while, and we as the syndicating bank, if we are fortunate enough to be awarded the mandate, must face the realities of the marketplace. I don't know that the market would be receptive to the terms offered for Maraka being the same as those for Nigeria or Algeria. Or better even. What do you think, John?"

John Howe was torn between how he thought objectively the market would respond to such terms, and the kind of answer he thought Tony Gould wanted. Chris watched the battle going on in Howe's jaw muscles; but at the end of the day, it was really no contest.

"With some fine tuning here and there, I think it could be done."

"What do you mean by 'fine tuning'?" Okubu said.

"I think the spreads and fees may have to be a bit higher than you suggest, sir."

"What would you propose then?"

"I'd like some time to think it through, sir. I'd like to talk to some friends at other banks. Without mentioning names of course."

"Of course. But how do you disguise a borrower like Maraka?"

"Oh, it's done all the time, sir. Pretesting the market. In addition," Howe continued, "I think we shall need a really excellent placing memorandum, Your Excellency."

"Meaning?"

"We're going to need rather fuller information on the state of the economy than we've had in the past."

"This is the first time, Mr. Howe, that I've ever heard anyone imply that the information we provide is inadequate."

It was certainly the first time he had ever heard John Howe imply such a thing, Chris thought. And he may never have heard such a thing from other commercial bankers either. But he supposed Mr. Okubu had not been in recent contact with the International Monetary Fund or the World Bank about the adequacy or reliability of the information provided by the Ministry of Finance.

"I did not mean to imply that the information we have gotten heretofore has been inadequate," Howe said, "for the uses for which it was provided. But a facility such as we are discussing is a quantum leap for Maraka and by any measure is a jumbo syndication for any borrower. I think the information we need will have to be a bit broader and a bit deeper."

"Mr. Howe, once we agree upon terms, Manhattan Banking can have any information it wants. Our economic consultants will be at your disposal. You have my word on that."

"Thank you."

"Now, Mr. Chairman, Mr. Kalama and I must be going." Okubu and Kalama rose, followed by the others. "Thank you for a pleasant lunch."

"Will you need a car, Your Excellency?" Miles asked.

"No, thank you, Mr. Vanderpane. It's such a lovely day and we have only a few blocks to walk."

Just before Okubu and Kalama got into the elevator with Gould and Fougere, the Finance Minister said, "I shall call in to see you two days from now—Thursday—for your answer, Mr. Chairman."

Vanderpane smiled and gave a little wave as the doors closed, secure in the knowledge that by Thursday, the answers would be provided by his minions. Then he returned to his office. Howe and Webb took another elevator to the eleventh floor to wait for Gould to return.

"What will be acceptable to them that will sell in the market?" Webb asked.

"Less than our terms, more than his," Howe said, not giving anything away when Gould wasn't there and he couldn't whirl and fizz.

"Can it be done?"

"Of course."

"How?"

"Maraka hasn't been in the market for a while." Howe was

39

beginning to sound testy. "A lot of multinationals have got a lot at stake there. There's a lot of liquidity around. Banks have to put that OPEC money somewhere."

"Why Maraka?"

"You'd prefer Sweden at three-eighths for a hundred years?"

"It might be a better risk."

"Risk and return are trade-offs, Webb. You know that."

"I was talking about absolute risk, John, not relative risk. Risk and return *are* trade-offs, and on that basis, there is no combination of spreads and fees that can compensate the bank for the risk it's taking in its exposure to Maraka."

They both nodded to Gould's secretary and went into his office.

"The market will say different," Howe said, sitting on the end of the sofa nearest the armchair that Gould invariably chose.

"What the hell does it matter what the other banks think? Bankers are sheep."

"Where do you think Okubu and Kalama are going now, Webb?"

"Again, what does it matter?"

"You've a stubborn streak, Webb. It's not doing you any good."

"And you have a curious way with facts, John."

"What is that supposed to mean?"

Tony Gould came in, followed by Max Fougere.

"John, what's the best we can do and still get a group together?"

"We can certainly keep the five-year grace; that's a giveaway. Spread, five-eighths throughout; commitment commission, three-eighths. There are two problems. No one is going to be happy with a cap on the legal fees of twenty-five thousand. The other problem is the management fee. No one will lead-manage unless that million dollars is shared equally. It's not so hot even then, because we'll have to give some of it away on the sell-down."

"So you're saying no skim?"

"That's right."

"Think the rest would be happy with an eighth on their underwrite? A hundred twenty-five thousand on a hundred million?"

"A bit happier than with a tenth. And everyone wants to get his hands on Maraka. We all have customers doing business there."

"We'll make the management fee fifteen basis points, skim two hundred fifty thousand, and give an eighth to the co-managers."

"There's not much left for the selldown."

"That's the way it's got to be, John."

"Okay, Tony."

"How about the risk?" Chris Webb said.

"Did you hear something, Max?" Gould asked. Fougere tapped his pursed lips with a finger and stared into space.

"Countries don't go broke," Gould said.

"But how about opportunity cost, Tony. A hundred and forty, maybe a hundred and sixty-five million bucks tied up in a dog. And how much will we have to cough up when we have to reschedule?"

Gould stared coldly.

"You've registered your dissenting vote, Webb. That's why you're where you are and why we're where we are. Thanks for giving us your opinion. I don't think we'll be needing you anymore today."

As he left Gould's office, Chris heard Tony instructing Fougere and Howe to draw up a term sheet and to brief Vanderpane prior to his next meeting with Okubu.

Ted Cutler, the head of the Central Credit Group, was smoking a cigar and reading a credit file. He was a big man, and the desk looked very small. The smoke rose past his thin white hair. Chris went into his office and sat on the sofa. An inch of cigar ash fell onto the credit file.

"You're pouting, Webb," Cutler said without looking up. "It's unbecoming."

"International Banking is about to commit to lead a billion-dollar syndication for Maraka."

"How much is our underwrite?"

41

"A hundred million."

"Final take?"

"Seventy-five."

"I was worried that you might be talking big money. You recommend we write it off now, or wait until the loan is drawn down?"

"For Christ's sake, Ted."

"Why do you get so exercised, young man? Once you learn that a banker and his money are soon parted, you'll be much happier."

"It's so goddamn stupid to piss money away like this."

"First stupid thing you've ever seen at Manhattan Banking, right?"

"Of course not."

"Well then."

"And all for self-aggrandizement."

"Young man, this is the late twentieth century. When ambition comes in the door, facts, conscience, ethics, and plain common sense all fly out the window. You're positively antediluvian. You've told Tough Tony you don't like it? And the cogent reasons why?"

"Yes."

"Have you put your disagreement and the reasons therefor in writing?"

"I will."

"Well, there you are, my boy." Cutler tapped cigar ash in the direction of his ashtray and missed. "Now let me tell you about one of our current crop of crackerjack lending officers.

"This person managed to get in to see me—a most unwelcome event, but not to be avoided because instead of protecting me from such mountebanks as you ought to have been, you were fooling around with Tony and his boys. This kid had the balls to make an oral proposal. I humored him rather than pitching him out on his ass. I asked him how the borrower was going to repay the loan. That stopped him for two seconds flat—these M.B.A.'s are good on their feet, which is not surprising, since that's what they think with—and then he said, 'What do you care, Ted, that's their problem,' all the while looking at me as if I'd just exposed myself. I told him I was sure he'd be much happier in an investment bank. *Then* I pitched him out on his ass.

"Look, Chris, with the peculiar loan approval setup we have, Gould if he cares enough can get any decision we make overruled anyway by going to Kincaid or Vanderpane. The best we can do in the circumstances is to try to minimize the damage. Now be a good boy and tell me the whole story."

5

Stewart hated to leave Hilary alone, but she had been too nervous even to have him around, much less to go to bed with him. As Paul drove him away from her compound, he could not rid his mind of the image of her standing in the middle of the sitting room watching the moth circle the lamp. The Volvo was going through the near-absolute darkness, the air conditioning running at high speed, when Paul jammed on the brakes and Stewart was thrown forward, putting out his arm just in time to prevent his hitting the back of the front seat.

"For Christ's sake, Paul, can't you be more careful?"

"I'm terribly sorry, sah, Mr. Stewart, that I have stopped so suddenly and have caused you to blaspheme, but there is something strange ahead."

Stewart looked through the windscreen. The road was dark all around except for the pool of the headlights straight in front of the car; but in the darkness farther ahead, he saw lights—electric torches he thought—waving this way and that. There didn't seem to be any particular pattern. Whatever it was, thought Stewart, it must be unpleasant, but if they turned around, there was no telling what might happen.

"Go ahead slowly, Paul," he decided. "I should have known you did what you did for a good reason."

"Thank you, sah."

The Volvo advanced slowly. Stewart sat on the edge of the back seat to the left of his driver, his elbows on top of the seat in front of him. Presently, he perceived that they were coming to a roadblock. He could see at least six heavily armed soldiers, two of whom kept their automatic rifles aimed, as far as he could tell, directly at Paul.

The car was closed because they had the air conditioning on. Stewart heard a clatter on the window to his left. A blinding light was shining into the car. When he opened the window, the barrel of a weapon was shoved at his face and a disembodied voice beyond the light said peremptorily, "Your papers."

Stewart handed out his passport, work permit, and identity card.

"Both." He meant Paul's as well.

"What's wrong?" Stewart asked, but he was ignored.

Both sets of papers were tossed back into the car, no attempt being made to hand them back. They fell at Nick's feet. The barrel of the weapon was withdrawn and the light was turned off. They were waved through.

A quarter of a mile beyond the roadblock, Stewart let out the breath he hadn't realized he'd been holding, and his heartbeat began to return to normal speed. It was only then that he allowed himself to be terrified over some bloody nervous fucker just out of the trees with a submachine gun held against his cheek. "What the hell was that about, Paul?"

"There were rumors tonight, sah. It was said that guerrillas had raided a police station in the city."

"Nothing else?"

"No, sah. I've heard no more. Just that. Guerrillas have raided a police station in the city."

It might or might not amount to anything, Stewart thought,

but this was the first time since he had been in Maraka that he
had been subjected to a roadblock and a heavily armed one at
that. There had been no telling how many more soldiers there
had been beyond the pool of lights.

Promptly at five-fifteen, Miles Vanderpane summoned his
driver Tommy and they left for Garrison. By the time the car was
creeping up the FDR Drive toward the George Washington
Bridge, the chairman was asleep. When he woke refreshed at six-
thirty, they were just turning into his driveway. They reversed
the ritual they had performed in the morning: Miles received his
attaché case from Tommy and returned Tommy's copy of the
Post.

The front door of the house was opened by the housekeeper as
he approached.

"Good evening, sir."

"Good evening, Mrs. Wilkes."

He put his attaché case onto the hall table and, as he did every
evening, looked interrogatively at Mrs. Wilkes.

"Mrs. Vanderpane is in the sitting room, sir."

"Thank you, Mrs. Wilkes."

Vanderpane went upstairs to his bedroom. He took off his coat
and tie and brushed his teeth. He put on a paisley ascot, a blue
velvet smoking jacket, and some well-worn dancing pumps, and
descended to the sitting room.

Samantha was reading an enormous tome—Peter Drucker or
someone like that—and offered her cheek to Miles.

"What would you like for a cocktail this evening, Sam?" he
said at the drinks tray.

"Make me one of your lovely martinis, Miles." She was wearing an Oxford-gray tailored pantsuit and a white blouse with a
loose bow at the neck and, he thought, looked very fine.
Straight, slim, a figure that could be compared favorably with
those of women twenty years her junior. Excellent woman that.
Wonderful helpmate. Rather romantic her asking for one of his
martinis. Miles Vanderpane felt stirrings he had not felt in a very

long time. He mixed the martinis carefully and got them well chilled before he poured them, straight up, with a twist.

He gave her a drink and took his own and sat in his favorite chair.

She sipped and looked at him with sparkling eyes. "Delicious as always, Miles."

"Thank you, Sam." He wondered if there would ever be any chance that they could get back to the way they had once been, back to their old footing of equality.

"Tell me about the Finance Minister."

His heart sank. He hadn't wanted to talk about business, but Sam was an irresistible force. He told her about the lunch.

"And what have you decided?"

"Fougere and John Howe are coming to see me tomorrow to discuss terms."

"Whose terms?"

"Our terms, Sam."

"Tony Gould's, more likely."

"I've told you the arguments for doing it, Sam. It's a little hard to see how we can avoid it." He felt defensive, which is not what he wanted to feel in his own sitting room; she sometimes had the same effect on him as Tony Gould had.

"No dissenting votes?"

"No. Well, yes, one, if you want to call it that. Chris Webb from Central Credit."

"He reports to Ted Cutler?"

Vanderpane nodded.

"Well, I'm glad to see there is somebody with some sense. What were his arguments?"

He supposed she had no idea how wounding she could be. "He said he thought that Maraka's debt burden was growing too quickly. And that they were going to have a revolution in the next year or two."

"And how did you answer his points?"

"We said that a rapidly growing debt burden was normal in a developing country and that revolution was irrelevant."

47

"Irrelevant?" She could not keep the incredulity out of her voice.

"Irrelevant to the repayment of loans."

"Miles, from all I've read, Maraka is going to have a debt service problem very soon. And one of the reasons is that the politicians are skimming so much off every transaction into their Swiss bank accounts that the country's balance of payments has been seriously eroded."

"Webb said something like that."

"Webb was right."

"What can we do, Sam? Really, a bank can't afford to be a fair-weather friend. And how about all our multinational customers who are depending on us to finance their sales in Maraka? I agree with Tony Gould there."

"Dear, dear Miles," she said quietly, "when are you going to see that Tony Gould is leading you around by the nose? He's after your job, Miles, and if you're not careful, he's going to get it."

Miles was depressed. It seemed that he and Samantha had this conversation, or some variation thereof, at least once a week now, and it was not something he really wanted to think about. He knew that Tony Gould was a force to be reckoned with, but he didn't know what to do about him.

"Miles, if the Maraka loan succeeds and makes a big splash, you'll find that it was due to Tony Gould's initiative, perspicacity, and aggressiveness. And if it goes sour, it would not surprise me if ultimately you were blamed."

But in spite of her gloomy prediction, Sam came as always to his aid. Although he had to admit he didn't know quite what she intended, her words at first troubled him, and then comforted him.

"Miles, I want to give a small dinner party here. Just a few people from the bank. Tony Gould and his mousy little wife, Maureen. Ghastly. Sounds like an Irish housemaid."

"Are you sure you want to do this, dearest?"

"Absolutely. And I want the Houstons and the Pelletiers."

"Whatever you'd like, dearest."

"It's not what I'd like, Miles, it's what will do you the most good. And believe me, it will do you a world of good. I want a couple of friendly directors to see what that little turd is really like."

Samantha's eyes were glistening with excitement; so much was she taken with her idea, although she revealed very little of what she was thinking to Miles, that she told Mrs. Wilkes that dinner was to be delayed a half hour, and she asked him to make her another martini.

When he sat back down, feeling rather mellow and comfortable himself, he said, "Most peculiar little thing happened at lunch today. Nothing really to do with what we've been talking about. But we had three visitors from Maraka, one of whom was never introduced, and whom everyone ignored."

Samantha put her drink onto the coffee table. Vanderpane hurried on. "There were Okubu and Kalama, as I told you, and this third fellow. Very black, nodded pleasantly, said nothing, stood in a corner throughout the meal absolutely unnoticed as far as I could tell. Since he hadn't been introduced, I made no gesture to include him. Do you think I should have?"

Samantha looked carefully at her husband, then leaned over and took his hand.

"Do you feel well, Miles?"

He melted at her touch. "Never felt better. Physically, that is. I won't pretend that all this talk about Tony Gould hasn't upset me."

"That third man, Miles," she said. "A bodyguard, do you think?"

"That's it, Sam. Clever girl. I'm sure that's what he was."

Webb stayed at his desk until nearly seven, recording his objections to the Marakan loan on a yellow legal pad, citing a source for every fact and coming to what he thought was the inevitable conclusion. And he knew it would do no good at all.

When he had finished the draft to his satisfaction, he locked it in his desk, put on his raincoat, and walked to the elevator.

He caught a Madison Avenue bus at Fifty-third Street. It was

49

early enough so that most of the people on the bus looked normal, except for a young black in a knitted red, green, and black cap who was spread-eagled across all the seats in the last row and who stared ferociously at nothing. No one went near him, but Webb thought he looked too far gone on whatever it was he sniffed or injected to be any problem to anyone. He wondered if his forebears had been kidnapped from Maraka by slave traders.

By the time he got to their apartment on Eighty-third Street, he was in a real depression.

"Little Boy Blue," Catherine said, kissing him lightly on the lips when he came in. He grunted and took off his raincoat and hung it in the closet.

"Would you like to hear about my day, sweetheart?" she said. "I can tell about yours by looking at you."

Webb grunted again and sat in the living room. Their cat, William of Orange, looked at him and walked away, sensing his mood.

"Let's go to Teddy's tonight, Chris."

"Goddammit, Cath, we're going to go broke eating out. You ever going to cook anymore?"

She tossed the newspaper he had brought her onto the coffee table.

"Goddammit, Chris, I had a hell of a day and I goddamn well don't goddamn feel like cooking goddammit. And if you want a nice home-cooked meal just like mother used to make, you can goddamn well make it yourself."

The whole thing was said virtually without heat—with a kind of quiet exhilaration almost—which told Webb that she was very serious and very tired, and confirmed what he already knew, which was that he was being stupid and self-indulgent.

"I'm sorry, Cath. That place gets to me."

"How about Teddy's?"

He looked at his wife for the first time since he had come home: at the short dark-brown hair and the intelligent blue eyes, and the dimple in her chin, and he loved her very much.

"Sure," he said.

Teddy's was an old-fashioned New York neighborhood bar,

with draft Budweiser, hamburgers, homemade French fries, and no Muzak. Occasionally someone came in to play the upright piano, a jazz musician between gigs, just for the hell of it. Teddy's certainly didn't pay him. The place was an anachronism, from the wooden booths and the red-checked tablecloths and the horseshoe-shaped mahogany bar, to the two beefy Irish bartenders, George and Brian, who were in their mid-fifties—hardly the skinny androgynous types in tight designer jeans in the singles places who got really short-tempered when you interrupted one of their *intime* conversations by asking them for a drink.

Webb mourned for his lost New York, the one he knew in the early sixties, when people still had a sense of community. When people had not yet withdrawn behind the locked front doors of their buildings, behind the locked front doors of their boxlike apartments with paper-thin walls and their neighbors' marital problems and cocktail parties in their own living rooms; when the people you talked to were not always wondering if you were important and how you could be used.

Who had unmade New York? The what of it—taxes, overborrowing, the influx of the poor and unskilled, the lack of maintenance of the city fabric, the ass-backwards welfare system, the political theft, the bureaucratic theft—yes, there was all that. But someone was responsible—someones really—the crooks, the incompetent, the thoughtless, all those who never considered the consequences.

New York was now a public relations triumph, where developers ignored the spirit of zoning laws, destroyed the grand and replaced it with the grandiose, and got richer and richer doing it; where overpriced boutiques with arrogant salesclerks closed at lunchtime to keep out the riffraff, while the rats gnawed the foundations and ran down Park Avenue, and the potholes were so deep they destroyed buses and cars. Big apple, my ass.

There was no booth free so they sat at the bar.

"Hello, Catherine," George said. "Hi, Chris. Usual?"

They both nodded, and George drew a pitcher of Bud.

"Make any bad loans today, Chris?" the bartender asked as he poured their first glasses from the pitcher.

51

"Yup," Webb said into his glass.

"Honey," Catherine said, and put her hand on his arm.

"If you say nothing and something goes wrong, you're blamed. If you're wrong, you're criticized. And if you're right, you're never forgiven."

"You're talking about your Maraka meeting?"

"Yes. No. I'm talking about the bank. Maraka is just the most recent symptom."

"They're going to make the loan?"

Webb nodded. "George, can we have two burgers, medium rare, with lettuce, tomato, and mayonnaise, French fries on one."

"Coming up," George said.

"Yup, Cath, they're going to make the loan." He told her about the meetings.

"But, Chris, why should you worry about it anymore? You told them what you thought and they decided otherwise. It seems to me that's all there is to it. How can you be blamed?"

"That's not what's bothering me, Cath. What bothers me is that decisions are made without reference to facts so obvious you trip over them. Someone is right because of his position, not because he knows anything. And I've never known us to think about doing anything more wrong than this loan to Maraka. That money will go into a lot of big-deal projects that are never going to be finished, while the president and the generals and the ministers all pay themselves enormous commissions for arranging all the deals and put the money into bank accounts in Switzerland."

"But why should the bank want to make such a loan?"

"Because it's big and flashy. It'll attract a lot of attention to the bank and the people who put the deal together, and they think it'll make a lot of money. Gould will give a lot of press conferences, and will opine with great wisdom on practically everything. And he'll get some more praise in meetings of the board and move one step ahead in his drive to become chairman. And when the thing goes belly-up two years from now, no one will remember that Tough Tony was the guy pushing it. Some poor bastard will get dumped on and a lot of officers and lawyers will be going to meetings to reschedule Maraka's debt, at great cost to the bank. All for Tony Gould's ambition to be chairman and management's refusal to consider anything but short-term results."

Brian brought the hamburgers and filled their glasses again and they began to eat.

"Why should your corporation be any different from any other corporation, Chris? Last week we made a two-million-dollar offer for a piece of soft-core pornography written by someone who couldn't put together a coherent note to the milkman. Today we found out we lost. The book got two and a half million. How many first novels will not be published now? Short-term results are all that matter to managements the world over. All Tony Gould is doing is reading the signals he gets from the bank's management."

"It's all bullshit."

"Of course it's all bullshit. It's not worth worrying about, sweetheart. And it's certainly not worth getting sick over. The thing to do is to maintain your integrity and your principles and always do what you think is right. And the hell with the rest of it."

"The Emperor has no new clothes."

"Never did," Catherine said.

"Have I told you you're my favorite editor?"

"Not for a week or so."

"And that I love you?"

"Not this evening."

"Then you're my favorite editor and I love you."

"Well, that's neat about the last part, but I'm not sure about the first part."

They walked back from Teddy's through the cool April night in silence. Catherine was right, of course. It wasn't worth worrying about. Ted Cutler had said the same thing. But Chris couldn't exorcise the depression.

Catherine squeezed his hand. "I don't like the way you're breathing, Chris. Holding your breath and then expelling it forcefully. You're trying to blow off the pressure. You're letting yourself be eaten up by this thing."

"I'll get over it, honey," he responded, conscious for the first time that he had been breathing oddly.

"I'll have to put you to bed and give you Aunt Catherine's Magic Treatment."

"Sounds positively incestuous."

Ben Kincaid was round and soft. He had thick sandy hair and little dark eyes set close together. He was from Alton, Illinois, by way of MIT and the Harvard Business School, and he was president of the Manhattan Banking Corporation.

Ben Kincaid saw the future as clearly as he saw his digital watch. He would succeed Miles Vanderpane when Miles took early retirement, and he was going to have Tony Gould made president. Then he was going to get the board to create the position of vice-chairman and he was going to make two of them. And Tony Gould was going to learn that succeeding Ben Kincaid as chairman was not going to be a shoo-in.

Tony Gould, who didn't know the rest of Ben's plans, knew that Ben wanted him to be president. But he thought that Ben's idea of president and his own differed. President meant nothing if he weren't chief executive officer. He had discussed this philosophically with two directors who were CEOs themselves and would understand, two directors who seemed to listen intently to his ideas about the bank. He didn't care if he were made chairman or president, as long as he also became CEO. For the time being, however, he was happy to let Ben dream his dreams, whatever they were.

At six-thirty, Gould went across the floor to Kincaid's office to keep the appointment he'd made earlier in the day. Kincaid was sitting in an overstuffed chair by the extension to the telephone he had on his desk. He was reading *Women's Wear Daily*, eating peanuts from a bowl resting on the arm of his chair, and drinking Dr. Pepper from a can. He was in shirt-sleeves that were rolled up to midforearm, and his feet were propped comfortably on the coffee table. Gould looked diffidently through the open doorway.

"Come in, Tony." Kincaid waved the paper. "What's up?"

Gould briefed him on the Maraka loan and the discussions surrounding it. He was organized, clear, succinct.

"So we're going to be financing some more wogs." And roared with laughter. "Correct that. Same wogs, more financing." And roared again.

Gould chuckled politely.

"Anything else on your mind, Antoine?"

"Ted Cutler's group is a bit . . . I don't think they're as constructive as they might be."

"Well, Tony, you know what their mandate is. In a way they're supposed to be the corporate sons of bitches. Good for everybody. Keeps everybody on their toes. You want some Dr. Pepper?"

"No thanks, Ben. No, that's not what I mean. But you can do a job like that in a positive way or you can do it in a negative way. Maybe it's not the whole credit group. But take the Maraka deal. It's a chance to get the syndication boys back on track, get some good earnings, protect balances, satisfy a lot of multinational corporations who are customers of ours, demonstrate that we know which end is up. And all I get from a guy like Webb is obstruction."

"Webb? Chris Webb? Seems to me he's a pretty bright guy. Pretty savvy too. What happened, Antoine? He ask some embarrassing questions?"

"Wouldn't argue with you at all, Ben. He is bright. But maybe he's been in that job too long. Lost some perspective. Taken the job of being a corporate son of a bitch too seriously."

"Meaning?"

"Meaning maybe he needs a transfer. Back to international banking. He did a hell of a job for us before. No reason why he can't do one again—once he shakes the cobwebs out of his head. I think he needs some experience in the field."

Kincaid's eyes seemed to grow smaller and more close together. "I'll think about it, Tony," he said finally. He looked at his watch. "Time to drag these old bones home. Can I give you a ride uptown, son?"

"Thanks, no, Ben. I'll be here another couple of hours or so."

"So be it." Kincaid rose from his chair and went to his desk. He opened his attaché case and upended his in-box into it and snapped the case shut. He punched the intercom. "Henry, tell my driver to get his ass in gear."

"Yes, sir," said the intercom.

"Good night, Tony. If you want some Dr. Pepper, there's a lot more in the icebox. Help yourself to the nuts."

"Good night, Ben. Thanks."

For the next hour Tony Gould prepared the report on first-quarter results that he was going to give to the department two days later. He intended to come down hard on expenses, which had been increasing at a faster rate than revenues; but while the department wasn't doing badly, the bank as a whole was not doing well, particularly because of the lack of growth in earnings in Domestic Banking, and increasing loan losses in both departments.

He then outlined a few ideas for establishing a regional banking office in Africa, to service all of sub-Saharan Africa. There was no question that Maraka was the place for it, and with the new syndication on everyone's mind, no better time to broach the subject. He would tackle Vanderpane and Kincaid about it at morning coffee, and made a note to that effect on his calendar.

Maybe the computer liquidity project was the job for Webb, he thought. No, he would only start complaining about the math. No, Tony thought, he'd arrange something altogether different for Chris Webb; he'd second-guessed Tony Gould once too often.

Gould left the bank at twenty minutes past eight, waving good night to the night security people who knew him well. He found a cab on Madison Avenue and reached his apartment twenty minutes later.

Maureen, wrapped in a printed cotton bathrobe, was in the study watching television.

"Hello, Maureen." He leaned over and kissed her forehead.

"Hello, Tony. Good day?"

"All in all, I think so. Yes. Fairly satisfying. Have you eaten?"

"Yes. There's some stew in the oven for you."

"Thanks. How are the kids?" he said and walked out of the room.

"Sally has set herself up as a child prostitute and John has been kidnapped," Maureen said in a monotone.

Gould went into the kitchen and pulled the casserole from the oven. He put the tepid stew onto his plate, poured a small glass of red wine, and cut a slice of French bread. He sat at the kitchen table at a place that was already set. While he ate he thought about his scheme for reorganizing the Far East/North Division. They needed shaking up: they were getting too comfortable. Success was making them soft. Ten minutes later he noticed that his plate was empty. He left the plate and the glass in the sink and walked out of the kitchen, turning out the light.

He went back into the study, where Maureen was still watching television. He wondered vaguely how much television she watched and whether she had been in her bathrobe all day.

"I think I'll turn in, Maureen. It's been a long day."

"Good night, Tony. Every day's a long day, isn't it?"

He hesitated a moment, but kissed her forehead anyway, deciding she had not meant to be sarcastic, and left the room. Maureen Gould stared at the television screen.

When he changed into his pajamas, the pang of regret he felt when he contemplated his limp penis was fleeting; all of that had been part of his life that belonged to his adolescence and was now past. Tony put on a video recording of his speech in March to the American Financial Executives Association concerning future developments in international capital markets. He felt it had been one of his best performances, and he wanted to critique it again. Within a few minutes, however, he was asleep.

57

6

One morning a week, very early, before the temperature went above eighty, Nick Stewart played forty-five minutes of tennis at the Maraka City Club with Tom Fraeser, the Bankers Trust representative. Fraeser was doing him a favor: he was much too good a player for Nick, he was fifteen years younger, and even the beard he wore didn't slow him down.

As they walked off the court, Nick told Fraeser about the roadblock.

"Nasty," Fraeser said, "especially for someone like you who has to jump-start his pacemaker every morning. I heard about the guerrilla raid last night too, but every Marakan I talked to clammed up about it."

Stewart opened the peeling door into the locker room. "By the way, Tom, we may have a deal for you."

"If you're talking about the jumbo, Nick baby, I think you can forget about us. We're up to our term limit on Maraka. And not everyone, including your present interlocutor, is overjoyed about the risk anyway."

Stewart shrugged and went to shower before he returned home.

When Ahmed brought his breakfast on the veranda behind the house overlooking the fortified garden, Stewart asked him about the raid on the police station.

"I know nothing more, sah," Ahmed replied.

"That's not like you, Ahmed."

"Truly, sah. There was a raid in the capital. Nothing more." And withdrew with more than the usual deference. It suggested to Stewart while he ate his mangoes that Ahmed knew a hell of a lot more than he was letting on.

Nick scanned the *Maraka Observer*, the English-language daily, while his coffee cooled. There wasn't anything about the raid; but no doubt the paper had been printed too early for the incident to have made the morning news.

For a long time, the government had maintained that the guerrilla activity was sporadic, poorly organized and equipped, and confined largely to the grim northwestern provinces (large manganese deposits), where the guerrillas were strongly resisted by the People's Army, informed on by the local populace, and in fact could hardly have existed at all except for their sanctuaries in the rain forests across the border in Nigeria. The raid on the police station might have been cosmetic, or it might have been something more—perhaps the Army's stout defense was losing weight. Would it at the end of the day make any difference to Manhattan Banking or to getting the loan done? Stewart thought not, but he thought also that he would mention the raid to Fougere when he talked to him later.

Stewart was in the office by eight o'clock. He found a Telex from John Howe and Max Fougere outlining the terms that were going to be offered to the Finance Minister; he thought they were rather fine terms, but he had long before learned not to question or worry about the wisdom of New York in these matters. Most of the time they were right anyway, and the few times they were wrong, an appropriate scapegoat was found. If they were wrong about Maraka, the scapegoat would not be Nick Stewart; he'd been dancing too long to Tony Gould's tune, because it got him what he wanted. When it ceased to do that, he would tell Manhattan Banking Corporation and Tony Gould to get stuffed.

He drafted a letter to Colin Mackintosh of the United Bank of Maraka increasing his line of credit and left the handwritten sheets on Miss Temba's desk. Then he returned to his own office. He rang Hilary's home number; no answer there, nor was anyone yet at her office—probably on the way.

He was comfortably settled in his chair with his feet on the desk, plowing through a week's *Financial Times*, when the phone rang.

"This is George Maguire, Nick. You got some time to drop by this morning?"

George Maguire represented Childs Construction and Engineering, a big American firm that never bothered with anything smaller than airports or cities. They were at present extending Maraka City harbor and putting in a new runway and terminal at Maraka International Airport. They were very big customers of Manhattan Banking.

"Sure, George. What's up?"

"Like to talk about the new deal you guys got on your plate."

"About ten?"

"Super."

They might not be able to feed their own goddamn population, but Stewart had to admire their organization. The pressure was beginning to come in from all sides. Just in case there was any backsliding. Shit, he didn't need any persuading.

He heard Jocelyn Temba in the outer office, and wandered out to see if the mail had come in. Most mornings, she gave off a kind of glow, having been well serviced the night before. But today, he was taken aback by her appearance. She looked drawn and worn, and older than she was. He thought briefly that perhaps she had taken on one of the whips-and-chains Germans;

but he realized that there was something deeper. Miss Temba was worried.

"Good morning, Jocelyn. How are you?"

"Very well, Mr. Stewart."

He looked at her as she sat at her desk inspecting the blotter with great interest.

"I must say you don't look very well."

At which Miss Temba threw her head back and laughed loudly and forcedly, with no smile. "I think I ought to be getting more sleep, Nick, if you know what I mean. Come, why don't you buy me a cup of coffee?"

She rose and took his arm and led him out of the office. There were several strange things going on. First was the warning look she gave him with her large, dark, dark eyes, which would have quite overwhelmed Stewart except for the fear he saw in them. Second, she had never called him Nick. Then—despite the sexual fantasies he had entertained about Jocelyn Temba—he had never shared a glass of water, much less coffee or anything else with her. And she had never, ever touched him.

They rode the lift down in silence. When they reached the stifling street, he followed her across to the dusty park on the opposite side. They walked slowly along the dirt path that led through the tattered palms. She held his arm and walked closely to him, in such a way as there would be no doubt in the mind of any observer that they were physically intimate.

"I'm sorry to be so familiar, Mr. Stewart."

He shook his head at her apology.

"You have heard about the raid last night on the police station?"

Indeed he had; thought nothing of it.

"It was . . . it was someone close to me, Mr. Stewart."

Good Christ. "I'm sorry, Jocelyn. I'm not quite certain—"

"Someone I know very well—please don't ask me who, Mr. Stewart, for your own sake—someone I know well led the raid. There were policemen killed. I am afraid, Mr. Stewart. I am afraid they will try to get revenge."

61

"I can't see how they can hold you responsible, Jocelyn."

"Because I have nothing to do with what happened? That doesn't matter to them, Mr. Stewart." The strain showed in her face. "I'm sorry, Mr. Stewart. You perhaps have not been here long enough to know how things work here. I'm not even so much afraid for myself, but for my mother, or my son."

Stewart was surprised that he knew so little about her that he had not known she had a son. Well, after all, she had joined the bank as Miss Temba. He wondered briefly if he could do anything for her, through the bank, perhaps, but decided not. It was a shame to think that such an excellent example of womanhood, at the moment pressing closely to him from shoulder to hip—he stole a glance at the breasts pressing against her thin blouse—should get herself into such a pickle.

"You may be worrying over nothing, Jocelyn."

She laughed again, without mirth, and walked ahead of him, disappearing around a corner of the path. When Stewart turned the corner himself, she was nowhere to be seen. He stood for a moment in the oppressive sunlight, the smell of dust and human excrement in his nostrils, and decided to turn back in the direction they had come. There was a black man in the path not far behind, who stepped aside when Stewart approached, and nodded and smiled. Nick nodded in return. He never saw Jocelyn Temba again.

Of course, he did not know it at the time. He assumed simply that she was much too upset to work and had gone off to be alone. The modest anxiety he felt he forced himself to ignore.

Nonetheless, his anxiety increased when he called Hilary's office just before his meeting with Childs and learned that she had not come in yet.

George Maguire was a large man, an engineer by training who, one felt, would have been far more at ease on a construction site with a hard hat on than he was sitting in an air-conditioned office behind a desk. He waved Stewart to a sofa, picked up a file from his desk, and sat in a chair opposite the sofa.

"You want coffee, Nick?"

"No, thanks, George."

"You all going to do this billion bucks that Maraka is looking for?"

"Now, George, you can't expect me—"

"Aw, cut the shit, Nick. Don't give me any of that confidential crap. Okay, we'll play it straight. Let's talk hypothetically. If you were approached by the Republic of Maraka to put together a billion-dollar deal, would you do it?"

"On the right terms, I think yes."

"What do you mean by 'the right terms'?"

"A combination of spread and fees."

"Ah."

"What on earth did you think I meant?" Stewart began to feel uncomfortable, despite the effective air conditioning.

"Never mind. We can go into that later. I think it's safe to say, Nick, that if old Manhattan Banking didn't go along on this one, we'd be mighty pissed off. So would a lot of other companies, I expect, but of course I can't talk for them. We might even decide to review our relationships with our bankers."

The events of the preceding evening, followed by Jocelyn Temba's peculiar behavior this morning, and—yes, Stewart had to admit it to himself—his inability to get in touch with Hilary, had begun to tell on him. Maguire's rapacious American ham fist pushed him over the edge.

"What's the matter, George? The Marakan Airport Authority becoming a bit slow in its payments?"

Maguire stood and walked over to his desk, but not before Stewart saw that the blood had drained from his face. Touched a nerve there, did I, George? Nick said to himself. Looking very pale, Maguire turned around.

"Shit goddamn, Nick, do you know how much dough there is to be made in this country? We got tenders out on ten projects, and we got a lot of competition for them. I could spend the rest of my career here."

"Do you want to, George?"

"Oh for Chrissake, Nick, stick to the point. Hell, yeah, they

63

got cash flow problems. But that's just now. When all these things start paying off, they're going to pay off big."

"I'll bet."

"Look, what the hell do you guys want?"

Stewart was beginning to wonder where this was all going to lead. He knew that he was not going to have anything to say about whether or not the bank did the loan, and Maguire was one of the guys in the driver's seat, because Manhattan Banking needed Childs Construction a lot more than Childs, with ten world-class banks on a string, needed Manhattan Banking; but strangely enough, George Maguire was beginning to sound a little shrill, almost a little desperate.

"Bankers always have one simple question, George, and that is, how are we going to get paid back? Maybe the answer isn't so simple though."

George Maguire was looking uncomfortable, and Nick Stewart was beginning to enjoy the rare sense of having the upper hand. He decided to press the advantage.

"Maguire, you once told me that Childs doesn't go into any venture unless it can see its way clear to earning twenty percent on a full equity basis. But you demanded eighty percent finance from us when you went into that joint venture that's doing the harbor. So if it all works out, you and your partners get a ninety-eight percent return on your investment and your bankers get a half percent *per annum* and take most of the risk. Frankly I think that's horseshit."

"All right, Nick. Okay. Let's talk turkey. What do you want?"

"I don't understand you, George."

"What do you want to support the deal? To make it fly?"

When Stewart realized what George Maguire was asking him, he had an odd sensation. He understood then that the pressure that was being brought to bear was not the kind he had anticipated, and was a lot more complicated than he could have imagined. He did understand that George Maguire, big and red and beefy in his big office with the air conditioning that never seemed to break down, was scared.

"Don't worry, George. I'll support the deal."

"I wasn't kidding, Nick. Anything—within reason, of course—you say, paid wherever you say."

"What's within reason?"

"Twenty-five grand?"

Stewart let the words sink in before he responded. He was enjoying keeping Maguire on edge.

"I'll get back to you on that, George."

Maguire insisted that they have a neat bourbon from his liquor cabinet to seal their agreement that Nick would support the deal in return for a consideration, although he was clearly upset that he didn't know what Stewart was going to ask for; and it was a matter on which Nick refused to be drawn.

Stewart walked back to his office through the dirt and heat and noise and stink, his stomach churning from the liquor and his mind a blank. When he reached the outer office, he remembered that Jocelyn probably wouldn't be back that day, and he went quickly through the mail that the office boy had left on her desk, but there was nothing of importance. Then he went into his own office, drew the blinds to prevent the sun from penetrating, and turned the air-conditioner up full.

At the end of a half hour of staring into the gloom, he thought he might make a stab at what was going on. Maguire was managing director of Childs Construction and Engineering Pte. (Maraka) Ltd., and in that capacity he had committed a lot of money (much of it owed to Manhattan Banking and other international banks) and Childs equipment and know-how to Maraka. And no doubt George had bribed his share of officials to get the business, and no doubt George had taken his cut also. But now he was frightened. And it was possible that George Maguire, with a lot of his people out in the bush, knew more than the rest of them. It was possible that George was beginning to realize that he'd made a mistake committing Childs so heavily in Maraka. And it might be that George was trying to salvage something out of it by ensuring that Maraka was in funds to make some payments. And was trying to cover his ass by saying that, for Chrissake, at the time Maraka was going belly-up, Manhattan Banking was lending them a billion dollars.

Stewart decided to skip talking to Fougere and to go direct to Tony Gould. He couldn't prove anything, but his doubts were strong enough to be voiced.

Hilary rang through.

"Where the hell have you been?"

"I was trying to be a reporter, Nick. Don't be annoyed with me."

"I'm not, old girl."

"Can we lunch?"

"I've booked a call to New York for around one."

"We'll make it quick. Let's go to the Wog's."

The Wog's, which was really called the Bombay Palace, was an Indian restaurant on the second floor of Stewart's office building.

"Good idea," Nick said. It was ten to twelve. "Meet me there now?"

"On my way," she said, and rang off.

Nick waited for her just inside the doorway of the Wog's and drank a Cheetah lager. She came rushing in, flushed and sweating, hair askew, and kissed him lightly on the cheek. They sat down immediately and ordered what they always ordered, which was kid vindaloo, okra, chana dal, and naan. The waiter brought a Cheetah for Hilary and a second for Stewart.

"Tell me what you didn't want to say to me over the phone."

"I've talked to all my usual contacts, Nick. None of them will say anything about this raid on the police station."

"Do you know if it's true that some policemen were killed?"

Her eyes grew wide. "No. I mean, I don't know. Where on earth did you hear that?"

"Miss Temba."

"Can I talk to her?"

"I don't know where she is. We went out for a walk in the park—oh for heaven's sake, Hilary, it was so that we could talk—and she . . . well, she just disappeared after we talked."

"What did she tell you?"

"Is this for attribution, or just deep background?"

"I'm sorry, Nick. I was being pushy. You don't have to answer if you don't want to."

In fact, he was weighing whether he ought to tell her any more, particularly as he sensed that they were being watched constantly now.

"Miss Temba told me that she was very close to the people who led the raid."

"Good God."

"And she was very frightened."

They were silent when the food was brought, and they began to eat. Stewart ordered two more Cheetahs and wondered whether he ought to tell her about George Maguire, but he decided against it. In fact, the more he thought about his conversation with Maguire the more unreal it seemed, and the less there was to talk to Gould about. After all, it was only an educated guess on his part about why Maguire should offer him a bribe. The man may have been in Maraka so long that he may have got used to giving bribes to everyone as a matter of course, as a way of doing business. Without some evidence, Gould would blow him out of the water. Once Tony had set his mind on doing something, he was not receptive to anything that would force him to think twice about it.

And Nick Stewart knew as well as Maguire knew that Maraka City was a hot, stinking, filthy, dangerous place, that he wasn't going to say a goddamn word to Tony Gould about any of it because his phone was tapped, and because Tony would hear about it anyway.

"I'm sorry, Hilary. I was off somewhere."

"I said, can you give me her address?"

"Whose address?"

"Miss Temba's."

"I don't know it. It's probably back in the office. If you're ready, we can go up now. I'll make some coffee."

Nick paid the bill and held the door into the corridor for Hilary. Just before the door shushed shut, he saw a large black man stand and leave his table before he had finished his meal.

The man on the switchboard was just taking the call from New York as they came in the front door of the office.

"Is it Gould?" Stewart said.

"No, sir. Only the operator."

"I'm not here."

"Yes, sir."

Stewart went into his office and unlocked the file drawer in which he kept the personnel records. "She lives in New Road, Hilary. That's not a good area for you to be."

"Never mind, Nick. I'll be careful. Where in New Road?"

"You're not being the good girl you promised you were going to be. And you're being followed, darling."

"I know. He's rather attractive."

"Hilary, do you think you might stop playing the plucky lass?" He held up his hand and scribbled on a pad, "These people mean business."

She read it and said, "Where in New Road, Nick?"

He consulted the file. "It says, 'gray house near the water pump.'"

She kissed him and left. "Don't you want some coffee?" he said, but the door clicked shut behind her.

Stewart asked that the call to New York—to Fougere this time—be put through again, and returned to his office. He spent an hour drafting a confidential memo to Tony Gould describing the conversation that he had had with Maguire and the conclusions that might be drawn from it. He was careful not to say that they were his conclusions, so that Tony wouldn't blow his top, but something told Stewart that he could be blamed if he said nothing. If Gould chose to dismiss it or ignore it, that was his problem, not Nick's.

At three-thirty, the operator rang through to tell him that Jimmy Moshu was on the line.

"Good afternoon, Jimmy," Stewart said heartily. *What the hell is it now, you creepy black bastard?*

"Good afternoon, Nick. Have you talked to New York yet?"

"Not yet, Jimmy," *as if you didn't know.* "In fact, I'm waiting for a call to come through now."

"I'll get off then, Nick. But after you've talked to them, do you think you could run up here to the Ministry?"

"If all goes well, Jimmy, how about five."

"That would be fine, Nick. But sooner if you can."

That mildest of hints again: *or else I shall make it unpleasant for you.*

"As soon as I can."

"Lovely. Good-bye."

In fact, his call to Max Fougere came through right after he had hung up.

"Nick, how are you. You rang Tony before?"

"I did, Max, but I couldn't take it when it came through. One of the hazards of the posting."

"It's your nickel."

"The billion-dollar syndication, Max. Just wanted to inform you that there's a lot of heavy pressure to have us commit. I've had drinks with a man named Moshu—"

"What?"

"Moshu. Jimmy Moshu, Deputy Finance Minister. Nice, intelligent chap, and very, very interested in having the bank do the deal. Virtually said it's time for Maraka's friends to stand up and be counted."

"Yes. Okubu took the same tack. Did they tell you about the oil?"

"Oh, hell yes. Very exciting development. It'll make a syndication a hell of a lot easier."

"Anything else?"

"Had a meeting with Childs Construction. *They're* looking to us to do the deal too."

"Yes, that fits. Tony thought the multinationals would be watching to see what we did. We all have a stake in Maraka, Nick."

"Absolutely."

"How's the political situation?"

"Stable, as far as I can tell. Government is functioning smoothly, Tena Maraka is in firm control."

"I missed that last part. You faded out."

69

"I said, 'Tena Maraka'—you know, the President, the Father of Maraka—'is in firm control.'"

"How about the guerrillas?"

"Nothing much, Max. The odd raid on a police station. Doesn't even make the papers anymore."

"I thought that was about the level of activity. Did you get the terms we are going to propose on the Telex?"

"I did, Max. Very fine, aren't they?"

"They are. But Maraka's becoming an oil producer introduces a new element. As if being one of the richest countries in black Africa weren't enough. I do want to make sure that our man on the spot supports the deal."

"I'm on the winning team, Max."

"That's fine, Nick. Let me have your agreement on the Telex, will you?"

"Will do, Max." Not bloody likely. "Never sign anything" was the first maxim of survival at Manhattan Banking.

After he had hung up, Stewart wondered if his simple-minded replies to Fougere's questions could take anyone in; but he had been helped by Fougere's own simple-minded questions, which were as insincere as Nick's answers, the only difference between them being that he knew that Fougere was insincere, and Fougere didn't know he knew. In any event, the secret police had gotten an earful of Manhattan Banking's support for Maraka.

The most important ministries—Defense, Finance, State Security (which is to say, the secret police), and Planning—were located in a series of identical, ugly, white blocks in a vast park on the hill below the pleasant proportions and wide verandas of the Presidential Palace, which used to be Government House when Maraka was a British colony. From the Palace on the hill that commanded a fine view of the city and the harbor beyond— and coincidentally provided an unobstructed field of fire at least to the long, low ministry buildings a quarter of a mile down the slope—the Father of Maraka, who had been in office since independence was granted in 1964, looked after the welfare of his people.

Nick had always enjoyed his visits to Government Hill because after his car had been allowed through the heavily guarded gates, they could drive along a pleasant road that wound through gardens that were well cared for, beyond the heat and noise and smells of Maraka City. The respite was always too brief, however; the trees and luxuriant plantings stopped and a smooth greensward began well in front of the Ministry of Planning. The car slalomed past and Paul stopped it in front of the steps leading into the Finance Ministry. Once again they had to produce their identification papers before Stewart was allowed out of the car and Paul issued a temporary parking permit and told where to put the car.

Once inside, however, Stewart was greeted warmly by Jimmy Moshu, who, Stewart was certain, must already have heard a tape of his conversation with Max Fougere.

Moshu's office was not large, but was well air-conditioned, and furnished with comfortable chairs covered in soft beige leather. From the large windows, Stewart could see the vessels in the harbor.

"May I get you something to drink, Nick?"

"A Cheetah would be fine, Jimmy."

"You really like it?"

"It's excellent. You ought to export it to the EEC. I think you could give the Continental lagers a run for their money."

"Really? Would you finance it?"

"Definitely."

"I must say that Manhattan Banking has precisely the sort of representative in Maraka we wish they all were." He took a bottle of beer and a container of orange juice from the small refrigerator flanking a bookcase behind his desk.

When Moshu was comfortably seated across a low table from Nick, they raised their glasses and said "Cheers," and Stewart asked, "But you don't drink Cheetah yourself, though?"

"No. I'm afraid I had more than enough beer in my under-graduate days at Oxford." Moshu sipped his orange juice with apparent relish. "By now you've talked to New York?"

Stewart nodded. "I told them I supported the deal, Jimmy. I

71

don't think they really needed my support, but the bank requires that the man *in situ* support the deal or it's no go. I cannot imagine there won't be a meeting of minds when Mr. Okubu sees Miles Vanderpane tomorrow."

"That's lovely, Nick. Thank you very much indeed for your vote of confidence in us."

Fighting back his tears, Nick said, "Have you shopped the deal around?"

Jimmy Moshu smiled as if he were humoring an imbecile. "Oh, yes. Mr. Okubu would not have been able to hold up his head before Tena Maraka if he hadn't."

Or keep it, I should imagine, Nick thought.

"Nonetheless, Nick, between us, I agree with you. There will be a meeting of minds, and I think Manhattan Banking will get the mandate. Let me get you another beer. There are a couple of other things I'd like to talk to you about. Do you have a bit of time?"

"Yes."

"Good. Is it cool enough in here for you? Good. I'd like you to meet General Ujimbu."

Stewart was startled. Ujimbu was Chief of Staff of the Armed Forces.

Moshu returned with Nick's second bottle of beer and settled back in his own chair. "I want you to hear some straight talk about our military situation. Okay?"

"The guerrillas?" Nick asked, in spite of himself.

"Precisely," Jimmy Moshu said.

Moshu said a few words into the phone at his elbow. Almost immediately the door to his office swung open and two junior officers, very smartly turned out in starched olive drab fatigues and shining brass and glowing black boots, wheeled in an easel, the board on which was covered with a dropcloth. With silent apologies they bowed themselves out of the room. Moshu sipped his orange juice and paid no attention.

The door opened again and a short broad man with considerably more brass at the collar of his fatigues strode into the room.

He had a large revolver strapped to his waist and carried a swagger stick. Moshu and Stewart rose together.

"Mr. Stewart, this is General Ujimbu."

"I'm happy to meet you, sir," Nick said, extending his hand. Ujimbu touched his hand lightly and said, "Pleased."

"Mr. Stewart represents the Manhattan Banking Corporation, General Ujimbu. They will shortly be asked to arrange a loan of one billion dollars for Maraka. One of the questions that will no doubt be in the mind of the participating banks will be the security of the state. Can you reassure Mr. Stewart on that point?"

"I believe I can, Mr. Moshu," Ujimbu said smiling. "Be seated, gentlemen." As they sat down he threw the dropcloth back over the top of the board with a single precise motion.

It was a map that Stewart realized was a greatly enlarged depiction of the northern and western border areas of Maraka. For the next half hour, with the help of the swagger stick and red and black felt-tipped pens, General Ujimbu described the infestations of guerrillas, their various strengths and political persuasions, the disposition of Marakan regular troops to counter the problem.

"I was fortunate enough, Mr. Stewart, to have observed the methods used by the British in Malaya. The Communists made the fundamental mistake there of alienating the peasants, a mistake they did not repeat in, for example, Indochina. We also do not alienate our peasants—positively coddle them, in fact—and we understand them. We have taken away all possibility of the guerrillas being able to become invisible among the peasantry because the peasants get nothing in return. Our troops are regulars and disciplined. They do not loot and rape; they protect. It is left to the guerrillas to steal and carry out reprisals for cooperation with the government." He smiled broadly at Stewart. "A refreshing change of pace, don't you think?"

"Indeed I do, General Ujimbu. You said that the groups were not all Communist—"

"By no means. The Communists, led by Arthur Ekaba, are the

73

best organized and the best trained by the Cuban puppets of Moscow, as all of Africa to its regret has come to expect. But there are others: power seekers, thugs, madmen, soldiers of fortune—curious those; there is a rumor that one of them has the same name as a classmate of mine from Sandhurst—some I think even genuine but misguided patriots not content to let the evolutionary processes of Third World development work their way. These, too, unfortunately, must be crushed. Unfortunate, because I think that if their energy could be harnessed for constructive purposes, it would benefit all Marakans. In any event, Mr. Stewart, thank you for your attention."

"On the contrary, General Ujimbu, thank you. I think your description was exceptionally thorough and persuasive."

"Do you have any questions, Mr. Stewart?"

"Only one really, and it's so minor I hate to take any more of your time with it."

"Anything at all, Mr. Stewart. My time belongs to Maraka."

General Ujimbu was so engaging, Nick almost regretted that he had said anything at all. But he pressed ahead. "Last night, when I was returning home from dinner, my car was stopped at a roadblock, and my driver and I had to produce our papers. That is the only time that kind of thing has happened to me in Maraka. Later I heard a rumor that a police station in Maraka City itself had been raided. Will you comment?"

"Indeed," General Ujimbu said easily. "There was a raid on a police station in the northern outskirts of Maraka City. One policeman and three guerrillas were killed. They were from the B Group—here—that I mentioned before. Very well trained, very heavily armed, Communist to a man. We dared think the unthinkable: that they had managed to pierce our defenses in a significant way. That was the reason for the roadblocks, by one of which you were inconvenienced. I'm happy to report that the precautions were found to have been wholly unnecessary, Mr. Stewart. The raid turned out to be exactly what most of us thought it was in the first place: pure image building. It turned out to be very expensive for the perpetrators."

While he was finishing his sentence, Ujimbu let the cloth

drop back over the map. "Will that be all, gentlemen? Then thank you."

The door swung open again and Ujimbu strode through. The junior officers came in again and wheeled the map out, once again bowing their apologies.

"Well, Nick, what did you think?" Jimmy said. "Another beer? No?"

"Utterly fascinating. No doubt the situation is in good hands. Very reassuring also, Jimmy. There are always one or two naysayers around that have to be convinced."

"I thought it would be useful."

"Indeed. In fact, if you don't mind, I shall return to the office now and make some notes. Good God, it's nearly seven. General Ujimbu is a spellbinder."

"Isn't he?" Stewart started to rise. "One other thing, Nick." He sat back down. "What are we going to do about your charming friend, Miss Ashton-Brooke?"

Stewart felt a sharp pain in his guts. He hoped he didn't show it. "I wasn't aware that anything had to be done about Hilary. She took your conversation very much to heart last night."

"She seems to have forgotten it today. This afternoon, one of our police patrols found her out on the New Road. Had to bring her straight back to her flat. Really, Nick, the place is not very salubrious for foreigners."

"I know that."

"I can't imagine what she was doing out there anyway. The whole area has been razed for development."

"I didn't know that, Jimmy. When did that happen?"

Moshu looked at him levelly. His eyes were opaque. "Why, this morning, of course."

Stewart said good-bye to Jimmy Moshu and was led out of the building by Moshu's male secretary. On his way out, he noticed that there were long, deep cracks in the masonry.

7

"**H**i, Chris. Come in. I need another couple of minutes to finish up here and I'll be with you." Kincaid was at his desk behind a stack of paper. Sunlight streamed into the office through windows that ran from floor to ceiling.

Webb sat on the sofa near the windows and looked desultorily through his file. He knew that Kincaid wanted to talk about Maraka—a "chin wag" he had called it—but he didn't know what the President wanted.

Kincaid stood and went to the refrigerator behind his desk. "You want a Dr. Pepper?"

"No thanks, Ben."

Kincaid popped the can and walked over and sat down, propping his feet on the coffee table.

"Chris, I understand that we're about to commit to do a big deal for Maraka." He took a sip of Dr. Pepper. "I don't know a hell of a lot about Maraka, especially about the warts, and I don't want to be embarrassed when a captain of industry starts talking to me about it. Now I understand that you know a lot about Maraka and that you have a dissenting view about the loan. Tell me why." Kincaid settled back and took another swig from his Dr. Pepper.

"They're going to have trouble paying the loan back. They're going to have trouble paying the loans back that they have now, without adding an extra billion."

"Why's that?"

"The economy is being mismanaged. They ought to be earning a lot more from exports than they are, and they're importing way too much of things they don't need. They spend money on prestige: the national airline, the national shipping company, that kind of thing. On the other hand, most of the population lives in poverty, if they are not actually starving. There's a wide gap between the rich and the poor and it's getting wider every day."

"Meaning . . ."

"Meaning there's a lot of corruption and a great deal of unrest in the country, some of which is manifested in growing guerrilla activity."

"Commies?" Kincaid, having finished the soda, was popping the sides of the can in and out.

"Some of it. Not all by any means."

"What is the source of your information, Chris?"

"Reports from our own Economics Department and our rep in Maraka. Magazines like *The Economist. The Financial Times. The New York Times.* State Department, IMF statistics, World Bank publications . . ."

"But nothing special. Nothing that anyone else—hell, everyone else—doesn't have access to?"

"No."

"And it's true that a lot of information is a little flimsy? Or secondhand, from a reporter who maybe has an ax to grind?"

"Yes."

"Now, Chris, I think you're a smart guy. I've never heard anyone say anything different, and you do a good job for the bank. But I think that Miles Vanderpane and Tony Gould and

John Howe and Max Fougere are smart guys too, and from where I sit it looks like a question of interpretation, of judgment, where four guys come out on one side and one guy comes out on the other. You know the thing about the bottle being half empty or half full? Well I think that's what it's all about then. I think old Tony's got a point when he says that all that heavy debt that looks bad now is going to look like chicken shit when the potential is developed. But goddamn," Kincaid whacked Webb on the knee with a pudgy hand, "you keep your independence, Chris. That's what you're paid for." Kincaid stood, and Chris stood with him. "Thanks for coming by, son," he said as Webb left the room.

Webb wondered as he rode the elevator back to his own floor what that had been about. It wasn't to learn about Maraka, but he was astonished that Ben Kincaid gave a damn about anything but golf and Dr. Pepper and his own career.

Kincaid, on the other hand, was standing at his window looking down on the ITT building across the street and thinking not so much about Webb or Maraka or anything at all except that Tony Gould was maybe making a big mistake, and that if it turned out that way, he had Tony by the balls.

On the morning that Thomas Okubu intended to return to the Manhattan Banking Corporation to receive the bank's final offer, Miles Vanderpane was too restless to nap while Tommy drove him into New York. Instead he stared out of the window at spring advancing up the Hudson River, his mind a total blank. It was curious that he couldn't sleep because he was exhausted. Samantha had been—well, the only word for it was vigorous— the night before, and as satisfying as the memory was, it was more satisfying at his age in concept rather than in execution. Occasionally he thought about what might have been; but he put his regrets aside. He had long before learned to avoid, and when he could not avoid, to ignore anything that hinted of bad or unpleasant news. Sam was a passionate woman; she had had lovers; but she was the mother of his children, now departed from the nest, and she had stayed with him, and that was what mattered.

Tommy swung the car into the left lane to pass another limousine that was moving more slowly. As they overtook the car, Vanderpane looked into the backseat. In the window was a black man, staring straight ahead. He was, in fact, the same black man who had accompanied Okubu and Kalama to lunch two days before and who had stood in a corner and said nothing. Miles could not help staring. As Vanderpane's car began to pull ahead, the black man looked at Miles and smiled and waved. The chairman sank back into his seat and began to shiver.

He felt that someone was staring at him, and looked up to see Tommy's eyes in the rearview mirror.

"You okay, Mr. Vanderpane?"

"Yes, of course, Tommy. Why do you ask?" His voice shook a little.

"You look awful white."

"I saw someone in that car we just passed. It gave me a start. It was someone I didn't expect to see."

"That blue Caddie with the diplomatic plates?"

"Yes, that's the one."

"Someone you know, Mr. Vanderpane?"

"No. Someone I saw once before. A couple of days ago. It was a surprise, that's all. I'm okay, Tommy."

But you look like death warmed over, Tommy thought. He hadn't seen anything like it since his Uncle Vito had found a dead cat on his porch in Brooklyn in 1945.

By the time they reached the bank, the color had returned to Miles Vanderpane's face and he was feeling a good deal better, although he was slightly nauseated. In his customary manner, he thanked Tommy for the pleasant ride, received his attaché case, and strode up the front steps. It was nine o'clock.

The elevator starter held the door open for him, and young officers stood aside to let him enter the elevator first.

"Good morning, Mr. Vanderpane," they said, crowding in after him.

"How are you?" he said heartily and collectively. If there were any answers he didn't hear them.

By the time the elevator reached the twelfth floor, Miles Vanderpane was alone. He got off, handed his attaché case to the guard who would take it to his office, and went into the sitting room where the senior management of Manhattan Banking took coffee every morning.

"Morning, Miles," Ben Kincaid said. "How's it going?"

"Fine, Ben, thanks."

"Good morning, Miles."

"Good morning, Bob, Tony, Ralph, Paul."

Kincaid's concession to the morning was to drink his Dr. Pepper out of a glass instead of a can. "Bob thinks the Fed's going to put an armlock on the money supply."

"Look at the numbers for the last four weeks. It's got to come."

"So the rates are going higher?"

"Yes. Still higher. And money's going to flow out of the savings banks, mortgage money is going to get harder to get, housing starts are off, industrial production is down, the dollar is down, unemployment is up, and inflation is way up. Pardon me, Ben, but your friend in the White House doesn't know shit from Shinola."

"He isn't any friend of mine. I didn't vote for the bastard."

"Miles, we need a regional banking office in Africa," Gould said.

"Another branch office, Tony?" Vanderpane's tone betrayed some impatience. He didn't like the way that Gould had shattered the relaxed mood of the informal morning meeting.

"It's the only way international banking can properly service sub-Saharan Africa. I'll have a detailed memo on your desk by eleven showing exactly what the needs are."

Vanderpane seemed content to let the matter drop at that point, which Gould was not quite ready to do. He sensed Kincaid watching him over the rim of his glass.

"And I think we ought to give serious consideration to putting the office in Maraka. Especially now, when we can get in on the ground floor with the jumbo."

As if he hadn't heard anything prior to Tony's mention of the new syndication, Vanderpane said, "Why don't you tell everyone about the loan we're about to propose to Maraka, Tony?"

Paul Swain, the head of domestic banking, listened politely to Gould's description of yet another spectacular deal and silently ground his teeth. Tony Gould's success was due entirely to his being in the right job at the right time. Swain's people worked hard and the business stayed flat. What the hell could they do? They couldn't drag the customers in by the hair.

Bob Sizemore didn't care what Tony was saying. His foreign-exchange traders and money dealers were big earners for the Manhattan Banking Corporation.

Ralph Hastings of the trust department kept in his desk a paper-clip chain that represented the number of days he had left until retirement. Mondays were best. On Mondays, he removed three paper clips.

"Five-eighths for ten years, Tony? For Maraka?" Swain said.

"Do we want the mandate or don't we?" Tony answered, irritation showing in his voice slightly. "The queue is a mile long for this one."

"And all that stuff you might have heard about the corruption and the guerrillas and the heavy debt burden is just crap."

Gould looked quickly at Ben Kincaid to see if he was being sarcastic, but Ben was in fact looking earnestly at Paul Swain.

"Paul," Miles said, "I do think Tony's people are on top of this one." Vanderpane smiled seraphically. "I'm very impressed with your people, Tony."

Kincaid stood. "If you all will excuse me, I've got some people from St. Louis to see. Bye."

The morning coffee session broke up shortly after the president left, and Gould, having established that the chairman had a sheet with the terms of the Maraka loan, returned to his office. He sifted through the calls that had come through in the previous half hour and had his secretary ring John Howe in London.

"I've run the terms by four banks, Tony. None of them seems very enthusiastic."

"You didn't tell them it was Maraka, did you?"

81

"No, of course not, Tony. But I have to say there couldn't be many African countries with the characteristics I described." And they would have been pretty bloody stupid not to have guessed, Howe added to himself.

"Who were the banks?"

"Citibank, Morgan, Bankers Trust, Conill."

"What didn't they like?"

"Mind you, Tony, none of them actually said they didn't *like* something. They were simply . . . unenthusiastic, as I said. They thought the spread was a little fine, based on what I described. They thought the tenor was a little long. And they definitely thought the management fee was off. Not enough to close off conversation, but everybody I talked to would like a reconsideration of the management fee."

"How much would fly?"

"No less than a quarter, Tony."

"Let me think it over, John. You talked to banks with some big ideas."

"They're a force in the market, Tony."

"I'll think it over, John." After he'd hung up, he remembered that he'd forgotten to say good-bye.

The day had turned cloudy. Gould stared through the window at the dark sky without seeing it. Howe knew his stuff. Well and good. But if they proposed a management fee of a quarter percent to Okubu, the mandate would go somewhere else, and so would all the fees and all the visibility of doing a billion-dollar deal for the Republic of Maraka.

Shit, the banks that Howe talked to knew the country he was describing. And they were trying to scare him off. Simple, garden-variety subterfuge. He ought to have recognized it more quickly than he had. In fact, Howe should have recognized it for what it was.

Gould gave a great sigh of satisfaction. There was no need to rethink the loan terms. What the other banks had said to John Howe told Manhattan Banking exactly what they needed to know: that the terms were bang on the market for Maraka. The deal would sell like hotcakes. And the last banks on earth that he would offer the deal to were Citi, Morgan, Bankers, and Conill.

At a quarter past eleven, Vanderpane called him to tell him that he had discussed the terms with Okubu and that the Finance Minister was arranging to have a signed mandate hand-delivered to the Manhattan Banking Corporation before noon.

8

N ick Stewart did not after all return to his office, but made some notes as Paul drove him home. He had difficulty concentrating. Although he would never have admitted it, he had been shaken by Moshu's story about Hilary.

As soon as he came in, Ahmed told him that Miss Ashton-Brooke was in the sitting room.

"You had better bring some whisky, Ahmed."

"Yes, sah. For Mr. Stewart. Miss Ashton-Brooke already has some."

Stewart looked at Ahmed's large warm brown eyes.

Ahmed lowered his eyes. "Miss Ashton-Brooke, sah, she was upset when she arrived."

"How long has she been here?"

"About forty-five minutes, sah."

"Thank you, Ahmed. You've done very well."

At which Ahmed smiled slightly. "Will you have anything else, sah? Dinner for yourself and the lady?"

"I think we'd better fend for ourselves."

"Very well, sah. I return soon with your whisky."

She was sitting in the big deep chair he always read in. The empty glass was beside her on the table. She was pale and she looked older, and Stewart thought that in a matter of hours she had ceased to be pretty and had become beautiful.

And he could see she was scared.

"Did they do anything to you, Hilary?"

"If you mean physically, no, they didn't do anything."

"What then?"

She stood and began to walk back and forth in the sitting room, her arms clutched tightly across her chest. She talked as if she were talking to herself.

"I finally got a taxi driver who wasn't too frightened to take me to New Road. He was frightened enough, and insisted I get out a half mile before we got there. So I walked through unbelievable squalor, with the people running away from me as if they'd seen a ghost and when I got to the New Road it wasn't there." She paused and looked at him and her eyes were shining as if there were tears in them. "It was gone, Nick. There was a lot of freshly scraped red clay with tread marks in it, and up what I supposed used to be the road there were two bulldozers pushing a lot of junk into a pile. I think it was whatever was left of the tin and wood shacks the people lived in. I would have gotten closer, but I heard this roar behind me and I turned around, and there was a jeep with four men in it—an officer and three other ranks. Two of them stood on either side with their guns waving in my face. The officer asked me what I was doing there. I was frightened, Nick, so I told them."

"You told them you were looking for Jocelyn?"

"That I was a reporter and was looking for Jocelyn Temba. The officer said no one named Temba lived in the New Road as I could see because no one lived in the New Road, which was being cleared for a new housing development. He asked me for my press card, which he's kept, and my identity card. He also has my passport."

"They can't do that. It's the property of HMG."

"Don't be absurd, Nick. They can and they do."

"Of course you're right. But let's talk to the Consulate."

"I think that's fine, Nick. I'll get them in a few days or weeks, after the consul has dealt with the Marakan bureaucracy. And in the meantime I can be picked up for entering the country illegally. My visa is in the passport."

"Don't worry, darling. We'll get you to the consulate."

"I don't want to go to the consulate, Nick. I want to get out of here."

"Hilary, old girl, I can well understand your feelings, but you're being a little irrational."

"There's another article in the paper on Thursday. It's not complimentary. I'm not sure the consul will protect me. Who knows who's in whose pocket in this evil place? Who knows whether the copper or the iron ore or the oil or whatever isn't more important to the consul than one Brit female, aged thirty-one, slightly used."

"Hilary—"

"I want to get out, Nick. I don't care about anything except getting out." She lay down on the sofa and folded herself tightly, her knees to her chest. "Or else they're going to kill me." She stifled a sob and went to sleep.

He didn't know how long Ahmed had been standing there listening, but the man suddenly materialized with his drink on a tray.

Stewart took a long drink and sat looking at the sleeping figure. None of it seemed real. Were they really talking about lending a billion dollars to this place?

Stewart thought that Hilary was probably exaggerating. Murdering a reporter for a world-class newspaper would raise a stink that nothing could eradicate. They were no doubt in the first stages of expelling her, which they would do when they picked her up on some pretext and found she had no passport or identity card. Standard practice.

Then he realized what a fool he was being. They wouldn't shoot her in broad daylight in downtown Maraka City. Hilary would just disappear. The police would investigate. "Sorry, we've found no trace of the poor young lady. Tena Maraka has taken a personal interest in the matter, but she has quite disappeared off the face of the earth. Brigands, no doubt. Could you sign here, please?"

So easy.

He woke Hilary, who rose as if she were drugged and followed him upstairs to his bedroom. He made her lie on his bed. He secured the heavy metal shutters in the bedroom and bathroom and, shutting out the light, left the bedroom and locked the door behind him. Then he pulled down the metal grate at the top of the stairs, and locked that.

"Ahmed. No one is to go upstairs. If anyone asks, I'm asleep up there."

"Understood, sah."

"I hope I won't be long. Please ring Paul for me."

Stewart was not a quixotic man to drive for and Paul could not resent the inconvenience for long. If Mr. Stewart wanted the car at that time of night—it was well past nine—there was a good reason for it.

George Maguire had a suite at the Intercontinental. It sounded over the house phone as if he had drunk most of his dinner.

"I want to see you, George."

"Shit, man, you know what time it is?"

"Yes, I do, George, but I want to discuss my invoice now."

There was a long pause, followed by a resigned exhalation. "Can't it wait until the morning, Nick?"

"No."

"Okay, okay, you don't have to get pissy about it. It's 304."

At Maguire's offer, Stewart poured himself a large whisky. George asked Nick to give him a Perrier, and he kept belching softly. Nick put a tape of country and western music on the tape deck and turned it up. They went out on the balcony and looked down on the sparse lights of Maraka City and at the lights of the vessels moored in the harbor.

"George, if you wanted to get out of here quickly and quietly, how would you do it?"

Maguire sucked at the Perrier and leaned on the rail, nodding toward the harbor. "Masters are more than willing to do some light passenger trade. This is all hearsay, mind. I hear that it costs a lot. Dollars, Swiss francs, or Deutsche marks. In a pinch they'll take sterling."

"That's my price then, George. One passage out."

"What the hell, Nick. What've you been doing? Laying Tena Maraka's old woman?"

"It's not for me."

"Who's it for?"

Nick gripped Maguire's forearm and said, quietly, "None of your goddamned business, you fat-assed Yankee son of a bitch. You owe me something and I'm here to collect."

"Jesus, Nick, don't get so worked up. Okay. No problem. It'll take a while."

"This is the tough part, George. It can't take a while. I want it done by tomorrow noon. Sooner."

"Shit, man, that's impossible. Nothing can be that important."

"It's important, George."

Maguire's eyes narrowed, and Stewart thought he may have gone too far and piqued the man's curiosity.

"Who it is and what it's about, believe me, George, has nothing to do with you. And if you can arrange it, I'll consider the invoice paid in full."

"You bet your ass it will be, Stewart. This ain't like buying a ticket to the opera."

Stewart put his hand on Maguire's shoulder. "I realize that, George. But this is a tough place to be, and we've all got to stick together."

The big man belched softly. "You'll get a call in the office tomorrow, Nick."

"Early?"

"Yes, early, goddammit. Now get the hell out of here. I got some arranging to do."

Stewart shook Ahmed awake from a sound sleep at the foot of the stairs and sent him off to bed. He lowered the gate behind him at the top of the stairs and locked it and unlocked the door to his bedroom. He could see Hilary in the glow of the spotlights from the compound. She was lying in nearly the same attitude as he had left her, and breathing evenly. He took off his clothes and lay beside her and stared into the twilight.

He had never known before quite how old she was. He was eighteen years older. He thought of how old she was when he was how old, and told himself that he was committing the cardinal error he vowed he would never commit again when he got his divorce (when Hilary was sixteen) and that was the fault of caring.

Nonetheless, he whispered a good night to her before he turned on his side and fell asleep.

Having left instructions with Ahmed to take breakfast to Miss Ashton-Brooke when she woke, but not to allow her to leave the second floor, and to ensure that no one else in the house knew she was there, Stewart got to the office by eight o'clock. The draft of his letter to Colin Mackintosh was still on Jocelyn's desk. If she didn't show up, he might end up typing the letter himself, since office temporaries were not easy to come by in Maraka City and were usually unreliable when one could get them.

He spent the next forty-five minutes going through the mail, although he could hardly concentrate. It was nearly nine when the call came through.

"Mr. Stewart," the operator said, "there's a call for you from Captain Pappas. He says you are expecting it."

"Yes, thank you. Put him through."

A deep voice, heavily accented. "Mr. Stewart, my owners have asked me to talk to you about the mortgage your bank has on our vessel. Can you meet me at the entrance to Albert Quay in, say, half an hour's time?"

"I think so, Captain." Best not to appear too anxious, for the benefit of whoever was listening. "Yes, that will be fine. See you then."

89

The entrance to Albert Quay was simply a gate in a cyclone fence beyond which ran a long jetty piled with crates and bales being off-loaded by deck cranes from a small cargo vessel tied alongside. There was a great deal of shouting, and the roar of machinery, and the growl of the forklifts. From the indistinguishable mass of men on the dock, some of it brown, and most of it black, a figure appeared that Stewart had not noticed in his survey of the dockside. He was a dark man of medium height, with a barrel chest and a large moustache. He bounced on his deck shoes when he moved and was dressed in a khaki shirt and trousers. He gestured to Stewart, and led him behind a crate.

"I am Pappas," he said, extending his hand and gripping Stewart's tightly. "I am master of the *Endymion* that you see behind. She is registered in Famagusta, twelve thousand tons, speed about twelve knots, more or less. Mostly less. I understand from our mutual friend George Maguire that you have a consignment of goods."

"That is correct."

"Where bound?"

"Where are you bound?"

"Ah, Mr. Stewart, that is difficult to say. We are tramping, you know. I only know the next few ports. Port Harcourt, Freetown—"

"Could you, when you put into Port Harcourt, invite the British consul aboard?"

"Of course, if he doesn't expect my poor little *Endymion* to look like Cunard."

"I'm sure he would understand, Captain Pappas. And you understand as well, don't you?"

"What do I understand, Mr. Stewart? What is this person?"

"A quite innocuous young lady."

"Ah." Pappas ran his tongue over his teeth behind his lips and then smiled broadly. "Young ladies are more expensive. They require looking after, if you understand, Mr. Stewart."

Nick was becoming uncomfortable dealing with Captain Pappas. Could he trust him? Could he trust Maguire? Did he have a choice?

"Ten thousand dollars U.S.," Pappas said.

"Mr. Maguire will arrange all that."

"Mr. Maguire did not indicate so."

"Okay. Then I'll arrange payment, Captain Pappas."

"I do nothing until I have received an authenticated Telex from my bank in Zurich, you understand."

"I understand."

"You must appear with the consignment at ten this evening."

"Not until then?"

"You would prefer we invite the immigration officials to observe, Mr. Stewart? I thought not. Put your car down there," he nodded slightly toward a gantry crane on shore, a hundred yards south of the quay. "Get out and walk up here, turn around and walk back. If anyone asks what you are doing, make a pleasantry. When you get to your car, your consignment will be on the water, on her way to *Endymion*. Mr. Stewart, don't look so worried. I'm an old hand at these things. I give value for money, as you British say." Stewart thought absurdly that he ought to tell Pappas that he wasn't British. "And there is no VAT." And laughed horribly. "Now, Mr. Stewart," Pappas continued, pulling some greasy papers from his rear pocket, "I have some quite meaningless documents for you to sign in case there are eyes witnessing our discussion. I shall give you a copy. On the copy you will find the name of a bank in Zurich, and the name of a man, and a number. Direct your payment to the attention of the man named, and quote that number. I shall know very shortly after that the funds have been received."

Stewart signed the document, which was closely printed in a language he did not recognize. Pappas tore a yellow copy out of the middle, handed it to him, and gripped his hand again.

"A pleasure, Mr. Stewart. Your consignment will be delivered safely. You have my word." Pappas turned on his heel and bounced away, and began to shout at the men in the bow of the *Endymion*.

Stewart had two problems, one far more pressing than the other. This was how to get ten thousand dollars to pay for Hilary's passage. The other, which was connected, was what he

91

could do about George Maguire. Maguire had already reneged on the money end of the deal. He was not a man to be trusted. Could he then trust him to keep to himself that the departing dry-cargo tramp *Endymion* would be carrying an unauthorized passenger? What could he possibly gain by telling State Security?

"Paul, take me to the United Bank."

"Yes, sah." He let in the clutch and started the air conditioning.

The wide road that ran perpendicularly to the docks was boiling with lorries leaving the vessels loaded with goods, or arriving empty to pick them up. As they passed Nigeria Quay, Stewart noticed a tractor with the name Childs painted on the cab being lifted aboard a very smart-looking cargo liner with a British flag at her stern. There were two other Childs tractors on the dock. The vessel was called *Orwell* and her home port was Felixstowe. The harbor development project that Childs was working on was a mile beyond.

It was eleven-thirty when Stewart asked at the reception desk in the dim banking hall of the United Bank of Maraka to see Mr. Mackintosh.

He came immediately, a short, thin man, with pale blue eyes and a crinkly fringe of fair hair around a bald head that was perpetually mottled with sunburn and peeling.

"What an unexpected pleasure, Mr. Stewart," he said taking his hand. "Please, come in, come in." He led the way along a corridor floored with broken linoleum to his office, which had walls of frosted glass.

"Can I give you some tea, Mr. Stewart?" Mackintosh asked, waving Nick to the one upholstered chair in the room, and sat behind his desk. His chair creaked.

"No, thank you, Mr. Mackintosh. I really shouldn't have come without notice, and particularly without your new line of credit letter. I do apologize for that, but my secretary seems to have taken a few days of unauthorized holiday."

"Think nothing of it, Mr. Stewart. I quite understand the vagaries of working in Maraka. And I know you are as good as your word and that the letter will be forthcoming in due course."

Mr. Mackintosh was kindness itself, but there were barriers in his eyes beyond which Stewart could not penetrate.

"That is good of you, Mr. Mackintosh. But I've come, in fact, because I have a bit of a problem."

Mackintosh simply nodded.

"I need a loan of ten thousand dollars."

"If it were only within my power, Mr. Stewart, it would be yours in an instant. But you may not know that we cannot make foreign-currency loans available to domestic borrowers without all manner of bureaucratic nuisance, and it would be useless in any event because it is only the largest national corporations that receive permission."

"This would be offshore, Mr. Mackintosh."

"That, of course, we can do, if it is a bona fide trade transaction. Permission for the foreign exchange is largely *pro forma* in those cases. Well, of course you know all this. What precisely is the transaction?"

"Is this in confidence, Mr. Mackintosh?"

"I'm sorry, I don't . . . oh. Yes, it is."

"I need to pay a master of a vessel for passage for someone who believes . . . his life is in danger."

Mackintosh held the arms of his chair and looked at the ceiling. He held that attitude for some minutes. When he looked back down, the benign appearance was gone, and in its place was a deep weariness and resignation.

"You realize what you're doing, if discovered, could make it go very badly with you?"

"Yes indeed."

Mackintosh looked away from Nick at the wall, and seemed to be pondering the matter. "Let me have the particulars," he said at last.

Nick passed him the yellow sheet. Mackintosh smiled briefly and mumbled, "Polish." Stewart pointed out the names and the number. "Yes, yes." Mackintosh looked at the paper a few moments longer, then nodded.

"I'm very grateful to you, Mr. Mackintosh."

"No need, Mr. Stewart. It's a difficult world. I wish your friend luck. Can I show you out?"

Nick had a hamburger and two Cheetahs at the coffee shop in the Intercontinental before he returned to the office. A small pile of unopened mail lay on Jocelyn's desk. It was her prerogative, and hers only, to open Mr. Stewart's mail. Nick stood in the middle of the quiet little room, and looked at the unopened mail and the gray cover on the typewriter and wondered if Jocelyn would ever show up again—the Jocelyn Temba who did not exist and who lived in the New Road, which did not exist.

The afternoon passed slowly. He opened his mail, most of which was from New York, and most of which he threw away. He typed the letter concerning the line of credit for the United Bank himself. He filled out his monthly expense statement and posted it to New York. A little after five, a call from Pappas was put through.

"The owners have agreed with the new terms," the master of the *Endymion* said, and rang off.

Partway there. He wondered how he could ever repay Mackintosh. Not the money; that he would get out of Maguire's hide. But Mackintosh had taken a hell of a chance. It was curious that when they were discussing the payment, he referred only to the problems it would cause Nick. Perhaps the Central Bank auditors were so inept they didn't bother him, and in any event he could blame Stewart for misleading him. Then too he might be up to his eyeballs already in peculation, and one more transaction wouldn't make any difference. Mr. Mackintosh wasn't the type, however; but there was more to him than Nick had thought.

At six o'clock, he received a call from Max Fougere. It was a terrible connection, but he managed to understand that Manhattan Banking had been awarded the mandate. When they hung up, Stewart called Jimmy Moshu.

"Excellent news, Jimmy," he began, oozing bonhomie. "Just as you suspected, Mr. Okubu has awarded the mandate for the jumbo to Manhattan Banking."

"That's very good news, Nick. I'm glad. You've worked hard

for it." Was he being a bit distant? "And thank you for letting me know."

"You're welcome, Jimmy. Well, I'll be off now."

"Just a moment, Nick. Have you seen Hilary Ashton-Brooke?"

Of course the little bastard knows, Stewart realized. She's being followed. "Yes, I have, Jimmy. She spent the night at my house."

"How did she seem?"

"Properly embarrassed, she was, Jimmy. I'd warned her, you'd warned her. I think she's properly chastised now, especially without her press card and her passport. Just to make sure she understood, I gave her a good spanking."

"A not entirely unpleasant task, eh, Nick?"

And they had a hearty man-laugh together.

"Taking those documents was a little harsh," Moshu said, "but it does underline the lesson. She can retrieve them by presenting herself at the Ministry of State Security."

"I'll let her know, Jimmy."

At eight o'clock Hilary and Nick drank a bottle of champagne that he had had in the fridge for a year and ate a cold supper that Ahmed brought on a tray to the bedroom. She was subdued but she had come to terms with the fear that had the previous evening sent her to sleep. While they ate, Stewart explained what they were going to do.

"Once aboard," he said, "the only thing you'll have to worry about is the captain, who is a lecher."

"I've known one or two of those in my time," she said, smiling.

Stewart drove the Volvo himself while Hilary hid beneath the line of the windscreen. He guessed that he would not be followed if they didn't see her in the car. The roads seemed more than usually empty and he hoped they would not run into any roadblocks. They arrived at the gantry a few minutes before ten.

He kissed her gently. "Good-bye, old girl. Take care of yourself."

"Nick, darling, I—"

He put his finger on her lips. "Now, Hilary, don't say anything you might regret later. And whatever you do, don't write."

He made sure the interior light would not turn on when he opened the car door, got out, and walked slowly toward the entrance gate to Albert Quay. The *Endymion* was brightly lit and the steam was up. As Nick approached the gate, he strained his ears for any noise behind, and thought he heard the click of a car door, but it was impossible to tell with the rumble of the ship's engines and the shouts and curses and laughter from the ship at the quay.

Nick looked along the dock through the locked gate and saw men standing at the ropes. A guard with a submachine gun moved into his line of vision beyond the gate. Stewart smiled at the guard. The guard returned the smile and motioned to him to move along with the muzzle of the weapon.

He turned and began to walk back to the car. There was a voice behind him that had the sound of command about it. At the same time, the noise from *Endymion's* engines increased, the lines were cast off, and she moved stern first into the harbor. While Nick watched, a man in white standing on the bridge made a thumbs up signal to the world at large. It could have meant anything at all; but Stewart knew the signal was meant for him.

He walked more quickly back to the car. After he had started it, he said, "What happened, Paul?"

His driver sat up in the rear seat. "It went well, sah. A man, very polite, foreign accent, opened the door and said, 'Come with me, miss.' Then Miss Ashton-Brooke she left the car and climbed over the edge there and I saw a small boat going toward the big boat. The little boat was not easy to see, sah, but I was looking for it."

While Paul talked, Stewart drove them away from the docks and along the empty roads. As they went along the edge of the city center, all the lights they could see—streetlamps, store windows, traffic lights, and the lights in the tower of the Intercontinental, which was the tallest building in town—went out.

Stewart thought nothing of it: one of the many short power failures that happened and made him amused when people like Tony Gould and Max Fougere talked knowingly about Maraka's infrastructure. But the lights were still out—all over town apparently—when they reached home ten minutes later, and when Nick cut the engine and the car lights and they were plunged into the deep tropical darkness, they could hear, far to the north, the faint but unique sound of machine-gun fire.

Ted Cutler knew that Tony Gould was standing in the entrance to his office, but he continued reading the credit file on his desk until Tony rapped on the open door.

"Hello, Tony. What can I do for you?"

Gould sat in the chair in front of Cutler's desk, a concession for him. He usually remained standing, or else he sat on the edge of the desk.

"I need some help, Ted. I need your cooperation."

"We aim to please, Tony," Cutler said, and settled back comfortably in his chair. He fished in his jacket pockets until he found a loose cigarette, slightly bent, which he lit with a kitchen match.

"Remind you of home, Tony?" he asked as the smell of sulfur filled the little room.

Gould either didn't understand the question, or ignored it; he thought that Cutler, who was getting close to retirement, must be getting senile.

"It would be helpful, Ted, if we were all pulling together on the Marakan jumbo."

"I don't know that anyone is doing anything else, Tony." An inch of cigarette ash rolled down his waistcoat.

"Your man Webb has made it obvious that he doesn't like the deal."

"That's his job, Tony, if he doesn't like something. His job is to say what he thinks and to state the reasons why, which I believe he's done both orally and in writing. If the collective wisdom of the bank decides that Webb is wrong and other people are right, so be it. The book is closed as far as we are concerned, and we go on to the next thing."

"But the book isn't closed as far as I'm concerned, Ted. I think Chris has for some reason gotten emotionally involved in this deal, and I think he would change his mind if he had firsthand experience. Everyone but Chris—including Nick Stewart, who's on the spot—knows this is a great deal; great for Maraka and great for the bank."

"What are you saying?"

"I think Chris could help us with the information memorandum. I know he'd do a bang-up job, and he would learn a lot that he can't pick up from the papers."

"Not a bad idea, Tony. Let me think it over. He's got a lot of other stuff to do."

"Sure, Ted. But Stewart and John Howe's people would really be pleased to have the help."

If Gould had gotten any more unctuous, Cutler thought, he would have slipped right out of the chair and onto the floor. He walked into Webb's office.

"Doing anything, Webb?" he asked.

"Nothing at all, Ted," Chris said. He had eight loan proposals to review.

"I thought not. Tony Gould would like you to go to Maraka."

"What on earth for?"

"He thinks if you got firsthand knowledge of the place, you'd become a true believer."

"Ted, first of all, as you neatly pointed out a couple of days ago, my opinion doesn't matter. In the second place, Tony's not that simple-minded."

"Of course he isn't. He wants you to cooperate whether you want to or not. And how can you do anything but cooperate if you're trying to flog the Maraka loan?"

"Who says I have to cooperate if it goes against my convictions?"

"My boy, if you don't cooperate, he gets you for being obstructive."

"So then I don't go."

"I think it's a pretty good idea."

"Ted, if you really want me to go to Maraka, I'll go, but I think the only thing that's going to happen is that I find firsthand evidence to support my convictions."

"I'm sure you're right. And that's why I want you to go, lad. I want to hoist Gould on his own petard. I'm getting mighty sick of his bully-boy management style."

"Well, while you're busy playing knight on white charger, Cutler, remember who you've chosen to be the fuse for the petard."

"Come, come, my boy, it will be a pleasant break from the humdrum to spend a few days in sunny climes."

"Get stuffed, Ted."

Precisely what Cutler would have said to Tony Gould if Ben Kincaid had not called and told him what Gould was going to propose, and had not said also that he thought it was in the interests of the bank that Chris Webb go to Maraka.

Webb's conversation with Ted Cutler took place at eleven-thirty. An hour later he walked to lunch at Dario's on Forty-sixth Street with his friend Jim MacLeod. MacLeod was a vice-president in the Corporate Division of Domestic Banking, responsible for middle market companies in Delaware, Maryland, and Virginia. It was a difficult market because middle market companies had with increasing frequency been seeking court protection from their creditors, but MacLeod had been very selective and as a result very successful; too successful in fact. When his customers reached a certain size, they were transferred from the Middle Market Group to the Large Multinational Group and were handled by different account officers, a graduation that not all of the customers appreciated. Through no intent of his own, most of them preferred to deal with MacLeod and the people who worked for him than with some M.B.A. they didn't know from some other part of the Manhattan Banking Corporation.

"I'm going to Maraka," Webb said.

"Is that anywhere near Red Bank?" MacLeod asked. He sipped his vermouth. "Whatever the hell for?"

"Gould thinks it would be a neat idea for me to help with the information memo for the jumbo. Cutler agrees."

"I'm getting worried about your friend Cutler."

"Ted thinks it would be better for the bank if I go, Jim. He's probably right. He's a good man."

"He's a good man, Chris. But he's only, what, a year or so away from retirement. He's fought the good fight and lost. He's not really interested anymore. He can't be. And when push comes to shove, with the best possible will in the world, and with an eye on his pension, I don't think he'll stand up for you."

"I don't believe that," Chris said; but he had paused before he replied.

"Trouble with you, Webb, is you're inflexible," MacLeod said and sat back while the waiter delivered two plates of *penne all'arrabiata.* Webb poured the Gavi. "In Manhattan Banking Newspeak, that means you're not agreeing with me. You've also misunderstood, which is a hoary old favorite. That translates as 'you had better not remember what I told you the last time we discussed the matter.'"

They ate in silence for a few moments.

"There has to be a better way of making a living," Webb said finally.

"There is," MacLeod said. "The problem is, neither of us can think of it."

It was a photograph that he had taken two years before in the gardens of the Imperial Palace in Tokyo. At the top of the picture was a footbridge with lampposts. Beneath the bridge there were shadows of varying densities, light on the broken surface of the water, light-colored flowers clustered on the grassy bank that could be seen through the arches of the bridge.

Webb slipped a piece of photographic paper into the easel and focused the enlarger while the lens was at its widest aperture. Then he put the grain magnifier beneath the lens and, looking into the magnifier, reduced the aperture until the grain was sharp.

He put the magnifier and the dummy sheet of enlarging paper aside and moved the red filter across the lens of the enlarger. He opened a drawer beneath the enlarger, removed a sheet of fresh paper from the package, and positioned it in the easel. He turned off the enlarger, swung the red filter away from the lens, and turned the enlarger back on.

Using a stiff piece of cardboard, he made ten test strips on the paper, exposing each strip two seconds less than the one before, so that at the end of the exercise the first strip on the left-hand side of the paper had been exposed for twenty seconds, and the last on the right for two.

He put the paper into the developer and moved it back and forth gently for nearly two minutes; he drained it and put it into the stop bath for thirty seconds; he left it two minutes in the fixer and then turned on the light in the darkroom. The ventilating fan hummed comfortably.

The picture looked pretty good, and his practiced eye told him it would probably be the fourth or fifth strip that would be best. He turned off the light and agitated the print gently in the fixer for another two minutes, then put it in the water-holding bath and turned on the lights again.

The deepest black and the most detailed white occurred in the fourth strip from the right; therefore, he would give the next print four units of exposure. He exposed the paper without manipulating the light, but he knew from the test strips that the shadows beneath the bridge would have to be dodged to bring out the detail he had seen in the negative, and he would have to burn the edges, particularly at the top, where there was a featureless sky above the balustrade of the bridge and the stark lamp-posts. He remembered the day well. It was a chilly Sunday in March with an overcast sky.

He made four prints before he was satisfied with two. While the two prints were washing, he rinsed all the trays and tongs he had used in a utility sink, dried them and put them away, and went upstairs.

It was a warm day and Catherine was sitting on the screened porch reading. William of Orange lay in a patch of sunlight on the warm boards, having exhausted himself eating.

"Hi," Chris said. "What are you drinking?"

"Iced tea. Want some?"

"No, thanks."

"Want anything?"

"No."

"How did it go?"

"Pretty well, I think."

"You ought to do a show, Chris."

"Maybe."

"Let me talk to Carl."

"I don't think I have enough prints for a show, Cath."

"Then do some more, sweetheart."

"God, time. I don't have the time."

They listened for a moment to the birds all around.

Catherine asked, "Do you want me to pack for you?"

"Thanks, darling. No, you'd forget my Clark Kent outfit."

"Do you really have to go?"

"Cutler agreed with Gould's suggestion. Gould wants to co-opt me. Looked me straight in the eye and said, 'I expect a constructive effort, Chris.' Cutler thinks I'll keep them honest. He doesn't know these people like I do."

He went back downstairs to the darkroom to turn the prints and to ensure that the water was still at the proper temperature. His arms ached with the inoculations he'd gotten.

When he returned to the porch, she said, "Why don't you quit?"

"And do what?"

"Take photographs."

"And what do we live on, darling?"

"My salary."

He drew his chair up to hers and took her hand. "Honey, we've been through this before. We can't carry the apartment *and* this place on your salary. And remember how trapped we felt in New York before we got it. You don't want to give it up, do you?"

"Rather than have you get ulcers or a heart attack? What do you think?"

He squeezed her hand and returned to the darkroom. The house in Brookfield was their weekend place. It wasn't big and it had taken them six years to get it the way they wanted because they couldn't afford to do it over all at once. But slowly the eighteenth-century house, which had been neglected for a very long time—probably was being neglected when Benedict Arnold was treating with Major André—took on new life. There was a small living room with a stone fireplace, a kitchen, a dining room that they'd added four years before, and two small bedrooms on half an acre that was mostly trees. One of the bedrooms Catherine used for an office, and on the weekend she read manuscripts. And there was the darkroom for Chris in the cellar. They had too much invested in the house, emotionally more than financially, to give it up.

He squeezed the water gently out of the washed prints with a sponge and put them on a nylon window screen to dry. By the time they were ready to mount tomorrow, he would be in London on his way to Maraka City.

Webb took the morning British Airways flight to London. It was a quarter to eleven when he reached the Athenaeum Hotel in Piccadilly. He ordered a steak sandwich and a bottle of lager from room service, hung up his suits and ties, and while he waited he continued reading *Phineas Redux*. He felt not unlike Phineas Finn, in being held responsible for solving problems precipitated by others, who were held responsible, as far as he could tell, for nothing at all.

He got up at seven-thirty after five hours of fitful sleep, which was all he could manage even after a long warm bath. By the time the waiter arrived with his breakfast, he had shaved and dressed. He ate at a window overlooking Green Park, which appeared dank and gloomy in the gray London morning.

Half an hour later he checked out, leaving his case with the hall porter. He walked through a chilly drizzle to the Green Park Underground station and took a train to Holborn, where he changed for the Central Line. He got off at Bank station and walked up Moorgate to Manhattan Banking House.

The receptionist phoned John Howe to tell him Webb had arrived. "Won't be a minute," she said.

Howe sent his secretary to fetch him, and she took him up to the third floor in the lift.

"Would you like a coffee, Chris? White, black? Good. Belinda, be a love and get us both some coffee." Howe was more expansive than the last time they had met. Perhaps he felt more at ease on his home turf; or when he felt he did not have to act like a performing bear for Tony Gould. Or it might be simply that he felt superior to Webb because it looked to him as if Chris had lost whatever battle it was that he had been waging. He could afford to be generous.

"When did you get in?"

"Last night on BA."

"All over jet lag?"

"No."

"Thank you, Belinda. And please ask Geoffrey to step in."

Webb sipped the tepid coffee while Howe opened a green folder on the desk. "Here is the offering Telex," he said, "that we will be sending out this morning to the banks on this list. From all we can gather, these are the banks with the greatest hunger for the business in Maraka."

Webb looked at the list. There were four American banks, and one each British, French, German, Japanese, and Canadian. They were being offered a lead-manager position for a hundred million dollars underwriting each. The amount wouldn't bother them: each of the banks was larger than Manhattan Banking.

The fee would bother them. They would after all get the eighth only on what they kept on their own books—the final take—which was true as well for Manhattan Banking. But Manhattan Banking was also skimming $250,000 for doing God knows what, and they were trying to do it in the big leagues. And some of the banks, despite the pressure from their multinational customers, might not even like the risk. Well, well, Chris thought, *on s'engage et puis on voit.*

Howe said, "By the time we've received all the expressions of interest, the information memorandum that you and Geoff are doing will be ready to send off. I can't imagine it will take more than a week."

"Who's coming from the Economics Department?"

At that moment, a tall young man came into Howe's office. His fair hair was shaped over his ears, and his eyes were pale blue and crowded rather closely at either side of an aquiline nose. His face was long and thin. He was wearing a double-breasted dark gray suit and a vivid blue shirt, with a predominantly red silk club tie.

"Chris, I don't think you've met Geoff Salcombe. This is Chris Webb, Geoff."

Webb rose and they shook hands and sat back down. Salcombe slumped in his chair and crossed his legs languidly.

"I was just asking John," Webb said, looking at Salcombe, "who in the Economics Department is joining us in Maraka."

"No one is available to go at the moment, Chris," Howe answered. "The idea is that we'll have someone vet the numbers when you come back."

"More to the point, John, is being able to ask the right questions and to recognize the implications of the answers. I'm not a trained economist. Are you, Geoff?"

"Good Lord, no. But one is not entirely without wits, old thing."

Webb saw immediately that Salcombe was another of Tony Gould's merchant bankers *manqué*, long on upper-class accents and the right connections and short on experience and brains, doers of deals who took fees and got on to the next transaction, forgetting or more likely ignoring the large exposure that the bank had just incurred on the deal they'd just done.

"Without an economist along, John, this exercise is a nonsense."

Salcombe sighed theatrically.

"The problem is, Chris, the economists we have are not businessmen," Howe said. "They're always crying doom and gloom, particularly about anything in the Third World. The reason why you and Geoff are doing the memo is that you're practical bankers. All the economists do is see the risks and ignore the rewards."

Webb recognized that the information memorandum was going to be another *pro forma* effort, in which the conclusion had been reached before they ever set out to gather the facts.

"Look, then, Geoff, I think you and I ought to spend some time with Henry Perkins before we leave tonight."

"Sorry, old man, I am frightfully booked for the rest of the day, except for lunch, which I understand John is buying us at one of his smart City clubs."

"John, can we see if Perkins can join us?"

"Of course," Howe said, without conviction. He called his secretary over the intercom. "Belinda, my dear, please ring Henry Perkins's secretary to see if there's a chance he's free for lunch. About one."

"I don't know—" he began, and his intercom buzzed.

"Yes, he is, John."

"That's fine. Ask him to join us here."

When he was alone, Webb found an empty office and rang Henry Perkins.

"I'm very sorry none of your people was free to join Geoff Salcombe and me in Maraka, Henry."

"It is a busy time, Chris. But none of us was invited either."

"But this memo is—or ought to be—basically an economic report."

"So it is. But you can always staple our last review to the back of the rest of the bumph. We did it in June last year. Look, Chris, don't misunderstand. I know what you're asking. I just prefer this department not get caught in any political crossfire. Can we leave it at that?"

"Can you have one of your people provide some guidelines so that we'll know what new information to look for?"

"Certainly. When are you leaving? Okay, it'll be ready by five."

John Howe's smart City club was reached by a steep, narrow staircase that smelled strongly of disinfectant. There was a small, dimly lit bar with an arched brick ceiling that opened onto a larger, more brightly lit dining room, also with an arched ceiling of brick painted white.

While they stood at the bar and perused the menu, Howe and Salcombe had sherry, Webb a glass of red wine, and Perkins a gin and tonic. Perkins was far heavier than when Chris had seen him last, two years before, and if possible, even redder in the face. His jowls hung over his collar.

Webb skipped the starter, while Perkins had whitebait, and the other two, potted shrimp. Salcombe and Perkins followed with grilled sole and a bottle of Muscadet, while Howe and Webb had rump steaks and a half bottle of Côtes du Rhône.

"Maraka is not the best country risk I've ever seen," Perkins said in response to Webb's question, and popped the last of the fried potatoes into his mouth.

"Nor the worst," Howe added.

"True as well," Perkins replied.

"But a billion dollars will improve the credit."

"Depends on what they do with it. What is the loan for?"

"Infrastructure," Salcombe said smartly.

"Coffee everyone? Port?"

"So, let us say they borrow a billion dollars and build, what, highways, dams, ports. None of those things generates foreign exchange to pay the loan back. 'But,' you say . . ." He paused and sipped the port. "Oh, that's very good indeed, John."

He took one of the cigars that was being handed round, cutting off the end carefully and lighting it with a wooden match.

"'But,' you will say, 'repayment will come from the sale of the raw materials Maraka has in such abundance.' Well, yes and no. One, can they mine the stuff or grow it? Two, can they get it to market? Three, will world prices for those commodities hold up, and how do those prices compare with what it costs them to produce those commodities? Four, what's the debt maturity schedule look like? Can they cover their current account deficit—what is the source of that deficit, by the way?—and their debt service? This year and next year and the year after that? If you can answer these questions satisfactorily—and I trust you all have an inkling you can, otherwise why would you go into such a loan?—then you'll be okay. I wouldn't mind another port at all, John, thanks."

Howe looked uncomfortable, Webb thought, although it may have been the heavy food and the stuffy atmosphere. Salcombe was much too pleased at being an important banker involved in a big deal to have noticed that anything significant had taken place.

Perkins sipped his second port and relit his cigar. "With proper management, there's no doubt in my mind that Maraka will be a real economic power in the future.

"Thing that always bothers me about country lending—not Maraka, but in general—is that commercial bankers don't make much impression on governments. Running a country's not like running a company; there are other considerations. Social and political. You can't talk to a finance minister like you talk to a finance director. You can't take a country into bankruptcy court. Right of offset? Sure, if there's anything to offset. You can't seize the assets you've financed in these infrastructure loans because they're in the country. What would you do with a railway or a dam anyway? You can't push a country around. Threaten to cut off their credit and see how fast you get your money back from the loans you've already made." Perkins was breathing heavily now, and sweating. "The only organization that seems to have any clout with countries is the IMF, and by the time they bring in the big guns—which doesn't always work anyway, for social and political reasons—it's too late, and you're only one member of the workout committee. Look at Zaïre. Or Turkey. What choice do you have except to reschedule?"

"And what are those rescheduled loans really worth?" Webb asked quietly.

"Must be getting back," Perkins said, rising heavily from the table.

At five o'clock, when he left the bank to get his bag at the hotel and then go out to the airport, Webb had a list of questions that the Economics Department had drawn up tucked into his attaché case.

He waited half an hour at the British Airways desk in Terminal Three at Heathrow for Salcombe to appear so that they could check in and sit together. He wanted to discuss with him what they were supposed to do, and how he thought they ought to go about it. When he decided he could wait no longer, he just managed to get into a no smoking cabin, but was put into one of the inside seats in the center section of a 747.

Chris had a suspicion about the reason he had not seen Salcombe, and when he encountered him on the way to the departure gate, his notion was confirmed.

"You're flying first class?"

"Of course, old man. We never fly any other way. Oh. I quite forgot those strange rules you have in New York. Look, perhaps we can get you upgraded." He was wearing a blue blazer and a beige turtleneck pullover.

"I thought we might sit together, Geoff, so that we could talk about what form the memo's going to take and to divide up the work so that we don't waste time when we get there."

"Just as well we're not sitting together, old thing. I shouldn't be much use to you at all tonight. I had a hell of a weekend, and today wasn't any better, and I'm simply exhausted. Looking forward to a good kip. What a bore, the plane is late already."

Webb handed him a copy of the memo from the Economics Department. "Well, do have a look at this before you have your kip."

110

Nuance was not Geoff Salcombe's long suit. He said only, "Thanks very much. See you in Maraka City."

Webb spent the first hour in the crowded, child-noisy plane (Abidjan, Lagos, Maraka City, Yaounde) reading. He was sitting between a large black woman in a print dress on his left and a thin man with a weathered look on his right. The man was wearing a short-sleeved khaki shirt and jeans and a hand-tooled leather belt with a large buckle that said "Wells Fargo."

When the drinks cart arrived, Webb asked for two Scotches, two glasses with ice, and soda. The man on the aisle asked for "Two bourbons, honey," in a strong southwestern accent, "no ice, no soda, no water, no nothing but a glass." He cracked both miniatures and poured them into the plastic glass and drank the whisky off in two drafts. He held up two fingers to the stewardess before she had moved beyond their row and received another pair of miniatures.

"Down the hatch," he said to Webb. "Where you going?"

"Maraka."

"Shit hole," said the man into his glass.

Chris opened his book and sipped his Scotch.

"Hey, no offense, buddy," the man said. "I was just glad to get out, that's all."

"Get out?"

"I got myself reassigned to Abidjan. Everything is better. The food, the women, the business, not necessarily in that order." He pulled the call button. "You going on business?"

"Yes."

"Well, you ain't a miner, and you ain't in construction, and you sure as hell ain't in oil, so you must be a banker."

"Right first time," Chris said.

"Nothing wrong with Maraka that a little good management wouldn't set right. But the niggers is just going to fuck it up. Oh, sorry, I didn't see her. There you are at last, honey. I sure would appreciate two more bourbons."

"I've heard they've just found oil," Webb said.

111

"Oh, man, if you only knew the times they just found oil. They always just find it when they're going to ask somebody for something. I've seen the reports. I say, maybe yes, maybe no. But they got a long, long way to go."

The stewardess was now handing out plastic meals on plastic trays.

"Hey, listen, old buddy," he said tapping Webb on the arm and leaning close to his ear. "There's a lot of money, I mean a *lot* of money, to be made in Maraka, but you have to know how to invest. You got to find out who to put on retainer. I could tell you who to talk to but you ain't in the oil business. I don't know who you grease in the banking business. What bank you with?"

"Manhattan Banking."

"You got somebody there, right? He'll know."

Webb wondered whether he ought to respond the way he wanted to, but decided that it wasn't worth it. Who was he to judge? The man was making a living in a tough way, one that drove him to put away three double bourbons in half an hour; he wouldn't understand the question; he would just narrow his eyes, and say, "Consequences? I don't get your drift, bub."

"God, this stuff is terrible," the man said, and threw his napkin across the food, and reached for the call button. By the time the stewardess arrived, twenty minutes later, he was asleep.

Webb read for another half hour after dinner, and tried to sleep himself. But although he was tired, he never managed to become fully unconscious. He kept going over the fact-gathering mission he was on, and the absurdity of it; and every time he heard a change in pitch in the engines he became watchful.

Webb woke when the plane landed at Abidjan. The Texan struggled to his feet and looked at him with bloodshot eyes.

"Nice talking to you, buddy," he said, and turned away.

It was past four in the morning when the plane landed in Maraka City. Webb was feeling stale and wanted nothing more than a hot bath and a bed. The humidity that met him at the cabin door was palpable: he felt as if he'd walked into a warm, heavy wet curtain. He went down the stairway sweating profusely and got into the airport bus. Salcombe was there already, leaning against an open window, yawning and fanning himself with a copy of *The Economist*.

"If it's like this at four in the morning, what do you suppose it's like at noon?"

The bus started with a grinding of gears. Perhaps fifty people had gotten off the plane at Maraka International Airport.

They drove toward a vast, low silhouette of a building, only one section of which was lit. On the way, they passed a shining 747 with the Air Maraka logo; there were blocks beneath the wheels and covers over the engines. When they arrived at the terminal, the passengers had to walk up a short escalator that wasn't working into the building, in which it was as sticky as it had been outside. Their health cards and passports were given cursory glances by men in uniform, all of whom wore pistols.

The baggage claim was littered with papers, broken glass, cans, and bits of rotting fruit. It took them twenty minutes to get their luggage, and while they waited, Webb and Salcombe made a circuit of the hall. A soldier with a submachine gun watched their peregrination.

After customs, which was as cursory as immigration and health, they passed into the front hall of the terminal. A tall, worn, tired-looking man waved to them. He was dressed in a short-sleeved white shirt and khaki shorts and looked as uncomfortable as they felt.

"Wish you chaps had picked a more convenient time to arrive. I'm Nick Stewart."

He led them outside to a white Volvo, put their cases into the trunk and unlocked the car doors. By this time, Chris felt as if he were sleepwalking and had no will of his own. He got into the backseat.

Stewart started off, turning the air conditioning up high. "I don't think you'll have any problem in a place like the Intercontinental, but to make sure, strip the top cover off your bed to be sure there aren't any scorpions inside."

"You're joking, old fellow," Geoff Salcombe said. His accent had become more public school when he heard Stewart's Australian lilt.

113

"No I'm not, sonny. Turn the water on *before* you put your hands under the tap, shake out your slippers in the morning, and for Christ's sake, double-lock your doors. Where the hell do you think you are, St. James's?"

Salcombe said nothing. "We're all tired, Nick," Webb said. "Thanks for the advice."

The night around was deep. Whatever else they believed in, the Marakans didn't believe in street lighting. There was no light around them at all. There was only the glow from the instruments on the dashboard, and the Volvo's headlights.

Webb dozed; for how long he couldn't say. When he woke, he saw a brightly lit sign on the left-hand side of the road, showing a photo mural of a man in gold-rimmed glasses and what must have been Marakan tribal dress. Beneath the picture were the words, "Tena Maraka welcomes you to our country."

"Who is Tena Maraka, Nick?"

"He was the father of Marakan independence, although why they needed one I can't say. Seemed to me the poms gave in pretty easily. Anyway, that's what he was before he learned to walk on water. Now he's called the Father of Maraka—that's what Tena Maraka means. There are some people who don't believe he exists at all, or else that there's just some mummy up there on Government Hill—you'll see that Wednesday—that they make juju in front of. I personally think he's alive and well and has the biggest Swiss bank account of all. Bigger than Mobutu's. Just saving for a rainy day."

When they were standing in front of the Intercontinental, before Stewart drove off, Salcombe cocked his ear.

"I say, what's that funny crackling sound?"

Stewart smiled. "I'll see you chaps in the office tomorrow. Today, I mean. For God's sake, don't come in early. Say about lunchtime. Just out the front door here go right, down to the first turning, right again. We're in Republic House. Across from a scruffy park. Can't miss it."

As they turned to go inside, a small man with bowed legs hurried down the steps to take their bags into the hotel. They checked in and were given adjoining rooms on the fourteenth floor. As they rose slowly in the elevator, the small man in one corner muttering to himself, Salcombe said, "Have you noticed the smell that seems to be all over?"

Webb merely nodded. He didn't want to discuss the shortcomings of Maraka in earshot of one of its citizens. The bellhop seemed to be paying no attention, however.

"And what was that crackling sound that the Aussie found so amusing?"

"I think it was gunfire, Geoff." Webb was so tired he hardly knew what he was saying. It certainly didn't matter.

"But you're not sure," Salcombe said quickly.

"No," Webb said. "I'm not sure."

Webb woke with a headache, and somewhat nauseated, and stared at the ceiling. In the bright glow spilling around the edges of curtains he did not remember drawing, he could discern the cracks above him, like cartographic notations in an unknown country. For a time he lay in bed, doing nothing, thinking about his stomach and listening to the rattle of the air conditioning. The room was cold and smelled damp.

It was nearly eleven-thirty. As Stewart had warned him, he shook out his slippers and brushed his teeth with the water the hotel provided in a carafe. The weak shower relieved somewhat the heavy headedness of getting to sleep at five-thirty in the morning.

After drying off, he opened the curtains. The atmosphere was thick, the humidity hanging in the air, obscuring what ought to have been a good view of the city and the country beyond, and nearly obliterating the horizon. Condensation covered the lower quarter of the windows, and there was mold around the edges where the frame didn't quite fit.

As he passed Salcombe's room, he knocked on the door but received no answer.

By the time he reached Republic House, his shirt was soaked through with sweat, and the smell of the city had made him feel distinctly unwell.

"Sit down, Webb," Stewart greeted him. "You look rotten."

Chris sat in a chair in the anteroom, breathing deeply in the cool, neutral air. "I wasn't quite prepared for the heat," he said. "Or the . . . the . . ."

"The stench. You get used to it. Where's your sidekick?"

Webb wondered whether the juxtaposition of the observation and the question was entirely inadvertent on Stewart's part. "I thought he was already here."

"No. I haven't seen him."

"He must not have heard my knock."

"Why don't we go back to my office." He led the way along the short, dim corridor. "Slept well?"

"So-so. Nick, that was gunfire we heard this morning?"

"What Salcombe was so worried about? Yes. The guerrillas have become a bit bolder recently. Nothing that amounts to much from what can be gleaned from the official and occasionally unofficial sources. But it's the kind of thing that has maximum PR effect and scares the hell out of the local citizenry."

"It doesn't do a bad job on a first-time visitor either. How firmly in control is the regime?"

Stewart rocked a little in his desk chair. "Pretty firmly, I'd say. Or some elements of it. The military seems fairly good. I met a bloke named Ujimbu the other day whom I'd be wary of if I were Tena Maraka. General. Very squared away. Ah, what the hell do we really know? Are you hungry?"

"Empty."

"Like Indian food?"

"Sure."

"There's not a bad place right downstairs. Too bad your friend looks like not joining us."

They took the slow lift to the Wog's and sat at a table overlooking the street, which as usual was jammed with cars. Stewart ordered two Cheetahs and thought about the last time he had been at the Bombay Palace.

"Here's your schedule," Nick said, handing Webb a single typewritten sheet.

"Cheers." They drank. Chris thought the beer was delicious. "Moshu?"

"Deputy to Okubu, whom you met. Clever chap. Keep your back to a wall."

"You're not coming with us, Nick?"

"I'll come for the meeting with Moshu, and the lunch. Which, by the way, will be pretty nasty. Then I'll leave you to the mercies of the Economics Section. Prawn curry all right with you? Lentils and paratha and lime pickle? What an accommodating bloke. You want another Cheetah?"

Webb nodded with some enthusiasm. The beer on an empty stomach had made him a bit euphoric. He wondered if Teddy's could get Cheetah.

"You'll notice the rest of the week, morning and afternoon, is blocked off for the Economics Section. That means simply that if you need that time they'll give it to you. It can run into next week too if you need it, but I suspect you may find that by then you've reached the point of diminishing returns, and are also wearing out your welcome."

"What about the economic consultants they had?"

"I was told their contract had terminated and they had all left," Stewart answered without irony.

The food that was brought smelled superb, and Webb suddenly realized that he was hungry. Stewart ladled some prawns and sauce onto Webb's plate. "I suspect you'll find this hotter than you're used to."

They ate for a few minutes without speaking. Then Stewart said, "I know what you do, Webb, but who is this poofter you're with? Is he an economist?"

118

"No. He's from John Howe's group. Syndications."

"That's pretty bloody strange to send two laymen to talk to the economists. Have some more lentils."

"Yes, please. I thought it was strange too. Howe's answer was that the economists are too pessimistic. They need practical businessmen like Salcombe and I are to put together the information memo."

"Too bloody much," Stewart said, and snorted.

"I want to tell you right away, Nick—no more, really, I'm absolutely stuffed—that I don't like this deal at all, and I think the bank is getting into a mess doing it."

"I'm listening," Stewart said, and pushed his plate a little.

"What I've read tells me this place is unstable, corrupt, and heading rapidly for severe economic dislocation and civil war. That's what I thought before I got here."

"Go on. I'm still listening."

"I've seen a lot of little things, and maybe some that are not so little. Things are not being maintained. There's a brand new 747 on the runway at the airport that doesn't look like it's ever been used. It's just sitting there costing money. Within an hour of our arrival, from the center of the capital city, I hear gunfire, which you tell me is caused by guerrillas. These look to me like symptoms of a pretty badly managed place."

"Let me give you another one," Stewart said. "The other night, most of the center of Maraka City was without power for almost eight hours. The guerrillas got to a power station and did some damage. Fortunately, there are a lot of technicians around to put things right."

"Well, Jesus, Nick, can you tell me what we are doing lending these characters a billion dollars?"

"Now hold on, young man; old fruit, as your colleague might say if he had managed to get out of bed. Much of what you say is true; not all. Also true is that this is one of the richest countries in Africa, all ripe for exploitation, and our customers are doing it. It doesn't matter who's in power, Chris, they're all after the same thing.

"Look, pal, if you've come here looking for negative things to

119

say about Maraka, you'll find them. But keep your eyes and ears open and you'll see other things too."

Webb liked Stewart, and wanted to trust him, but he had difficulty gauging the sincerity of his convictions. How much of what Nick Stewart was saying was for the record?

"What do you think is going to happen to Maraka, Nick?"

"I think there's going to be a coup. I think it could be bloody. And after it's all over, unless you get some wild-eyed leftist or visionary in, the possibility of which is pretty remote, life is going to go on just as before. The rich will get richer, the poor will continue to be ground into the dirt, the multinationals will continue to exploit the resources and to bribe the officials, and the banks will be paid interest and principal on the nail."

"The kinds of things you describe always end up badly. How can we condone them?"

"They don't always end up that way. And we're not condoning them, Chris, we're just making money out of them. Look. The mistake you're making is forgetting we're dealing with human beings. You're looking for perfection where none is possible."

"I'm looking for a little less imperfection, so we can get our money back."

Stewart shrugged and flapped his hand for the bill.

They rose silently in the lift. As Stewart opened the office door, he said, "There will be difficulties, Chris, but things will work themselves out."

"Perhaps. But I may have to write a dissenting report on the condition of Maraka that Tough Tony won't like at all."

"And what good will that do?"

He showed Webb into the musty office that was kept free for visitors and showed him how to use the air-conditioner and the intercom. Stewart then returned to his own office to deal with the telephone calls and correspondence that had accumulated during the day.

Webb spent the next two hours going through twelve months of publications from the Central Bank of Maraka and the Finance Ministry, looking for answers to the questions that Perkins's people had put together, and even his relatively untutored eye could tell that the reports were unprofessional and inconsistent, and, even if the data were accurate, they were out of date by the time they appeared. Publications of indigenous and foreign banks concerned with the economy of Maraka specifically or of West Africa generally were a little better, in direct proportion, it seemed, to their physical distance from Maraka. He found nothing new, certainly nothing that, viewed as objectively as he could manage, would alter his opinion. He thought about Stewart's warning, that it was easy to find negative things about Maraka, and he told himself he must keep an open mind or he would be no better than his colleagues who came to conclusions before they had any facts to support them.

At three-thirty, Salcombe appeared, sweating heavily, and dropped into a chair in front of Webb's desk.

"Been here long, old fellow?"

"Since lunch."

"Good heavens, don't mention anything to do with food. I have rather a gippie tummy and I haven't taken a thing. Have you made all kinds of executive decisions already?"

"I've been going through these," Webb said, pointing to the stack of publications.

"Have you drawn any conclusions?"

"There's not enough of substance here from which to draw any conclusions, as far as I can tell, except that we need more data and different data than I could find. I would like you to go through this stuff quickly to see if I've missed anything."

"Glad to, old chap. Where do I start?"

When Stewart returned to his office after lunch, he found that Moshu had rung up, asking him to call urgently.

He was put straight through. "What can I do for you, Jimmy?"

"Have you seen Hilary Ashton-Brooke?"

At last. "Not for three or four days, Jimmy. Why?"

"I thought you were . . . close," Moshu replied irrelevantly.

"Well, with respect, Jimmy, I don't own the woman, you

121

know. She often goes somewhere on assignment without telling me. She is a correspondent after all, and travels quite a lot."

There was a pause at the other end. "But you see, Nick, that's just it. She has never picked up her passport or working papers. So she cannot have traveled far. And without her papers, she may get into difficulty."

"That is worrisome. Perhaps she went off to be alone for a bit. You know your people frightened her rather."

"The security of the state is second to no other consideration. You will please remember that."

"I'm surprised you think that Hilary somehow threatened the security of the state, Jimmy. But I've no doubt about your point of view. I hope you don't think otherwise."

"Miss Ashton-Brooke must be found." Moshu was beginning to sound a little shrill.

"That is assuming she is lost."

"I'm rather surprised myself at your lack of concern, Nick."

"My dear fellow, I *am* concerned but I've rather a lot on my plate at the moment, what with the jumbo, and now I have the two chaps here who are going to call on you and the Economics Section tomorrow. Hilary is an adult who can look after herself."

"When did you see her last?"

"The night that she stayed with me. After your people had . . . escorted her back from the New Road."

The line went dead. It had occurred to Stewart to ask if Moshu knew anything about the disappearance of his secretary, but fortunately he had thought better of it. That might have put the bastard into a real rage.

For a few moments, Stewart stared at the white sky split by the dusty blinds drawn over the window, and wrapped himself in the sound of the air-conditioner while his heart slowed down. How could Moshu have missed hearing the pounding that was so clear in his own ears. Sooner or later, Nick knew, they would find out, and he thought he had better have a quiet word with the Australian consul.

Stewart was relieved and frightened at the same time, and he wished he had not told her to avoid contacting him. He wanted to know that she was safe. But he would know, soon enough, when she started writing again. If the papers were available, that is. The *FT* had not appeared since last Wednesday, so he had never read the Thursday article Hilary had mentioned.

And now that enough time had passed and he was no longer on his guard, there was also a matter that Stewart had to clear up with George Maguire.

At five-thirty, Webb and Salcombe appeared in his office. Salcombe sat on the worn sofa and arranged himself decorously.

"We're finished with the material you gathered, Nick," Webb said. "The rest has to depend on our talks with the Finance Ministry. There are a lot of holes."

"Dear chap, this *is* the Third World," Salcombe explained from the corner.

"Why don't you both have dinner with me at home tonight?" Nick said. "Salcombe and I will have to change your mind about Maraka, Chris. That is, unless old Geoff there hasn't already arranged a bit of bint for his evening's entertainment." And winked lewdly at Salcombe, who was alternately offended and pleased at being thought such a man of the world; ultimately, he blushed.

"You fellows go off to your hotel now and get some rest—if you're not used to it, and even if you are, this climate can be debilitating. My driver Paul will pick you up at eight. And Geoff," he added, "there'll be no need to dress."

On the way back to the hotel, Salcombe said, "I say, do you think Stewart was pulling my leg?"

"About what, Geoff?"

"About my thinking we might have to dress for dinner."

"Possibly," Webb said.

Salcombe's eyes widened perceptibly as Paul drove the Volvo past the guards with submachine guns into the courtyard in front of Stewart's house. Nick opened the door himself and greeted them as they got out of the car.

"I say, old man, is all that," Salcombe gestured toward the gate behind him, "really necessary?"

123

"No, Geoff," Stewart said. "It's just for show. As a representative, I only get two guards. Branch managers get four. Occasionally—just occasionally—there's the odd spot of burglary." They followed him through the front hall into the comfortably furnished living room. "Unfortunately we can't use the veranda at this time of year. The mosquitoes are the size of hummingbirds." Webb and Salcombe sat in the soft chairs. "What'll it be, gents? Don't worry about the ice. It's made of Evian and there's plenty of it."

He gave a whisky and soda to Chris and a gin and tonic to Salcombe. He took a neat whisky himself.

"What's the news from New York, Chris? People still talking about Vanderpane retiring early?"

"That's a rumor I haven't heard in months."

"One of the hazards of being in the field. Particularly this remote. All the rumors are stale. Old Vanderpane should retire. Turn the reins over to Mrs. Vanderpane. Ever met Sam?—here, let me top that up, Geoff." He put a healthy slug of gin into Salcombe's glass, and followed it with a thimble-full of tonic water.

"Who's Sam?"

"Mrs. Vanderpane, Samantha Vanderpane."

"No, I've never met her."

"There's a woman with a pair if I ever met one. And how is old Max?"

"The same as always. Quiet and smart."

"Smart, hell, old Max has a mind like a razor, and uses it like one."

Webb was wondering how far Stewart was going to go when his man, whom he called Ahmed, appeared to announce dinner.

They had a spicy hot chicken stew with peanuts and mashed yams to soak up the sauce. With it they drank pitchers full of Cheetah, and Stewart made sure their glasses were always topped up. Even though it was cool in the dining room, sweat was running down their faces and soaking through their shirts.

Nick told them stories about other places he had worked for Manhattan Banking and other banks—Hong Kong, Beirut,

Lagos—and Salcombe hung onto his words, punctuating them from time to time with "Smashing" or "Super," especially when he was describing yet another full, firm-breasted beauty he had conquered. Webb wondered if Geoff noticed that all of Stewart's conquests resembled one another strikingly.

They returned to the living room for their coffee. When Salcombe received his, he put it carefully on the table beside him and was asleep in a moment.

"These purebreds are good for short sprints," Nick said, looking at Salcombe with some distaste, "but they can almost never go the distance."

"That material we went through this afternoon, Nick, didn't amount to much."

"No. That's true, it doesn't. I think the best stuff you will get is whatever you guys glean in the next couple of days."

"Have you ever read someone in the *FT* called Ashton-Brooke?"

Stewart nodded.

"Of all the things I've read, his strike me as the most incisive, the least willing to compromise and to call black gray because the PR people say that it's gray."

"Hers. Her things. H. Ashton-Brooke is a woman." He rose and went to the drinks cabinet. "How about something more to drink? No?" He poured himself a large neat whisky. "H. stands for Hilary."

"You know her then?"

"Yes."

"Any chance of our talking to her?"

"No."

"Can I ask why?" Webb sensed that he was touching a nerve.

"She's not in the country."

"Will she be back, do you think, before we leave?" he persisted.

"Goddammit, how the hell should I know?"

The ferocity of the response made Webb lose interest in any further interchange with Stewart. He had been deliberately and obviously taciturn, and then, for no reason, simply blew up.

"I think we ought to be getting back now, Nick. It's nearly twelve. Thanks very much for dinner."

"I'll come back with you."

"There's no need, I assure you. Your driver took good care of us coming out and will no doubt do the same going back."

"I need some air to clear my head." He jabbed Salcombe awake. "Come on, Snow White. Time we take you home."

The three rode in silence with Paul back to the Intercontinental. The streets, Webb noticed, were almost completely empty, with just an occasional movement in the shadows, but nothing so substantial as a human form. The sound of the air-conditioner covered any noise from the outside.

Stewart came into the hotel with them, Salcombe walking between them like a somnambulist, and rode up to the fourteenth floor. Once Geoff was safely inside, Stewart said, "I'd like to have a word with you, Chris. Can I come to your room?"

When they were inside, he said, "I'm sorry that I snapped at you back at the house. I couldn't explain there because the house may be bugged."

It was Webb's turn to be surprised.

"Hilary—Ashton-Brooke, the reporter we were talking about—was worried that she might . . . get into difficulty over the articles she's written for the *FT*, so she got out. Shall we say extralegally?"

"And you helped her?"

"Yes."

"Doesn't all that say something about this place?"

"This place is better than the people who run it, Chris."

"Who run it now, and will probably run it in the future?"

"Perhaps."

Webb was sitting on the edge of the bed, his head buzzing a little with the alcohol he had consumed. He shrugged and shook his head.

"Good night, Chris. Paul and I will pick you both up at ten forty-five to go to the Ministry."

Stewart stood for a moment in the hall outside the door. It was twelve-thirty, but he wondered if old George Maguire was still up. He took the elevator to the third floor and walked along the corridor to Room 304. There were muffled voices and other noises coming from inside, but he could tell they were mechanically produced. He knocked on the door. There was no answer. He knocked again, harder.

"Who is it?" said a slurred voice.

"Stewart."

"Goddammit, Nick, I was asleep."

"I just want to watch your telly, George. You can go back to sleep for all I care."

He heard the lock turn. Maguire opened the door a crack and peered out with one eye over the chain to see who it was who had been imitating Nick Stewart. Stewart knew he was disappointed that the real thing was there. Maguire removed the chain, opened the door wider, and stood back to let him in. The room smelled strongly of cigarette smoke and bourbon.

There were a couple of low lights on in the room. George had one of the hotel armchairs drawn up in front of his video recorder. There was an ashtray full of butts on one arm of the chair and a half-empty bottle of Early Times on the floor. On the other arm of the chair was a glass with some bourbon in it. On the television screen, two unattractive Japanese were copulating gymnastically in pastel colors. The muffled sounds were badly simulated groans of pleasure.

"How the *hell* do they do that?" Stewart said.

"Cut the shit, Stewart. What do you want?"

Maguire stuck his thumbs inside the belt of his jeans and held himself up. His hands had disappeared beneath his stomach.

"Ten thousand dollars. Plus interest."

Maguire swayed a little. He was breathing hard and his eyes were blinking rapidly as if he was having trouble focusing.

"I don't know what the hell you're talking about."

"George—do you mind if I sit down?—the other day when I was down in dockland setting up the passage you arranged for me, but neglected to pay for, I saw some Childs tractors being loaded on board a ship. I thought that was odd."

127

"Not odd. If it's any of your fucking business, I had to send some stuff to Dakar."

"George, you've got bids out on ten projects in addition to the airport and the jetties. How can you afford to send equipment away? It's a wonder the authorities haven't made an inquiry already."

"It doesn't mean anything, Stewart. You can't prove anything."

"The vessel was called *Orwell* and she was flying British flag. No doubt it would be a simple matter to get a copy of the bills of lading."

"Fuck you." Maguire splashed some bourbon into his glass and stared at the television screen.

"Would Childs like to know you do business by bribery, George?"

"Ditto Manhattan Banking?"

"I think I can explain mine away pretty easily. I was helping someone in trouble. The money wasn't for me, even. It was for some greaseball ship's captain. I got nothing out of it. But you, George. Bribery is a way of life. Do you think Childs might like to hear about that?"

The tape had ended, but George was still staring at the television screen. He drank some courage.

"They weren't born yesterday. They know how business gets done."

"But they don't know officially, George. Maybe they'd like an inquiry from the SEC."

"Shit."

"Have it your way, old man." Nick got up and started for the door.

Maguire sighed heavily. "Hold on, Nick. Don't go away pissed off."

Stewart returned to the other chair. "You have anything besides pornographic tapes?"

"Oh hell yes. Only trouble is I've seen them all a hundred times."

"Can I pick one?"

"Be my guest."

Nick picked a Western that seemed to promise a lot of noisy gunfire and slipped it into the machine. When it started, he turned the sound up.

"Why are you taking equipment out of Maraka, George?"

"Have a drink, Nick." Stewart poured a small shot for himself. "Fact is, I think the place is fixing to blow up, and I want to save what I can. It can't be much, but it'll be something."

"Why do you think the place is going to blow up?"

Maguire was looking at the screen but he didn't see it. "We got a lot of people up in the bush. They see things. Hear things. The army is a mess. They haven't paid them in over three months, and they're really pissed off. These raids you've been hearing ain't a joke either. Far as I can tell, soon as they encounter a rebel group that's got more than bow and arrows, the army disappears. If they ever attack big, there's gonna be hell to pay."

On the screen, bodies and horses were dropping everywhere.

"How long do you give it?"

"Oh, man, what the hell do you think I am, a fucking fortune-teller?" Maguire sat up in his chair and then leaned forward, touching Stewart's arm. "Nick, all I want is to be left alone to do my fucking job in peace. I don't need no hassles. I'm so goddamn sorry I came here I can't see straight. But I really put my foot in it this time."

Nick was feeling dirty and worn out. It was past one o'clock. "George. The money."

"Yeah, yeah. Where do you want it? You got a Swiss bank account?"

"No." He couldn't have it transferred direct to the United Bank; it could get Colin Mackintosh in trouble. He couldn't think clearly anymore. "Put it into my account with Manhattan Banking in New York. When you're ready to do the transfer, call me tomorrow and I'll give you the number."

"Good night, Nick."

"I'll be waiting for your call. First thing, George."

"Yeah, right, okay," Maguire said without conviction, and closed the door behind him.

Stewart told himself to remember that Maguire had already cheated him once and was likely to do it again. He had probably been dealing in duplicity so long that, like the Soviets, he could no longer distinguish between truth and deception, and his view of things was different from that of normal people.

The lifts were no longer operating and he had to walk downstairs to the lobby. When he mentioned the problem to the man at the reception desk in the darkened lobby, the clerk simply shrugged and mumbled something about new security measures.

John Howe received the first Telex response to the offering Telex for the billion-dollar loan to the Republic of Maraka on Wednesday morning. It was from the London office of the Tokyo and Osaka Bank, accepting the invitation to join the syndicate as a lead manager with an underwriting of a hundred million, and asking no questions. A lot of Japanese firms were exporting to Maraka, or setting up joint ventures with Marakans for the assembly of automobiles or bicycles. It was an auspicious beginning, but not a real test.

The second response arrived not long afterward. It was from the Vancouver Chartered Bank, and was an unequivocal turndown, with no explanation. Howe would like to have called and asked them the reason, but it was too early in the game for that. He was not desperate; but he was worried. When no other replies had been received by five-thirty that afternoon, he called Tony Gould and caught him just before he went out to lunch.

"What else did Vancouver Chartered say?"

"Nothing at all, Tony. It was just a polite decline. Maybe not so polite. The Telex was kind of curt."

"I never understood why you wanted to approach the Canadians anyway."

"Vancouver has been particularly interested in Africa, Tony."

"I've got to meet some people for lunch, John. Syndicating this deal is *your* job." And hung up.

"You son of a bitch," John Howe said into the dead handset.

From the moment he met Jimmy Moshu, Webb was on his

guard. Moshu was at pains to make himself agreeable, to the point of unctuousness, but he could not conceal his dead staring eyes, weighing and judging every action and response, every effect of his own words and actions. During the brief meeting he had with Stewart, Webb, and Salcombe, and during the lunch, which was not as nasty as Nick had said it would be, Jimmy Moshu answered questions he wasn't asked.

"Why has production of copper fallen in the past two years, Mr. Moshu?"

"Call me Jimmy."

"Thank you, Jimmy. Why has production of copper declined, I believe by six percent in the past two years?"

"We plan to add a second rail line to Mewanga, in the heart of the copper mine area. That way we shall increase efficiency, with full ore carriers on the up line and empties returning on the down line."

"Yes, but—"

"Shall we have coffee? Marakan coffee, I might add."

After lunch, Stewart returned to the office, and Webb and Salcombe were introduced to Mr. Ngomo and Mr. Bhala, who led them through a large room full of ramshackle desks piled high with paper, and clerks moving the paper, sheet by sheet, from one side of the desk to the other.

Ngomo and Bhala were anxious to be helpful, but it was apparent early on that they didn't have answers and that they didn't know where answers could be found. Webb and Salcombe were given more recent statistics.

"But Mr. Ngomo, what accounts for the very large current account deficit, particularly when you have a trade surplus?"

"Ah, Mr. Webb, that is invisibles."

"Yes, Mr. Ngomo, but what are they?"

Mr. Ngomo looked at Mr. Bhala, who shrugged. Webb did not ask whether they thought the cause might be remittances abroad, disguised as invisibles: they were only functionaries, *apparatchiki*, in a large authoritarian machine. They did as they were told.

Maraka's need to borrow was growing rapidly. The country's

reserves of hard currency were running down, but as Maraka's imports were largely covered by the hard currency earned by its exports, the borrowing was required to finance the current account deficit and debt service. The new loan to Maraka would be used partly to amortize some of the existing loans to Maraka, partly to pay interest, and partly to salt Jimmy Moshu and Tena Maraka and Thomas Okubu's Swiss bank accounts, and if anything was left over, they might build another road to nowhere.

At five-thirty, Chris Webb and Geoff Salcombe thanked Mr. Ngomo and Mr. Bhala for their information and their time.

"Will you be returning tomorrow, gentlemen?"

"We shall be returning, Mr. Ngomo," Webb said, "but not right away. We shall need some time to put the information you have given us into perspective, and to frame the questions that will no doubt arise."

"Quite so, Mr. Webb. Whenever you are ready then. Mr. Bhala and myself are entirely at your disposal. Here is my card. When you ring, ask for that extension."

They were taken to the entrance of the Finance Ministry, where they shook hands with the two, and walked down the steps to the place where Paul was waiting with the Volvo.

As they drove off, Paul asked, "To the office?"

Webb said, "Yes, please," and Salcombe, "To the hotel, please," simultaneously.

"I think we ought to talk to Nick about our meetings," Chris said.

"Good heavens, old thing, I'm positively knackered."

"Think of it as good training, Geoff."

Salcombe agreed to return to the office, but he sulked all the way. Webb wondered what would happen to Maraka—and its creditors—when something—a major guerrilla offensive, for example—damaged or otherwise seriously disrupted the flimsy infrastructure they had now, so that all that copper and tin and cobalt bound for export could no longer reach the coast? Or if the prices of several of her commodity exports collapsed? Or if market sentiment turned against her, and she could no longer borrow hard currency?

132

When they got to the office, the door was locked and they had to ring the bell. Stewart himself let them in. He had taken his shoes off, and he was carrying a glass of beer.

"For God's sake, get those ties off before you die of heat exhaustion."

They went back to his office. He moved a pile of papers off the sofa and tossed them onto the coffee table.

"You chaps want a beer?" He took two out of the small fridge in the corner, uncapped them, and gave them each a glass. The glasses said "University of Pennsylvania 1964" on them.

"Where did you get these, Nick?" Webb said.

"They were here when I arrived." He slumped back in a chair and put his feet onto the coffee table. "Have you been enlightened?"

"It's a cosmetic exercise, Nick," Webb said. "It's strictly for appearances. I know more about the economy of Maraka than the two so-called economists we talked with today."

"Maybe you just have a different point of view."

"Nick, the data are a crock."

"Well, now, I don't know—" Salcombe began.

"The government is either being deceptive or else they don't have a clue as to what's going on."

"I would think it's the latter," Stewart said, "about the people you saw this afternoon."

"Either that or it's unhealthy to know."

"Perhaps."

"Maybe Maraka *is* a better place than the people who run it, Nick, but that has to be taken entirely on faith. There's no evidence. This country is being robbed blind."

"What has that got to do with our loan?" Salcombe said testily.

"They won't be able to pay it back."

"Countries don't go broke," Stewart said, looking steadily at Chris. "That's what our superiors believe. Correct that. Know."

"No, they don't go broke," Webb said. "They run out of foreign exchange."

"How about another beer?"

133

Webb nodded.

"Honestly, chaps, is this getting us any further along?"

"I think so, young man," Stewart said from the corner, where he was getting out three more beers. He opened a tin of peanuts.

"These are Marakan groundnuts. A British company I'm prospecting is expanding its plant to process and package these things, the demand is so great. I think they're super."

"They're fabulous," Chris said, taking a second handful. "Okay, Webb, where do we go from here?"

"The only way we can put out an information memo on Maraka is by pointing out the risks any prospective lender is likely to be taking. I'm thinking of the kind of thing that's done in U.S. prospectuses with speculative stock issues."

"There's no SEC looking over our shoulders here, Chris."

"Any other way would be dishonest, and I will not have anything to do with it."

"Tony is not going to like it. That's an understatement."

"Why should I care what Tony Gould likes or doesn't like?"

"Close your mouth, Geoff," Stewart said. "It's unattractive. You no longer value your job, Chris."

"Not at the expense of my integrity."

"Have you heard that, Salcombe? The last honest man." He drained his glass. "Nonetheless, we are committed. Contractually committed. Sent off a letter to Okubu, authorized signatory. Received a countersigned copy back."

"We're not committed if we can't put a deal together," Webb said. "Material adverse change maybe."

After they left, Stewart sat at the Telex machine and tapped out a message to the Payments Department of Manhattan Banking Corporation, instructing them to debit his account ten thousand dollars plus the interest figure Mackintosh had given him and to credit same to the account of United Bank of Maraka, Maraka City, Attention C. Mackintosh. Maguire had paid up; now Nick had to worry about how he was going to get his revenge.

Webb woke trembling and sweating in the middle of the

night, his heart racing. The room was cold and profoundly dark, and the air-conditioner clattered reassuringly. He had had a nightmare, one of those whose elements are so real that the conscious mind has to fight its way out of the fear. He had dreamed of a small black child overwhelmed in a sudden down-pour, washed away into an open sewer, floating on top, its mouth open, arms up like a doll, turning around and over in the slimy water. He tried to reach it but he couldn't, and though he realized it was only a doll, a scream was coming from its open painted lips.

On Thursday, John Howe received responses from the Rhein Main Landesbank AG and the Société d'Albi, both of which expressed interest, without commitment, and looked forward to examining the promised information memorandum in due course. British Commercial had not responded, nor had the four American banks. The syndication was falling flat on its face.

11

C hris Webb arrived at the office the following day at nine, having slept badly. He'd had another dream: he was going to lunch with Tony Gould, and as usual, he jumped down from the fifteenth floor to join Gould on Park Avenue. It seemed to him that he had done this often before, but he no longer knew why. There was an elevator in the building and there was no need to take such a chance of landing safely. And he concluded that it was dumb to continue taking chances for Tony Gould.

Stewart looked even more worn and tired than he did normally.

"You mentioned yesterday that we would probably reach a point of diminishing returns, Nick. I think we're there already."

"You don't need to go back?"

"There's no point in going back."

Stewart shook his head. What was the truth of Maraka? Webb saw a country whose blood was being sucked by a rapacious elite; Stewart saw a country with enormous potential, capable of providing a reasonable standard of living for its entire population. The banks, with their innate conservatism, would bet on, help to maintain, the status quo, with no understanding of the problems. Webb was right; Stewart was right; Manhattan Banking was wrong.

"What next?"

"I think we ought to go back to London and put together the information memo, pointing out the gaps in the data."

"You've discussed this with Salcombe?"

"No. The decision is unilateral and irrevocable. Salcombe is usually absent when decisions are being made."

At which Salcombe entered the room.

"Heard my name mentioned, chaps. At what momentous decision have I not been present?"

"We should get back to London," Webb repeated. "I don't think we're going to get any further here."

"I am forced to agree," Salcombe answered. "Those nig-nogs yesterday didn't know anything. My dears, *I* know more about the Marakan economy than they, and that means they're really in trouble."

Webb and Salcombe spent the rest of the day outlining the information memo, and in the evening, Stewart took them to Lee's Chinese Garden. It was meant to be by way of a small send-off; their flight to London was at ten-thirty the following morning. They all drank too much Cheetah, Stewart because he was depressed, having associated Lee's with Hilary, and Webb and Salcombe out of relief. In the middle of dinner, Stewart excused himself to go to what Lee called the Gents, which was a hole in the ground behind the restaurant, enclosed in moss-covered, jerry-built partitions that ran from shoulder to knee. The smell from the kerosene lamps by the back door wasn't strong enough.

As he was about to reenter the restaurant, he felt a light touch on his shoulder. It gave him a start, but it was only Colin Mackintosh blinking in the feeble light from above the door.

"I'm sorry I startled you, Mr. Stewart. I saw you inside and tried to get to you before you came out, but I was too late."

"And so you waited for me." It was more a statement than a

question. "I don't think I've ever seen you here before, Mr. Mackintosh. And I come here rather a lot."

Mackintosh returned his gaze steadily. "I wanted to acknowledge receipt of your repayment in a less than formal manner."

Stewart nodded.

"And to suggest that you might be more than ordinarily cautious for the moment."

The touch on the shoulder was nothing compared with Mackintosh's somber words. "What do you mean?"

"I hope I've made myself clear, Mr. Stewart," Mackintosh said, and disappeared around the side of the restaurant. For the first time Stewart realized that if one went the way Mackintosh had, he could avoid being photographed by the coppers across the road.

"Nick, old thing, you look as though you've seen a ghost," Salcombe said when he returned to their table.

"Not exactly," Stewart said, "but the bog outside does have a way of putting you off your food. Look, would you chaps mind if I took you back to the hotel. I'm about beat."

Paul drove them to the hotel, where they found that the lifts were not working and they had to walk up fourteen floors. Stewart spent the short ride home wondering what on earth Mackintosh had been talking about. But if he had wanted to frighten him, he had certainly succeeded.

Stewart went with them to the airport in the morning. After he had seen them through immigration there was no point in staying around, and he left, but he felt he had just lost something. He had nothing to look forward to but a drink that evening with Jimmy Moshu, and a cookout for a bunch of bankers on Sunday afternoon at the house of a representative from an Australian bank, at which he knew already that he would drink too much and feel generally sorry for himself.

When Nick arrived at the bar of the Intercontinental at six, he found that Moshu had preceded him and was sitting in his special corner, surrounded by the semicircle of empty tables. It

must have cost the hotel a bundle in lost booze revenues whenever Moshu or those of his kidney came to have a drink.

"Can I offer you some white wine, Nick?" Moshu said, reaching for the bottle in the bucket next to him.

"Not tonight, Jimmy, thanks. I'll have a whisky and soda. No
ice and not a hell of a lot of soda."

Moshu nodded to the waiter. "So your colleagues have left
already?"

"Yes," you bastard, as you well know.

"Presumably they found what they came for?"

"I assume so, Jimmy. I never know what these back-office
types are looking for anyway. In any event, I did not discuss it at
great length with them. And they are under time pressure."

"Quite." Moshu nodded. "And you have heard how the syndication is going?"

"No, not yet, Jimmy. It's a bit early to tell, isn't it?"

If Moshu responded, Nick did not hear him. He was watching
a well-put-together young blonde weave her way delectably
through the crowded tables ahead of the geriatric patient she
seemed to be with.

Moshu followed his eyes. "Excellent taste again, Nick."

Stewart winced inwardly and closed his eyes briefly.

"'A thing of beauty is a joy forever.'"

"You've lost me."

"You're not a literary man, Nick." For some reason, Moshu
was finding that enormously amusing.

"Not in the least."

Moshu turned sober. "Do you know where Miss Ashton-
Brooke is?"

"I don't."

"Are you worried?"

"She's an adult, Jimmy. She has to take care of herself. But,
yes, I am worried a little. I haven't heard from her for a week."

"Would you like another drink, Nick?"

"No thanks."

"I must be going then. You'll let me know about the syndication as soon as you hear, won't you?"

"Without fail."

"Good night, Nick." Moshu rose and left the bar, one man preceding him, and two following. Nick thought, either Moshu is losing status or they've become budget-conscious. The last time he had seen that performance, Moshu had had four bodyguards.

Stewart sat at the corner table picking at the groundnuts and feeling depressed. He ordered another drink and standing up told the waiter he would return. He went down the steps, through the lobby, and out into the sticky air to where Paul was leaning against the Volvo.

"No need to stick around, Paul. I'm going to be awhile. I'll get a cab here. Ask Ahmed to leave something in the fridge."

"Very good, sah."

Stewart returned to the table, where his drink had been placed, and contemplated the condensation on the outside of the glass. He finished the drink and ordered another. Derek Houndswell, the English production manager of United Aluminium, stopped at the table.

"How are you getting on, Nick?"

"Super, Derek, old man. Couldn't be better. Take a pew. Drink?"

"Gin and tonic." The waiter nodded and left. "How is the loan going, Nick?"

"That's what everybody asks me, Derek. I don't know. I expect to know on Monday. The offering Telex just went out last Monday."

"Quite," Houndswell said. The drinks arrived, and he took a large draft.

"Everyone is terribly interested in how the loan is going. Why is that, Derek?"

"Natural, I suppose," Houndswell answered, and took a smaller sip.

"Well, perhaps, Derek. In normal times in normal places.

This is neither. What I think is that everyone is waiting to see what the market reaction to Maraka is."

"Perhaps."

"And they're not sure of the outcome the way they used to be."

"Maybe. Do you suppose I might have another?"

"Nothing to it, Derek. On Manhattan Banking." Nick waved to the waiter indicating another round. The semicircle of tables around the corner had already filled up.

"Derek, do you think Maraka is going to blow up?"

Houndswell removed his gold-rimmed glasses and polished them on a handkerchief. "I think they're going to go through one or two bad patches. Is that what you mean by 'blow up'?"

"What kind of bad patch?"

"Guerrilla activity, coups d'etat, instability, that sort of thing."

"Jesus, what was that?" Nick said rhetorically. The sound of an explosion some distance away had silenced the bar. Fifteen or twenty people rose and went down the steps. The rest looked from table to table. No one said anything for a while.

"Case in point," Houndswell said, attempting to be sanguine, but his voice was shaking and his hand was shaking as well, as he reached for his drink. "The odd terrorist bit. But things will come right in the end."

"What makes you think so? Seems rather an increase of activity lately."

They could hear the police Land Rovers roaring past, hooters screaming.

"This country is far too rich for the West to let it go, Nick. Too many resources and too many companies have too much at stake. We'll get out of it what we want to, and the risks are worth the return. MI 6 and the CIA are hard at work."

"And how about the KGB?"

Houndswell shrugged.

The buzz of conversation began again in the bar, aided by the return of the curious, who had found nothing further than that a car had exploded on Main Road. The air conditioning in the bar whirred and thumped and the police vehicles went by in the road outside the hotel. There was supposition that the car had been from one of the embassies.

"Must push off, cobber," Houndswell said, tapping Nick on the knee and rising. "Going to Ben's on Sunday? Good. Thanks for the drink. Drinks."

Stewart had another drink after Houndswell left. He felt as if the world were closing in on him. He looked around the bar, but there were very few women, and none of them unaccompanied. He wondered what had happened to the delicious blonde he had noticed before: probably feeding broth to her date and wrapping him snugly in a woolly blanket while he feebly fondled a boob and tried to remember what it was all about.

It was too early for the black whores to show up, and they weren't much to look at anyway. They were the kind of thing that would attract George Maguire when he wasn't too drunk to see.

Nick stood and threw a handful of notes onto the table and walked unsteadily out of the bar and down the stairs. In front of the hotel he got a cab, an elderly Nissan that wheezed and rattled. All the windows were open and the breeze was warm and moist. The taxi was diverted off Main Road, where there was a blockade of Land Rovers, beyond which he could see a twisted lamppost.

Stewart paid off the cab and walked through the gates into his own compound, nodding to the two guards who leaned languidly against the wall, their submachine guns resting on straps across their stomachs.

"Can I get you something for dinner, sah?" Ahmed asked after he had come in. It was very quiet in the house except for the hum of the air-conditioners.

"Hasn't Paul spoken to you?"

"I have not seen Paul, Mr. Stewart."

"Have you seen the car?"

"No, sah. Did you not come in the car?"

"No. I came by . . ." Nick felt suddenly as if he couldn't breathe.

Ahmed started forward. "Mr. Stewart, sah, are you unwell?"

Nick held up his hand. "I . . . did you hear the explosion, Ahmed?"

"Yes, sah. We have heard it was a car."

And they both understood. Ahmed put out a hand and caught Stewart under the arm.

"Shall I ring round to the hospital, sah?"

"Yes. Yes, Ahmed, do that, will you? Will you help me into the sitting room first?"

When Ahmed returned a few minutes later, Stewart was staring into space.

"There is no information, sah. They refused to speak to me."

"Thank you for trying, Ahmed."

"May I bring you a whisky and soda, sah?"

"Yes, thank you, Ahmed."

He rang Moshu's private number.

"There was an explosion in a car on Main Road tonight, Jimmy, not long after you left the Intercontinental."

"Yes, Nick, I heard it."

"I think it may have been my car, Jimmy. Can you find out for me?"

"Why do you think that?" Moshu asked him quietly.

"Because my driver has not returned home, and it's not like him."

"Ah. I'll ring you back."

Moshu called nearly an hour later. Stewart had not touched the drink that Ahmed had brought him, nor had he eaten.

"I am informed that it was a car registered in the name of the Manhattan Banking Corporation, Nick. Number plate 1878V."

"And the driver?"

"I am informed it was a forceful explosion."

It was a moment before Stewart could respond. His voice was shaking.

"What caused it?"

"It was a terrorist, Nick. It appears he destroyed himself in the process. His scooter was too close when the bomb went off. Was your driver a family man?"

"Yes."

"May I offer my condolences?"

Stewart lay awake for most of the night, the vision of Paul's wife hunched over in grief after he'd told her still in front of his eyes. Toward light, stupefied from lack of rest and from his own grief, he slept fitfully, remembering at last that Colin Mackintosh of the United Bank of Maraka had warned him to be careful.

By Sunday afternoon, Chris Webb, working in his hotel room in Piccadilly, had completed a twenty-eight-page handwritten draft of the information memorandum. Salcombe looked in three times: late Saturday morning he read what Webb had written thus far, said "Smashing," and went away, promising to bring Webb a bottle of wine that afternoon; about four-thirty he appeared with a bottle of red wine for Chris and a long-legged, long-haired brunette in tight designer jeans and a furry pink sweater for himself—"my mentor" Salcombe said of Chris introducing him to the woman and insisting he try the wine. About noon on Sunday, he appeared again with a copy of the *Sunday Times* and an invitation to lunch after he had read the rest of the draft.

"You can't really include all this, old thing."

"All what, Geoff?"

"This business: spotty economic data, unexplained deterioration in reserves, the possibility of revolution, the exploitation of the populace. Anyone truly interested in Maraka would know all that anyway, to a greater or lesser degree. You've just chosen to emphasize the negative, and that would kill any deal, not to mention one for a billion dollars."

"Possibly."

"Probably."

"Very well, probably," Webb said. "On the other hand, anyone who chose to go into the deal would know exactly the risks he's taking."

"He'd know one man's opinion of the risks he's taking. Bit too much value judgment in this for my taste, old chap. Afraid I can't sign off on it."

Webb shrugged. "No problem as far as I am concerned. As long as it doesn't cause you one."

"Not another word about it. Shall we have a pizza and a lager? Or something rather more grand?"

Miles Vanderpane was still dressing when Samantha, wearing a well-cut red silk dress that emphasized her height and went well with her dark hair, descended to the living room. She had just mixed a small martini for herself when Charles and Rosalie Houston were shown in by Mrs. Wilkes.

"Samantha, darling," dumpy Rosalie cooed, "so long. How nice to see you," and kissed Samantha's cheek.

"So glad you could come, Rosalie," she cooed back, unable to keep herself from parodying her guest. "What *have* you done to your hair?" which was obviously dyed and thinning.

"You've noticed," Rosalie shrilled. "I told Charles you would."

Charles Houston, who was president of a newspaper chain, was a tall man with gray hair, whose amusing, attractive features were slightly asymmetrical. He was heavy in the body, indicating the well-built youth who had played football for Hotchkiss and Princeton. She liked the way he looked at her when they greeted, and she enjoyed the firmness of his hand on her shoulder and the well-remembered scent he used, but she had difficulty believing that she had ever taken this man as a lover. How he used to pout when he couldn't have his own way. How meager was his intellect.

"Miles will be down in a minute. Charles, will you get something for Rosalie and yourself from the bar?"

Rosalie had begun a detailed description of their week in Japan when Mrs. Wilkes appeared with Grace and Ernest Pelletier.

"How lovely to see you, Samantha," Grace said, stumbling slightly against a chair. "Hello Rosalie, hello Charles." Poor Grace, so intelligent, so unattractive, so inappositely named, married to such a stick of a man. Ernest Pelletier, Vermont-bred, thoughtful, sober, slow, was chairman of the board of the family paper company. He greeted Samantha chastely by shaking her hand.

Pelletier and Houston were outside directors and unwavering supporters of Miles Vanderpane: Miles's and Ernest's fathers had been best friends, and Miles was on the board of the paper company; Charles and Miles had been roommates at Princeton. They were old, old, immutable, and well-placed, connections: Houston was chairman of the auditing committee of the bank and Pelletier served on the executive committee with Vanderpane and Kincaid.

Miles came into the room then, rubbing his hands, looking happy and relaxed, positively cherubic, in fact, Samantha was pleased to see, in time to get glasses of white wine for Grace and Ernest.

Fiona appeared then, looking very fetching in a black uniform with a white organdy apron, to hand round the cheese canapés. Samantha watched Charles watching Fiona with amusement: she could never understand why he had married Rosalie, whose attractions were modest at best, or why, after the children had both moved to the West Coast, as far from their mother as they could possibly be, he had stayed married to her.

It did not surprise Samantha that the Goulds arrived forty minutes after the appointed time, when everyone else was well into his or her second drink and when they had all settled into a comfortable conversation among six people who had known each other a long time—in the case of Charles and Miles, over forty years, and Miles and Ernest, even longer—who knew each other's strengths and weaknesses, and who did not threaten each other. The entrance of Tony and Maureen Gould introduced a discordant element that Samantha had foreseen and that she was delighted was so apparent.

Gould preceded his wife into the room, his face wreathed—

with an effort—in a smile, his eyes blank behind his glasses. Samantha had forgotten how slight Gould was—he was easily the shortest person in the room, for his wife was taller as well— and how pale, and she supposed that his height had a lot to do with his power need. The man undoubtedly had an aura, but she liked him none the more for all that.

She took his hand warmly in compensation and called him Tony.

"Have you met my wife Maureen, Samantha?"

"Once much too long ago. How are you, dear?"

Maureen Gould was another surprise. If in Samantha's mind's eye, Tony Gould had been taller than he was, Maureen, pushed into the background, had been shorter. She was, in fact, discernibly taller than her husband, and made no concession to that fact by continuing to wear heels. She was fair, with short light brown hair, large dark eyes, and a rather wide, tense mouth. Her eyes looked slightly haunted, which Samantha could have predicted, knowing what she did about Tony Gould. The woman—Samantha had almost called her a girl because her youthful appearance belied her age, which must have been no less than late thirties—was slim and graceful and vulnerable-looking, and Samantha felt maternal toward her.

She allowed the Goulds time for one Dubonnet and then nodded to Mrs. Wilkes, who left the living room and returned almost immediately to announce dinner.

They sat down in the candlelit dining room to figs and Parma ham. Miles was at the head of the table, with Rosalie on his right and Grace on his left, and Ernest Pelletier was at the foot. Samantha was to his left, with Gould on her left, and Maureen Gould across the table between Ernest and Charles. Mrs. Wilkes moved silently around the table pouring Gewürztraminer.

Rosalie began talking about the hostages in Iran, and Charles added several uncomplimentary remarks about President Carter. Samantha asked Tony Gould how the Marakan syndication was going in a low voice, but not so low that Charles couldn't hear if he paid attention.

Gould was clearly taken by surprise, and said, "What do you

147

know about Maraka?" in a clumsy way, and smiled to cover his mistake.

"Why Tony, don't you think I should interest myself from time to time in my husband's work?"

"No, I didn't mean that, Samantha. What I meant was, what do you know already?"

"About the country," she said, smiling with understanding, "rather a lot."

"It's a bit early to tell about the syndication," Gould said. He knew by this time that it was not going well. "The first reactions have been cautious."

Fiona removed the plates from the table while Charles talked about Martha's Vineyard with Maureen and watched Fiona simultaneously.

"Does that come as a surprise, Tony?" she asked.

"Not really," he said.

Mrs. Wilkes brought in a standing rib of beef, and while Miles played paterfamilias with a carving knife and a serving spoon for the roast potatoes and green beans, she poured a Châteauneuf-du-Pape.

"Do you have children, Maureen?" Samantha asked.

"Two," Tony said.

Samantha patted him lightly on the arm. "Now Tony, let me talk to Maureen. What are their ages, dear?"

"Sally is ten—"

"Nearly eleven," came from Samantha's left. They both ignored it. "—and John is eight."

While they ate, Maureen Gould spoke quietly and intelligently about her children, recognizing that they were not representatives of the Second Coming and so she loved them all the more. She had no visible reaction to her husband's interruptions and corrections.

Her cheeks were flushed becomingly in the candlelight, which also gave the large dark pools of her eyes an air of mystery. With the wine and the sympathetic listeners around her, the tenseness of her mouth disappeared, and more often than not her mouth curled around her observations in an engaging smile. Tony was unaware of the miracle that was taking place, being now heavily engaged with Charles Houston in a discussion of the quarterly provision for loan losses.

Samantha watched Maureen talking animatedly about the poor condition of the New York public school system with Ernest, disagreeing with him in a charming way. Her neck was a smooth white column, and her rather modest blue wool dress clung to her small firm breasts. Her fingers were long, with well-kept nails, and each gesture was supple. How could she have married the obscenity next to me? Samantha wondered. How could she go to bed with him?

There was a buzzing in her ears and she could no longer hear the conversation, which faded in and out like poor radio reception. She did not stare because she didn't know what would happen if she did. But Samantha realized then that she was passionately in love with Maureen Gould; had never felt such a powerful attraction to either man or woman; in fact, had never wanted anyone as much as she wanted Maureen Gould.

"I'm sorry," she said to Tony.

"Miles asked if you'd like some more."

"No thank you, dear. Mrs. Wilkes, I think everyone needs more wine."

After the crème caramel, they took coffee and brandy in the living room. Having the farthest to drive, the Goulds were the first to leave.

"And what did you think of Tony Gould tonight, Ernest?" she said, pouring coffee.

Pelletier shook his head. "Good fellow for the trenches, Samantha, but I thought I was in a board room, not your dining room. Not the sort of man for the GHQ, I think."

She made sure everyone had the drink he wanted and went to sit on one of the small sofas with her coffee. Miles and Rosalie and the Pelletiers were in conversation, and Houston came to sit beside her.

"You look as smashing as ever, Sam."

"Thank you, Charles."

"When are we going to bed together again?"

"How did you get on with Tony Gould, Charles?"

"Good heavens, Sam, you don't have your hooks into him, do you?" He looked aghast.

"That's truly disgusting," she said severely.

"No offense, darling. I was just asking, that's all. You've got too much taste. Even if I do say so myself."

"You always were conceited, Charles. You never *have* recovered from that one touchdown you scored against Yale."

Houston chuckled, but in truth, the sound of cheering that he remembered in Palmer Stadium grew fainter every year. "Now that young man is undeniably intelligent and energetic, but he's too big for his little britches and he's playing a dangerous game."

"You've seen that, have you?"

"Hell, yes, he's anything but subtle."

"I wish you could make Miles see what you see."

"Sam, you know as well as I that Miles is not the sort of person to believe evil of anyone."

"Too true, Charles."

"But Ernie and I and most of the others will watch out for him. Good God, it's past midnight! Past our bedtime." He leered at Samantha and squeezed her knee as he got up from the sofa.

"Mrs. Gould seems rather nice."

"Oh yes," he responded absently, "very nice."

But you're not going to have her, Charles, she thought, because I am.

After their guests had left, Miles and Samantha sat side by side on the sofa drinking weak Scotch and sodas.

"Nice party, Sam," Miles said languidly. "I do enjoy the Houstons and the Pelletiers. Did it accomplish what you wanted it to, do you think?"

"And what I hope *you* wanted it to also, Miles."

"Yes, well, I don't think Tony was so bad tonight, dear."

"He's not much of a guest, Miles. He has no conversation, and his ambition shows all over him."

"I guess he *is* limited, Sam, but such fellows have their uses, you know."

"Miles, you're hopeless," she said, squeezing his arm. "Mrs. Gould, on the other hand, is very pleasant."

"She is rather, yes."

Samantha closed her eyes and thought about the lithe figure of Maureen Gould. She leaned over and kissed Vanderpane on the cheek and darted her tongue into his ear.

"My dear, I am really quite tired," he said. "I don't know that I'm up to anything tonight."

Samantha leaned her head on his shoulder. "I'll do all the work, darling. You won't have to do anything but relax and enjoy it."

On Monday, Webb returned to Manhattan Banking House in Moorgate. He turned over the draft of the information memo to John Howe's secretary, who had been expecting it, and went into Howe's office. Salcombe was already there, looking through a file of Telexes. He handed Chris a message from the British Commercial Bank Ltd. formally declining the invitation to become a lead manager.

"I rang them twice after I received it on Friday," Howe said. "As far as they are concerned, the spread and the management fee are too low, and they can't quite see what we are doing that is worth the other lead managers conceding us a quarter-of-a-million-dollar skim. I think what they're telling me is that this isn't all that easy a credit and it's a mistake for Manhattan Banking to think we can go it alone."

"How about the rest of the banks?"

Howe simply nodded toward Salcombe, who handed Chris the file. "The Japs said yes, the Frogs and the Krauts say they might be interested, the Canadians said no."

"How about Union Guaranty, Cal Trust, and the rest?"

Howe said, "They haven't answered and I don't think they're going to bother. We've really screwed this one up."

"What did British Commercial mean by difficult credit?"

"They didn't say that. They implied it wasn't going to be easy, but they were talking about the size of the deal, not about the creditworthiness of the borrower."

"Wait till you see Webb's memo," Geoff said.

"Dammit, I should have stuck to my guns," Howe said, ignoring him.

"So either we drop it, or we have to increase the spread and the management fee."

"And share it equally. No skim. Tony is not going to be amused."

"Nor will the Marakans."

Howe sat back in his chair and tapped on the desk with an index finger. "How was your trip?"

"Most educational," Webb answered. "The country is as badly managed as some of us thought. The bureaucrats don't know any more than we do, and in one or two cases less, the ministers are busy feathering their own nests, and you can hear gunfire from the center of town. No doubt my worthy colleague Geoffrey will have a different interpretation of the events he and I witnessed."

"Right you are, old thing," Salcombe said brightly.

"We have to talk to Tony, Chris. Will you sit in?"

"Sure. When? I want to see if I can find this Ashton-Brooke who writes for the *FT*."

"I'll book the call for two. I don't want to tell him the news just after he's got into the office. He doesn't like surprises, especially first thing in the morning."

Chris called the *Financial Times* and asked if there was any way he could get in touch with Hilary Ashton-Brooke. He was told she was no longer with the *FT*, and referred to a wire service, which he called. He was switched to an extension that was answered by a woman who said, "Ashton-Brooke."

"This is Chris Webb from the Manhattan Banking Corporation."

"Did Nick ask you to call?" she said immediately. "Is he well?" Her voice sounded somewhat strained.

"Yes," he answered, leaving it up to her to decide which question he had answered. Judging from the nature of her inquiries, Chris realized that Stewart had been rather less than forth-coming about his relationship with Hilary Ashton-Brooke.

"That's awfully good to hear. And what can I do for you?"

"If possible, Miss Ashton-Brooke, I'd like to talk to you about Maraka. Can I buy you lunch?"

"Why not?"

"Where can we—"

"You know Ludgate Hill? There's a pub called the Bell and Magpie about halfway up toward St. Paul's on the left that does a decent steak and chips. Best to get there about twelve."

The Bell and Magpie was a large room with a bar to the right of the entrance and a counter set with place mats on the left in front of a grill. There were already ten or twelve people at the bar when he arrived a little past twelve. He ordered a pint of lager and leaned against the bar and watched the door. A few minutes later, a very attractive young woman in a rumpled skirt and sweater rushed in and looked around in a nearsighted way. Webb waved tentatively.

She smiled and came over. "You're Mr. Webb?" she said and extended her hand.

"Chris," he said, taking her hand. "What can I get you?"

She pushed back the wisp of hair that had fallen over one eye. "A half-pint of what you're drinking would be fine, thanks. Shall we sit down?"

They moved to the counter and sat on stools and ordered minute steak, egg, and chips.

"I want to talk to you about the situation in Maraka."

"First tell me about Nick. You said you've just been in Maraka City. The trade-off will be that everything you tell me will be off the record. You said on the phone that he was well. Did he seem worried at all?"

"Actually, Miss Ashton-Brooke, I hardly know him. I don't think he seemed worried. He looked rather tired, but I think maybe that place would make anyone look tired."

"That's true. On the other hand, Nick looks tired most of the time. It's part of his appeal: his Weltschmerz. What can I tell you?"

"As you know, Manhattan Banking is putting together a large syndicated credit for Maraka. I have read a lot about the country, your articles among many others—they can't have made you very popular there—and I've just been in Maraka in connection with writing an information memo for the syndication effort."

Two steaming plates with minute steak and a fried egg and fried potatoes were put in front of them, and they began to eat.

"My conclusions," Webb continued, "are that while the country is obviously rich and in theory ought to be able to handle easily the debt service on a loan such as ours, it can't do so in practice, through mismanagement of the economy, instability—"

"Misappropriation of funds," she added.

"*Und so weiter.* That goes with Weltschmerz. It seems to me that the only conclusion one can draw is that one has to proceed with caution in dealing with Maraka. Many of my colleagues differ with me about the degree of caution necessary. My question to you is, on the basis of your experience in Maraka, what do you foresee happening over the next year or so? Let me get you another lager while you think it over."

When he returned with their beer, she said, "I think the neglect and abuse of the populace and the looting of the country by the regime has made revolution inevitable." She leaned her cheek on her hand and looked at him thoughtfully. "I don't know who will come out on top, but I wouldn't think it a particularly auspicious time for a large government loan."

"The answer to that—which I don't necessarily ascribe to—is that the form of regime in power is essentially irrelevant. If they want to be able to get the funds they need for development, they cannot repudiate their loans."

"That's logical, I suppose," Hilary responded, "but it must be expensive from time to time when the logic doesn't operate. You can't deny though that the banks and the foreign companies in Maraka would be more comfortable with a right-wing dictatorship than with a left-wing one?"

"I wouldn't deny it at all," Chris said. "But there's nothing the least bit profound about that point of view. Corporations make more money by and large when they're relatively free of interference and government regulation—"

"By keeping government ministers well greased."

"Perhaps. I trust not always . . . and when the society is stable. Instability is not good for business. Neither are left-wing governments."

"Who interfere by nationalizing the companies, and demanding that resources not be exploited except for the benefit of their own people; that kind of interference."

"If developing countries existed in a vacuum, Miss Ashton-Brooke—Hilary—then I'd be inclined to agree with you. But there is too much grabbing for power and money and influence in a country like Maraka by left and right—not to mention however East and West are playing it for whatever advantage—to ascribe pure motives to anyone. And the real losers are always the people."

Hilary looked thoughtful. "I once went to interview a woman—Nick's secretary, as a matter of fact—who I learned knew something about a guerrilla raid that had been made on a police station. When I got to where she lived, I found that the entire area had been bulldozed out of existence. My passport and working papers were taken away from me by the police simply because I was in the area. You're right. The people are the losers."

"Was this recently?"

She nodded.

"And that's why you left?"

"Yes."

Webb remembered that Nick had helped her leave Maraka. "But you haven't written about it yet."

"No, not yet. I can't. It would endanger Nick. I will though."

They finished their beer together and Chris paid the bill.

"Good-bye, Chris," she said when they parted at the door. "I'll be watching Maraka closely." And turning, she began walking rapidly downhill toward Ludgate Circus.

•   •   •

155

Stewart knew that Tony Gould had decided that Manhattan Banking was going to syndicate a jumbo loan for Maraka, and that nothing was going to be allowed to interfere with the process. Gould wanted to do a big visible deal that would put his department and particularly himself in the first level among American world-class banks, up with B of A, Citi, Chase, and Morgan, and ahead of Man Han and Chemical and Bankers Trust and Conill. For all Tony cared about risk, the borrower could have been as easily Papua, New Guinea or Norway had they offered themselves at the right time and had the characteristics to attract the kind of attention that Maraka could. As a result, anyone telling Gould what he didn't want to hear would get a little tick mark against his name in Tony's mental black book.

There was no doubt, however, that the bank ought to be made aware of certain things: the car of course they knew about; there had been no reaction. But Nick thought they ought to know the kinds of things that people with a lot of experience in Maraka—Maguire and Houndswell—were saying. Unlike Chris Webb, Stewart drew no conclusion; he was inclined to agree with the optimistic view expressed by Derek Houndswell, but it was not an opinion he was likely to express *en clair* to Gould or Fougere. They could draw their own lessons.

There was also the matter of Colin Mackintosh's warning. He would keep that to himself for the time being; nor would he mention the disappearance of Jocelyn Temba. He thought that the bank post to New York was relatively safe, but he couldn't be certain. Best to leave the really controversial stuff out of memos.

As telephoning was out of the question, Stewart spent a morning in his office drafting and typing a confidential memo to Gould, recording Maguire's remarks about the condition of the army and the fact that a major construction company was removing some of its equipment because of the dangers it perceived; recording also Houndswell's comment that although it would go through one or two bad patches, Maraka was too rich and Western companies had too much at stake there for the West to let Maraka go. Nick did not use Maguire's or Houndswell's names,

nor did he identify their companies; but he indicated that he
thought Houndswell was the more reliable by a long way. He
sealed the memo in an envelope and tossed it into the priority
mail sack that his messenger would take to the airport in mid-
afternoon. He also sent a short telex to Gould calling his attention to the memo that was on its way. He then went to lunch
with the branch manager of the Credit Lyonnais.

Toward the end of the afternoon, Nick received the kind of
Telex that was known in the bank as a Ghoulogram:

RE MEMO IF ABOUT NEW CAR YOU CAN FORGET IT
AS NOT IN THIS YEARS BUDGET GOULD

"Tony, I have you on the conference phone because I have
Geoff Salcombe and Chris Webb with me."

Gould made no acknowledgment.

"We're calling about the Maraka jumbo."

"So I assumed."

"It's not going well, Tony. The only bank that's accepted our
invitation is Tokyo and Osaka. British Commercial has told us
that the spread and fees are too low, and they've been very
waspish about our skim. The American banks haven't even answered, and I don't think they're going to."

"That's the problem. What's the solution?"

"I think we have to go back to the Marakans and give them
the facts of life."

"Which are?"

"We have to go back to the terms I mentioned in the beginning: three-quarters throughout and a quarter percent fee."

"And a skim?"

"A skim won't fly, Tony. The fee is going to be shared *pari
passu.*"

"Have Nick go to Okubu and tell him what the story is. Then
we'll see what we can salvage out of this fuckup."

Howe closed his eyes, and Webb watched his hands growing
white as he gripped the arms of his chair.

"Did you learn anything in Maraka, Webb?"

157

"I learned a lot, Tony; but nothing to make me change my mind." From the window in Howe's office, Chris could see the tops of the trees in Finsbury Circus.

"You'll be amazed to learn that I'm not surprised. Pick up your phone, John."

Howe picked up the handset, listened for a couple of minutes, replied with an inaudible monosyllable, and hung up. His face had turned bright red and his hands were shaking.

"Tony isn't pleased with our performance," he said.

Webb thought, welcome to the company of those who have been led down a garden path by Tony Gould. But he said nothing.

"What is the status of the info memorandum, Chris?"

"It'll be done by the end of the day. I'll take a copy with me back to New York and have it vetted by Gould before you release it."

"Gould? Why does it have to be vetted by Gould?"

"Because I have been very specific about what I believe are the risks entailed in lending to Maraka."

"Oh shit, you can't do that."

"Why not?"

"How the hell . . . look. Everybody who knows the country knows it's risky. You don't have to rub their noses in it."

"Exactly what I told him," Salcombe said.

"Goddammit, Chris, isn't this job hard enough without you types mucking about?"

"I sympathize with your position, John, believe me. But I didn't ask for this assignment. Tony Gould shoved it down my throat because he thought that I might be forced into the fold somehow. He was wrong. If Tony doesn't like the memo, he can change it. But two years from now, maybe less, I'll ask you what the present value of our Marakan assets is."

"Okay, Webb, go your own way. Don't cooperate. See how much damage you can do. I told you before that it wasn't going to do you any good. If we price this deal where I thought we should have in the first place, we can place it easily. Unless you muck things up. What is your game, Webb?"

"There isn't any, John. That's why you can't understand it. Maraka is a corrupt, repressive country that is in economic decline because it is being mismanaged and looted by its rulers, and it is on the brink of political chaos. I do not think it wise for the bank—or anyone else for that matter—to increase its exposure there. If that's a game, then that's the one I'm playing."

Howe had had a bad ten days and looked it.

"We'll let Tony decide," he said, his voice shaking.

"Absolutely. Let Tony decide."

At a quarter to six, the memo was finished and corrected. Webb looked for Howe, but he had already left. He gave the original to Geoff Salcombe for reproduction later, and kept three copies for himself.

"John wasn't feeling well and went home," Salcombe told him. "Whenever something doesn't go right, it goes straight to his stomach. *En tout cas*, old fruit, I enjoyed the trip to Maraka. I'll see you in New York one of these days."

Ted Cutler was packing his pipe. It was Wednesday morning in New York. "Goddamn, Webb, who the hell do you think you are, Zane Grey?"

"I still have jet lag, Ted, and I'm tired. What are you saying?"

"This cowboy stuff in here. The page on risks. It's beautiful. Gould is going to hit the ceiling."

"He may have already. I dropped a copy off with his secretary this morning."

Webb described his talk with Henry Perkins, the London economist, his trip to Maraka, his discussions with Nick Stewart, what he had seen and heard, and his lunch with Hilary Ashton-Brooke. At the end of an hour, Cutler's phone rang. His secretary told him that Mr. Gould was on.

Cutler asked that Gould be put through, and after a moment, he said "We'll be right up." When he hung up, he was absolutely jovial. "Tony wants to discuss guess what."

Tony was not raging up and down his office when they arrived. He was relaxed, nearly serene. When he spoke, it was quietly.

159

"Do you regard page twenty-one as a constructive part of the information memo on Maraka, Ted?"

"Page twenty-one?" Cutler said, fumbling with his copy to Gould's obvious but contained annoyance. "Which is that? Ah. Why yes I do."

"In what way?"

"It leaves prospective lenders in no doubt as to what they might be getting into. *Might*. It doesn't say they will have a problem, it says they *might*. If they choose to ignore what we call at Manhattan Banking a *caveat*, that's their lookout. They can't say afterward we didn't tell them."

"Ted, we're trying to syndicate a billion-dollar deal for Maraka. We need a lot of assistance from everyone concerned, and it's going to turn out to have been a most worthwhile exercise. I won't even mention the return we get from it. But it will also greatly enhance our existing relationship with Maraka and with the multinationals that do business there, and have tremendous PR fallout. Such things as this page twenty-one in a memo that is supposed to go to everyone who might be interested in doing the deal—which after all is only one man's opinion—"

"Supported by a lot of authority," Webb said. But Gould was in excellent form today. He didn't miss a beat.

"And with a lot of argument to the contrary also. What I'm trying to say is that all this does is emphasize the negative and can't help our syndication effort at all. And since we're committed to doing the deal, I think page 21 is going to have to come out."

This was Tony Gould at his very best, the voice of reason and moderation, seeking in his own calm way the solution that would best see them on their way. If he had been expecting an argument from either Cutler or Webb, he was disappointed. There was no point in discussing anything with someone whose conclusion was already drawn before the issues had been raised and who was impervious to reason. Webb had realized some time before, although he had never before verbalized it, that while Tony Gould sounded eminently logical, all he was in fact was mathematical.

.   .   .

The *maître d'hôtel* of La Reserve on East Sixty-fourth Street, who considered himself a connoisseur in such matters, and preferred his women young, decided that he could easily make an exception for the two who were lunching at one of his better tables. Mrs. Vanderpane was of course a regular, and he had admired her often. The other woman was new, younger, tall, willowy, with dark eyes and a lovely wide expressive mouth; he wouldn't mind seeing her again at all. Together they easily formed the most decorous table in the house, which was filled with those who were called the Beautiful People by someone who surely must have been joking.

"This is the first time in a long time that I've been out to lunch like this, Samantha."

"You must get out more frequently, Maureen."

Maureen finished her Dubonnet and felt somewhat wicked. "It's difficult with the children."

"Have you thought of getting a nanny?"

They were served smoked salmon, and the *maître d'hôtel* himself poured the Cassis that had been chilling in the bucket beside them. The women were as attractive up close as they were from a distance. Mrs. Vanderpane was a marvel, looking easily ten years younger than she was.

"I have, Samantha, but Tony doesn't approve. This salmon is lovely. So is the wine. Tony thinks that the children should have mother's influence."

"How about father's?"

"He's working awfully hard. He sees them as much as he can. Which isn't a lot."

"That *is* too bad. It's certainly not good for the children." Samantha noticed with satisfaction that Maureen was nodding in agreement. "But then, I suppose Tony must enjoy what he's doing."

"Tremendously."

"And that after all," Samantha said, looking steadily into Maureen's eyes, "is what matters."

"I'm sorry, Samantha, I'm not sure I quite understand what

you're saying." But it was more the look than the words that had confused her.

"May I be frank with you, my dear?"

"Please."

"Wouldn't you like your life to be as satisfying as Tony's?"

"Of course."

"Is it?"

Maureen wondered where it was all leading. But she kept reminding herself that this woman was the wife of her husband's boss. "My life has many satisfactions."

"But I dare say, my dear, that you are not getting out of it what Tony is, who after all is pursuing a career that seems to be his single greatest interest."

Somehow, Samantha had managed to say all this to her without offending her, and it was obvious to Maureen that Samantha liked her, and that fact had nothing to do at all with her being Tony Gould's wife, nothing to do at all with the Manhattan Banking Corporation.

"No, Samantha, you're quite right. I'm not getting out of my life what Tony is getting out of his."

"And why not?"

"One of us must make sacrifices."

"And why must it be you?"

"I'm sorry, Samantha. I . . . he's the breadwinner."

"Maureen, darling, what do you do with all this nice bread that Tony is winning?"

Maureen was grateful when the filets of sole were placed in front of them because she had no response. The *maître d'hôtel* noted with appreciation the delicate curve of Maureen Gould's neck; as did Samantha Vanderpane.

They spent a few moments tasting the sole, which was excellent. Maureen sipped the wine and had her glass refilled instantly.

"Does Tony satisfy you, my dear?"

Maureen blushed to her hair. "He's a good provider."

"That's not what I mean, my dear. You know that's not what I mean."

Maureen was confused. Samantha was asking her offensive questions, but she could not possibly have been kinder or more charming, and what was more, she *cared*, and no one had *cared* in such a long time. The whole experience was such a departure from her quotidian existence that if asked she would have said she was enjoying herself; and finally, her curiosity was piqued.

"If you mean sexually, Samantha," she ventured, "the answer is no." She went on hurriedly, "That wasn't always so. But it has been in recent years. Tony is . . . Tony's very involved with the bank."

"Have you ever thought of taking a lover?"

My God, the woman is bold. "Yes, I have. Of course, I have. Thought about it, that is."

Samantha touched her wrist lightly, and wondered whether Maureen felt the same electricity that she did. "I know I've said outrageous things, Maureen, but I hope you'll forgive me. I've said them because I care for you so very, very much and I want you to be happy."

The things she had said had been outrageous, and Maureen did forgive her; for the first time in years someone had asked her how *she* felt about things and had listened to the answer. It was dazzling; but she wondered why she was being pursued.

When they had received their coffee, Samantha said, "Miles and I keep a little apartment on Seventy-eighth near Fifth that we use whenever we're in town. Will you have lunch with me there next Tuesday?"

Maureen replied that she'd be delighted.

"Excellent. About twelve-thirty? And, Maureen, darling, don't worry about anything."

Maureen blushed to think that the puzzlement she was feeling had shown, but she was relieved as well. She was certain that Samantha was saying that she needn't worry about the fact that her husband was chairman of the institution for which Maureen's husband worked. The bank was irrelevant to their friendship.

"Lovely as always, Jean-Pierre," Samantha said to the *maître d'hôtel*, and put ten dollars into his hand.

"Thank you very much indeed, Mrs. Vanderpane," Jean-

Pierre oozed, and admired her bone structure. "Madame," he said, and nodded as Maureen passed. She was a knockout. The parts didn't go together very well—her breasts were too small for the rest of her—but it added up to a woman. And he loved wide mouths on women.

It was an early May day, with the sun shining, the sky blue, and the air soft and reasonably clear. Samantha kissed her on the cheek, and they parted at the corner of Sixty-fourth and Madison, Maureen deciding to walk home. She was not given much to sustained introspection, but she embarked on it now, turning the questions over and over, as if she were holding a prism up to the light.

Why should anyone concern herself about her as much as Samantha Vanderpane, a woman who hardly knew her? Did she feel sorry for her? That wasn't much of a compliment. It had to be more than that—hadn't it? Yes. And why not? Maureen knew herself imperfectly, but she knew enough to recognize that fourteen years of marriage to Tony Gould had left her self-esteem in rather a bad state. Tony was not the sort of person who made one feel good about oneself. She wondered what he was like in the office.

But that was off the subject, which was not Tony but herself. As she waited for the light at Seventy-second, she put her mind into neutral, and only recognized after she had crossed that letting her mind go entirely blank was a habit she had developed to cope with her reality. At present she was using it to avoid examining one of the questions she had posed to herself that she had not really wanted to consider. But the softness of the air and the slight effect of the wine she had drunk at lunch made her feel quite good about herself, so that she was carrying herself straighter and walking with longer strides.

She had detected the strong sexuality in Samantha. She had sensed it at dinner the other night, but it was diffused. Alone with her, she noticed that it pervaded the atmosphere. She wondered whether Samantha went both ways: AC/DC as they used to say in college. Could it be that Samantha had a crush on her? She immediately rejected the idea, but recognized the rejec-

tion for the kind of conditioned reflex she had been brought up
to have whenever such things were whispered about. Could it be
that Samantha had a crush on her? Why not indeed? As she
approached their apartment building, she had an imaginary
scene with Tony:

"I've taken a lover, Tony."

Tony rages up and down the living room. "I'll kill the son of a
bitch," he shouts.

"It's Samantha Vanderpane, Tony."

Tony is shocked. He either faints or tries to figure out how he
can use this revelation to advance his career.

The doorman tipped his cap to her as he held the door and
wondered what Mrs. Gould was smiling about. It wasn't like her.

On the hall table Maureen found a bouquet of anemones from
the florist shop in the Westbury Hotel. With the bouquet was
Charles Houston's personal card: "These will not solve the problems of education in the inner city, but hope they will make you
feel better when you think about them. Enjoyed seeing you Saturday and hope we shall meet again soon. Best, Charles."

Maureen laughed aloud.

T homas Okubu's office was twice the size of Jimmy Moshu's, and Stewart thought little Okubu looked even smaller behind his vast desk. Okubu motioned to him to sit in one of the chairs in front of the desk. Moshu then sat in the other.

"Thank you for sending a car, Your Excellency," Nick said. "I think you know why I am without my own transportation?"

"Oh, indeed. Mr. Moshu has told me about the . . . incident. I am truly sorry." He sipped a glass of mineral water, which was the only thing on the desk. "The hooligans who have created the atmosphere in which such things are possible will be stamped out. In the meantime, innocent people suffer." He sighed gently. "But you've come to report about the Euroloan, Mr. Stewart."

"I have, Your Excellency."

"And how is it progressing?"

"I'm afraid we've run into a spot of bother."

The temperature in the room dropped, but no one had touched the controls of the air-conditioner.

Okubu sipped the mineral water. The silence lengthened.

"And what precisely is the problem, Mr. Stewart?"

"Our initial indications are that, while the market is receptive in general to a Marakan jumbo, it is not receptive at the present pricing."

"And what does Manhattan Banking think the pricing ought to be?"

"The indication seems to be three-quarters over the offered rate throughout and a management fee of one-quarter percent flat. And although we will try for a billion, the underwriting will only be for six hundred million."

"And although you were totally wrong before, we should trust now that you are right. I am not pleased, Mr. Stewart. Maraka is not pleased."

This was spoken quietly and without emotion, but Nick could feel the menace behind the words.

"Let me go on a moment, Mr. Stewart. Manhattan Banking was given a mandate to syndicate a billion-dollar loan, fully underwritten, for us. You have not carried out that mandate. I remind you that one of my options is to reopen the bidding for our loan, and to drop Manhattan Banking altogether."

"If I may, Excellency? Thank you. We have had a meeting with the interested parties. They exhibit much more interest at the level I have just mentioned."

"If you will forgive me, Mr. Stewart—I am not speaking personally, now—but we are fast learning that Western banks are a pack of thieves. You're nearly as bad as the multinational corporations. You are taking advantage of Third World nations because we are in the position of supplicants now. You loot us and expect us to be grateful. You use us as pawns in the geopolitical games you play with the Soviets. No wonder some of us turn to the Socialist bloc. But remember this, Mr. Stewart, we will not always be pleaders at the tables of the rich, especially a country like Maraka. You should none of you forget the lesson of OPEC."

167

Stewart thought it best to let Okubu's lesson in modern political theory pass without comment.

"With respect, Finance Minister," he said, "I must take exception to your previous comment that we were totally wrong. I believe the terms we are now proposing are the terms Mr. Howe originally put forward."

Okubu moistened his lips. "Certainly not as to the amount of the underwriting. The rest of your point is irrelevant, Mr. Stewart. Manhattan Banking wanted the mandate and did what it thought necessary to get it."

He sat very still, well back in his tall, black leather chair, staring into space, the fingers of his right hand resting lightly on the edge of his desk.

"Prepare a letter, Mr. Stewart, with the new terms. I will discuss it with my colleague Mr. Kalama at the Central Bank and then I will countersign it. But do it quickly, Mr. Stewart. The development of Maraka cannot be allowed to be impeded by the misjudgments of foreigners who do not have her interests at heart." He nodded to Moshu, who stood immediately.

"I'll see you out, Mr. Stewart," Moshu said.

Okubu nodded to Nick as he rose but he did not offer his hand. Nick and Jimmy Moshu walked through the hallway and down the steps to the car that was waiting to take Stewart back to his office.

"Nick, a bit of advice. There had better not be any more 'spots of bother,' as you called it, or I think things will go very hard for Manhattan Banking in Maraka."

"Forewarned is forearmed, Jimmy. Thanks."

As the car drove away he waved through the side window to Jimmy Moshu standing on the steps of the Finance Ministry, and retained the image in his memory for a very long time after: a black man in a well-cut beige tropical suit with a white shirt and a dark blue tie, standing against the intense white wall of the building, which was in sunlight, the sky beyond a deep gray with the coming rain.

All things considered, Stewart thought, it had not gone badly; it had gone so well, in fact, discounting Okubu's blustering, that

168

he wondered what they were so anxious about. At a meeting of the banks they had originally invited into the syndicate, on the other hand, poor, ambitious John Howe had been put through the shredder for bringing to market an oversized, underpriced loan for a borrower such as Maraka, and then to have the balls to expect a skim on the deal as well. The final insult was rubbing his nose in an underwrite of only six hundred million, with the rest on a best-efforts basis.

Stewart's meeting, in contrast, had even had moments of comedy. He particularly relished a man who skimmed a percentage off everything he touched reviling the banks as thieves. But Okubu had given in much too easily for someone who only a month before had pushed around the chairman of the Manhattan Banking Corporation and the head of its department of international banking.

He booked a call to John Howe as soon as he got back to his office. While he waited, he took off his shoes and opened a bottle of Cheetah. When the call to Howe was put through, he had just opened a second bottle, and was trying to forget about the bomb that had killed Paul. Had it been, after all, merely a random act of terrorism?

"I've been to see the Finance Minister, John, and he's agreed to our proceeding on the terms we've discussed. He wasn't happy about it."

"None of us is, Nick."

"I'll send him the letter and let you know as soon as I've got back the countersigned copy." The letter had been prepared already in London and sent to Stewart, who had only to date and sign it.

He was sitting with his feet up on the coffee table, staring through the blinds at the gray sky, and well into his third beer, when Mackintosh rang.

"I was wondering if I could buy you a drink, Mr. Stewart?"

"Be delighted, Mr. Mackintosh."

"Lovely. Six at the Intercontinental?"

Stewart had never seen Colin Mackintosh outside his office at the United Bank of Maraka, except for the strange encounter

169

one night behind Lee's. He had certainly never seen him in the bar at the Intercontinental. Business over drinks after work was not his thing. Five o'clock came and home he went to wife and kiddies.

When Nick arrived at the Intercontinental a little past six, Mackintosh was already there, some pink fluid in a glass in front of him, and sitting in a particularly noisy part of the bar, although there were quieter tables still available.

"Don't you want to move to a quieter spot, Mr. Mackintosh?" Nick said.

"After all this time, I think you ought to call me Colin."

"Colin, then. Don't you—"

Mackintosh shook his head. "What will you have, Nick?"

When the waiter had gone to get his Cheetah, Mackintosh leaned close to him and began to speak as if he were telling him a particularly delicious joke. What he said was,

"You're not out of the woods yet." And smiled broadly.

Stewart looked at him as if he were mad.

"I told you that night I saw you at Lee's to be careful, but I couldn't know at that time what to look out for. I have learned since—"

The waiter appeared and poured Stewart's beer. Nick sat back, lifted his glass to Mackintosh and took a long draft. He replaced the glass on the table and leaned forward.

"I have learned since that it was not a terrorist who blew up your car and killed your driver."

Until now, Nick had never known what was meant by blood freezing.

"Oh, yes, Nick, quite sure. State Security. It was a warning. You've blotted your copybook."

"They must have found out about my shipment."

"No doubt."

Nick suddenly saw himself in the same room, over in the corner with the semicircle of empty tables around it, with Jimmy Moshu.

"'A thing of beauty is a joy forever.'"

Mackintosh stared.

"Do you know the line, Colin?"

"It's the first line of a poem by Keats."

"And what is the poem?"

"Endymion, I believe."

"I'm certain," Nick said. And he remembered how amusing Moshu had thought it was. And now Paul was dead.

"What are you, Colin?" Nick said.

Mackintosh chuckled without smiling and shook his head. "Very nice seeing you, Nick," he said standing, "but I'm afraid I've got to be off home to my dinner. Can I drop you? No?" He hadn't touched his drink.

With a little wave, Mackintosh walked awkwardly through the tables and out the door of the bar.

How had Moshu found out? It would not have made sense for Mackintosh to have told him because Mackintosh was involved, although there was no telling what a man might do to protect himself and his family. In fact, how did Colin Mackintosh know so much, this mild little expat bank manager who could not go home to Surrey because of his black wife? Or it could have been—must have been—George Maguire. He was the only alternative. But what could Maguire have gotten out of it?

He thought briefly of charging upstairs to Maguire's room and dragging him away from his pornographic videotapes and confronting him; but it would do no good. Nick felt worn out, and left the bar without finishing his last beer.

On the following day, Stewart signed the letter containing the new terms and had his messenger hand-deliver it to the Ministry of Finance. As things went in Maraka, he did not receive Okubu's agreement to the terms and conditions, despite the Minister's requirement for haste, until after the weekend, part of which he spent in bed with a bottle of duty-free whisky and the British Caledonian air hostess who had brought it. He had picked her up in the Intercontinental bar on Saturday night.

"Now I know why it's called a lay over," she said when she left on Sunday afternoon. It had been a perfect liaison: no ties and no regrets.

Stewart rang John Howe on Monday morning to tell him of

the receipt of Okubu's agreement, and followed up with a confirming Telex. During the course of the brief conversation, his phone went dead for nearly a minute.

On receipt of Stewart's call, Howe sent out the new offering telex, and by the end of the week, the entire six hundred million dollars had been underwritten by Manhattan Banking and the original nine banks, each taking sixty million. The attempt to syndicate another four hundred million was begun, but no one was under any illusions that the billion dollar mark would be reached; the consensus was that they would reach seven hundred fifty million. The information memorandum less Webb's page of warnings was sent out to all participants.

On Tuesday, Maureen went to the handsome six-story building on the north side of Seventy-eighth Street in which the Vanderpanes kept their apartment.

The doorman nodded when she gave her name, and told her the Vanderpanes were on the top floor. She rose slowly in the carved and mirrored elevator that had a leather-upholstered bench at the back.

The elevator opened directly onto the entrance foyer of the apartment, and Samantha, slim and straight in a blue ruffled blouse and beige slacks, met her as the doors opened. Maureen felt a little dowdy in her light cotton print dress, but Samantha greeted her warmly.

"Maureen, darling," she said, embracing her. "Come in, come in."

The living room was long and narrow, done with light fabrics and deep soft chairs. There was a dining area at one end, and a terrace ran the length of the room.

"What can I get you to drink, dear?"

Maureen had thought about this engagement for the past week. And she had resolved to change her situation. She did not see the reason any longer to play the role of neglected wife and harassed mother.

But she was nervous.

"A martini, Samantha, thank you."

172

"I wish Miles were here to make one of his very special martinis for you," Samantha said, and Maureen thought briefly that she had made a dreadful mistake about her; but instinctively she knew she hadn't. "I'll do my best."

Samantha was surprised and a little dismayed that Maureen had asked for a martini; she hoped she had not become attached to a secret daytime drinker. But when she watched Maureen walking gracefully the length of the living room, her heart beat a little faster and she knew she had overreacted.

"Would you like to see the rest of the apartment, my dear?"

"I would very much, Samantha, yes. But not right now. The terrace looks so delicious."

"Then by all means let's go out and enjoy it."

Samantha took a glass of white wine and they went out to sit in white deck chairs. The air was warm and there was a gentle breeze coming from the direction of the park.

"I've been thinking of what you said to me at lunch last week," Maureen said.

Samantha kissed Maureen's face with her eyes. She wanted to hold her in her arms, but it was too early for that yet. She sipped the wine. "And what have you been thinking, dear?"

"That you are absolutely right. That I am carrying too great a burden in support of my husband's ambition, and that I'm not getting any of the rewards. I don't mean the material ones. They are clearly there, and limited only by my lack of interest in them. What I mean are the emotional rewards."

"And the physical ones?"

Maureen took a deep breath. "Yes, and the physical ones. I think it simply uncanny how you, who know me hardly at all, could have put your finger squarely on the source of my discontent. There has to be something more to life than cleaning up after children and a . . . yes, after our lunch, after the past week, I can say it. A selfish husband. Tony is very capable, very talented, Samantha, but he's interested only in himself." Samantha noticed that the glass in Maureen's hand was shaking a little. "And I have come to the point where I can no longer tolerate his

173

. . . his arrogant assumption that I identify only with his interests. How did you know, Samantha?"

Samantha looked down at her hands. "I *felt* your problem, darling, the instant you came into the room the other night. For some reason, I am on your wavelength, and I recognized how unhappy you were. I am a woman after all, and I understand."

"Oh, Samantha, I know how much of a woman you are."

Samantha smiled at this ingenuous statement, but she was in truth a little disconcerted. Had she not been intending, sooner or later, to seduce Maureen Gould, she would have felt almost as if Maureen were seducing her.

"Can I get you another drink, dear?"

She was not surprised this time when Maureen answered in the affirmative, because the poor lovely thing was very tense and unhappy.

"Thank you, Samantha," she said and took the full glass from her, their fingers touching briefly. "I have been thinking also about your asking whether I had ever taken a lover."

"Maureen, darling, I am embarrassed about that. I do hope you'll forget I ever said such a presumptuous thing."

"I will not forget it, Samantha. I don't want to forget it because it was very important. And there is certainly no need to forgive you. I have stopped lying to myself. And I've come to a decision."

Samantha's heart was beating rapidly.

"I am going to take a lover."

But before Samantha could respond, Maureen continued. "I received some flowers from Charles Houston," she said.

I knew it, Samantha said to herself. To Maureen, she said, "Charles is very nice, dear; and occasionally even thoughtful. But he is essentially an undergraduate. He's a sixty-year-old undergraduate. And a selfish lover."

Maureen knew she should not be surprised, but she felt surprised nonetheless. She had so much to learn and so far to go. But her resolve was strengthened. She looked directly at Samantha, her mouth curved slightly in a smile that the older woman understood with her heart before she heard the words.

The air seemed sultry, and the rest of the world was far away from that terrace.

"You know, Samantha, somehow I recognized that about Charles Houston as instinctively as you knew all those things about me." Maureen leaned forward and took Samantha's hand. Again, Samantha felt the electricity in Maureen's touch. "I still want a lover, my dear. I need a lover. But I don't want Charles Houston." Here the pressure increased a little on Samantha's hand. Maureen was breathing rapidly, as if she had been running and couldn't get quite enough air. "In fact, I don't want a man at all, Samantha. I want a woman who can know me and understand me as you have. I want you." The last words were uttered in a quiet voice that was husky with her nervousness. There were tears gathering at the corners of her eyes. Samantha kissed her gently on the lips.

Nick woke suddenly, sweating heavily. The power was off again and the room was stifling. Although it was pitch black in the room and he felt as if it were the middle of the night, he could hear the sounds of heavy traffic from the road beyond his gate, and thought he must have overslept.

He got to his feet and went to the window and opened the shutters. He had not overslept: it was dark out and the traffic he had heard was military.

He lay in the dark for a long time, unable to sleep because of the heat and the noise, and wondered what the hell was going on.

When Ahmed brought his breakfast to the veranda, Nick asked him what had happened during the night. There was no *Maraka Observer* that morning.

"There was a coup, sah."

Stewart nodded for him to continue.

"A revolutionary council has taken charge of the government and put Tena Maraka under its protection."

They should shoot the old son of a bitch, Nick thought.

"Where have you heard all this, Ahmed?"

"It was on All-Maraka Radio very early, sah."

"Did they say why Tena Maraka had to be protected?"

"No, Mr. Stewart. They said that the revolutionary council must cut out the cancers from the political body of Maraka. They said that they will bring to justice the bloodsuckers of the people."

"Who forms this revolutionary council, Ahmed?"

"Military people, sah. Many names I don't know. Led by General Ujimbu, Mr. Stewart."

"Ah." Evidently the military wasn't getting a big enough cut of the dash, or was tired of sharing it with government incompetents. On the other hand, they might be genuinely worried about the guerrilla activity, and realized they couldn't keep the army together fighting for the bloodsuckers of the people; although, listening to Ujimbu's briefing, you'd never have thought he was worried.

After breakfast, he rang the Australian consul.

"Good of you to call, Mr. Stewart," the consul said cheerfully. "I don't think there's anything to worry about at the moment. There was very little fighting or disruption. Family quarrel, I'd call it. By the by, if you get a chance, could you pop around here to the consulate?"

Nick promised he would try to come at eleven that morning.

It looked as if the Marakan jumbo was going to have another attack of indigestion.

He walked to work through air nearly dripping with humidity. There may have been fewer cars on the road, and fewer pedestrians, but the streets were still crowded, and except for the number of armed troops in battle dress on every corner, one would not have known that anything had happened.

There had been no mail delivery, however. He went through the routine Telexes that had missed the power failure and asked Andrew, his man on the switchboard and the reception desk, what was going to happen. Andrew declared that he didn't know, but whatever it was could be no worse than what had gone before, but he doubted very much whether it could be any better either.

When it was nearly eleven, he got a cab in front of the Inter-continental and went to the Australian consulate.

The consul, who was called James McKee, showed him to his office and gave him a cup of coffee.

"The coup went off like clockwork, suggesting to me that it had been in the works for some time. As I understand it, it was the Capital District garrison that led it. That's Ujimbu's personal command. I am told that he is moving quickly to consolidate his position, and that he has had oaths of loyalty from nearly all the major units around the country. What that means remains to be seen. The fact that the colonel of a regiment says he supports Ujimbu doesn't mean that the regiment supports Ujimbu, and could mean only that the colonel is playing for time. The Capital District garrison supports Ujimbu because all of the officers—field grade and above, at least—have gotten rich under his leadership. The reason it will be touch and go for a while is that those kinds of loyalties don't extend beyond the area immediately around Maraka City.

"My guesstimate is that he can pull it off if he gets the time—if the guerrilla units are not a lot larger than we have been led to believe and if they hold off making a major assault. The army has a tenuous hold in the northwest."

"I've heard the army is poorly paid and disgruntled and likely to disappear if anything serious takes place."

"That's sound information about some units. It depends on the political acumen of the officers. But if Ujimbu is as clever as we think, he'll know whom to grease."

"What happens to the former ministers, Mr. McKee?"

"What always happens in these situations, Mr. Stewart," the consul answered.

Nick had a vision of Jimmy Moshu standing on the steps of the Finance Ministry in his tropical suit and waving and smiling his phony smile.

"In any event, Mr. Stewart," the consul continued, "I'm asking all our compatriots here to call in every day. If we don't hear

177

from you, we shall register our official concern with the government."

By the time Stewart returned to Republic House, it was nearly noon. He had had two urgent calls from John Howe. He asked Andrew to get London for him, and while he waited he watched from his window the helicopters like angry insects taking off from the military strip not far out of town and fly away toward the north until they disappeared in the haze. The low clouds were gray and thick, heavy with rain. The approaching rainy season may have been the reason for Ujimbu's timing; perhaps he calculated that the rains would impede any guerrilla offensive or, heaven help us, even a countercoup.

Howe came through. He sounded on edge.

"For God's sake, John, there's nothing to worry about."

"I hope you're right, Nick. Ever since I heard the news this morning I've been waiting for everybody to bail out of the jumbo."

"Nobody's going to bail out, lad." Howe clearly needed massaging.

"This thing has been jinxed from the start."

"No such thing, John."

"Can you tell me what's happened?"

"You probably know more about it than we do. There are no English papers today, and no English-language broadcasts. Everything I know is word of mouth." He gave Howe a shortened version of what the consul had told him, leaving aside his speculations on the means by which Ujimbu would go about consolidating his position.

"You met Ujimbu once, didn't you, Nick?"

"Yes I have. Most impressive fellow."

"And everything is calm?"

"Looks almost normal, except there are a lot of soldiers around."

"I read they were going to try the former government for crimes against the Marakan people."

"I was told the radio called them bloodsuckers of the people,

178

so I wouldn't be surprised." Jesus, the language of twentieth-century revolution was flatulent.

"And that means people like Okubu."

"No question."

"My God."

"Look, my boyo, there's no point worrying about anything. So far I don't see anything worth worrying about, and I've no doubt that's the same message the Cal Trust and Illinois reps will be giving their head offices. As soon as I've heard from the new lot, John, I'll let you know."

"Gould is going to blow his stack."

Stuff Gould, Stewart thought. "Why, John? Because the political and social developments in Maraka are not going according to his personal timetable, whatever the hell that may be?"

At three that afternoon, Nick received a call from Colonel Ngoa, of whom he'd never heard, asking him to come to the Ministry of Finance.

"We are aware of your lack of transportation, Mr. Stewart. We'll send a car."

The car was a Land Rover in jungle camouflage driven by a sergeant, who was accompanied by a young lieutenant. The officer saluted Nick as he got into the backseat.

The greensward on the approach to the ministry buildings had been chopped up by the tracks of armored vehicles, three of which—a tank and two half-tracks—they had to go around as they approached the Finance Ministry. Higher up the hill, Stewart could see an armored car outside the Presidential Palace. Otherwise, the familiar buildings looked exactly as he'd last seen them.

He was taken along the corridor by the young lieutenant to the office that used to be Okubu's. There were a lot of officers in the corridor and, with their boots sounding on the uncarpeted stone floor, the impression of a great deal of activity. There was a lot of paper now on Okubu's old desk, and the man who sat behind it was much bigger than Okubu. He greeted Stewart courteously, with a pronounced British accent.

"I am Colonel Ngoa. General Ujimbu has asked me to talk

179

with you concerning the loan that your institution is putting together for the Republic of Maraka."

Nick nodded and remained silent.

"We want to assure you, Mr. Stewart, that Maraka intends to honor its commitments, present and future. The needs of Maraka—to address some of which you are arranging the loan on behalf of the people of Maraka—are unchanged. In addition, we believe that Maraka is better able to cope with the threats to our security, now that the army is fighting for the people, and not for a clique of cutthroats whose only interests were self-interests."

Nick nodded politely and noted the use of the past tense.

"General Ujimbu has also asked me to convey to you that he considers that the Manhattan Banking Corporation has made an agreement with the Republic of Maraka, not with the maggots who temporarily occupied these positions, and, just as we intend to honor all our commitments, we expect you and the other banks who have underwritten the six hundred million dollars to honor yours."

"I have no doubt that we will honor our commitments, Colonel Ngoa," Stewart said, not dreaming of saying anything else. "What may prove a bit more difficult is getting beyond the original six hundred million dollars."

"That's as may be, Mr. Stewart. You will do your best, we're certain. That *is* what 'best efforts' means, isn't it?

"From now on, any matter that requires the attention of the Ministry of Finance should be directed to me. Unless you have any questions, then, I won't detain you further. Thank you for coming."

On the silent ride back to Republic House with the officer who again saluted him, Stewart wondered briefly and not too seriously whether he ought not call it a day, hop on a plane to London, and have the bank call the whole thing off. But that would be as dumb as John Howe was being. Maraka had suddenly become a bit more interesting, particularly now that he didn't have to deal with that turd Jimmy Moshu anymore, and he thought he might like to stick around to see the end of the show.

When he got back to the office there was a Telex from Hilary:

ARRIVING BA 026 SATURDAY STOP ARE YOU FREE FOR
DINNER QUERY

"Idiot girl," Nick said, crumpled the Telex and threw it across the room.

He rang John Howe to tell him of his visit to Ngoa. It only made Howe fret more.

"If any of the banks rescinds its underwrite, we're really in trouble."

"No, you're not, John. First off, it won't happen. Second, if a couple of banks pull out, and the deal collapses, all bets are off anyway. We can claim material adverse change. And at the end of the day, you haven't lent them the money."

"But what about our present exposure?"

This character sounds as if he joined the bank two weeks ago, Nick thought. "It's already there, John. If there's a problem, it's still there, no matter what we do."

"What am I going to tell Tony?"

Ah, at last the problem emerges. "Tell him anything you like, John." With which Stewart hung up. He was tired of Howe's whining and need for reassurance. Perhaps he would think the connection had been cut off.

The noise in the Intercontinental bar at six o'clock seemed louder than usual. It was as if a great weight had been lifted from everyone; they had all been waiting for the other shoe to drop, and it had, and everything was just fine. He hoped they were right.

Stewart joined Derek Houndswell, who was standing alone at the bar, and ordered a whisky and soda. Houndswell reminded him that the last time they had met was the night Stewart's car had been blown up.

"Did they ever tell you why they thought terrorists were going after you?"

"It wasn't terrorists, Derek. It was the fucking State Security."

"Good God, man, what on earth did you do? Ask them to cover their overdraft?"

181

"Nothing I can think of, Derek."

"Well, the accounts are now being rendered, aren't they?"

Nick had only partially heard the last sentence, having been distracted by the arrogant strut across the bar of a young coffee-colored black woman, very trim fore and aft, who was with one of the red-faced beefy oilies, a kind of up-market George Maguire.

"Sorry, Derek, I didn't catch that."

"You know those helicopters that have been taking off all day?"

"Yes?"

"Good heavens, man, you don't know what they're doing? The enemies of the people are being flown up north over the jungle and just pushed out."

Nick put his drink carefully on the bar and said "Excuse me." As he was leaving, he knocked over a barstool.

He walked slowly, but deliberately, across the room, through the entrance, and turned left along the corridor to the Gents. He pushed his way in, locked himself into a stall, and vomited. In his mind's eye, he saw Jimmy Moshu in his beige tropical suit screaming and turning over and over beneath the helicopter, first one Gucci loafer flying off, then the other.

Maraka was a living nightmare. This is what Ujimbu thought would ensure stability and consolidate his position. When the neutrals—the non-Communist opposition out in the bush, for example—saw how the good general was dealing with those who might have some different ideas about the future of Maraka, there was no chance of compromise. And no chance of any real stability for Maraka.

He rinsed his mouth out and washed his face and returned to the bar.

Houndswell was still there. "I'm sorry, Nick. I didn't know you'd take it so hard."

"Not your fault, Derek. I've just been dealing with some of those people you've told me are being pushed out of helicopters. You couldn't have known. Never mind. Let me buy you another of those in return for some more prognostication. You were right last time."

Stewart signaled another round to the bartender.

"A period of consolidation, my boy," Houndswell said. "This chap Ujimbu has his head screwed on right. And as far as I can tell, a good group around him as well. I think they'll pull the country together and the economy is going to go full-speed ahead. Make no mistake about it, Nick, this coup was great for business. The middle class, small as it is, are happy as clams. They think that Ujimbu is going to let them keep what they earn by the dishonest sweat of their brows. Had nothing like the coup taken place, the country would have disintegrated eventually through a combination of internal and external pressures."

"Don't you think he may be assuring instability by dealing so uncompromisingly with the opposition?"

"Not to be too cold-blooded about it, old man, what better way is there to neutralize the opposition than by eliminating it? There are a lot of old scores being repaid as well."

Yes, Nick thought, the whole thing is beginning to resemble the standard garden-variety pattern. Ujimbu will make revolution inevitable.

But to Houndswell he said, "Does anyone know what's happened to the Father of Maraka?"

"I've heard he's still up in his castle on the hill under the protection of some of Ujimbu's handpicked troops. The translation is that he's under house arrest. He's still too much of a hero to these people to be got rid of, the symbol of Marakan independence. He'll be brought out and dusted off for state occasions and that's all Ujimbu will ever let him do. The old thief will never see those funds he was putting aside in Switzerland against a rainy day."

Stewart stared into his whisky and soda. He didn't want to finish it. He didn't want to do much of anything.

"Tell me, Nick," Houndswell said lightly, "how did you learn that it wasn't terrorists who blew up your car?"

Even through a brain numbed with weariness, an alarm bell

sounded, and he knew that he shouldn't tell Houndswell the truth.

"George Maguire told me."

"The Childs chap? How the hell would he know?"

Stewart shrugged. "I didn't ask. Probably something he heard let slip. He was thick as thieves with people in the former government. Maybe they let him know accidentally on purpose. Sorry, Derek, I'm worn out. I'll be off now. Thanks for the crystal-ball gazing."

"Can I drop you, Nick?"

"Thanks very much. I'll just grab a taxi out front."

Hilary came out of the customs hall carrying two small cases and dressed in a white short-sleeved blouse and beige slacks. She was looking rumpled after the long flight, but a lot healthier than she had just before she'd left. He waved and walked quickly to her and kissed her lightly.

"I'm so glad to be back, Nick," she said with a question in her eyes. "Are you happy to see me?"

"Of course," he said, busying himself with the bags. He straightened up and said, "Where to now?"

"Can we see if there's anything left in my old flat?"

She followed him outside to a white Mercedes. He put the bags into the boot and unlocked her door. He turned the air conditioning and the fan to high and they started off.

"It's rented," he answered. "The Volvo was blown up, and Paul along with it."

"My God, Nick, no. When did it happen? Why?"

"It happened a little while after you'd left. Because you'd left. It was a sign of disapproval from the government."

Rain started suddenly, very heavy, and stopped just as suddenly. The sky was the color of pewter.

"I'm so sorry, Nick," she said quietly.

"You were in danger, Hilary. We had to get you out. It wasn't your fault."

They drove a little in silence.

"But are you really happy to see me, Nick? Because you seem so different somehow."

"In an ideal world, I'd be delighted to see you. It is not an ideal world and part of me is not happy to see you. Maraka is a dangerous place."

"Less so than it was before, surely."

"Is that why you've come back, Hilary? To confirm a preconception? Is that the way journalists work?"

"You're being cruel, Nick."

"I'm sorry. I don't mean to be. But I think this place is frightening. The country is falling apart."

"That's not what it looks like to others."

"I don't care what it looks like to others."

"Nick, don't let's argue. I am so happy to see you." He thought, but it's not me you want, it's Maraka.

Hilary's flat had been searched. There were clothes strewn onto the floor in the bedroom and broken glass in the sitting room and the kitchen. Her radio and her camera and all the liquor were gone.

"It could have been worse," she said. "I never expected the camera and so forth to survive anyway."

They threw everything in the refrigerator into trash cans without looking too closely at it and left the door of the fridge open to air it out.

They returned to the bedroom, where the shutters were still drawn against the heat. She turned on the air-conditioner and took off all her clothes.

"Very nice," he said.

"Don't you want me, Nick?"

"Sure, Hilary. But not right now."

She pulled all the sheets from the bed and added them to the pile on the floor and lay back on the mattress.

"You *are* different. You've become remote." She turned her back to him and began to sob.

He sat on the mattress beside her and stroked her shoulder.

"There's no need to carry on like this, Hilary."

185

She cried harder. He rubbed her side and her hip and could no longer remain disinterested. She felt the change in his touch and turned and helped him out of his trousers. He took her roughly.

When he lay beside her, staring at the ceiling, she said, "At least part of you hasn't changed. But it could have been nicer. Captain Pappas would probably have been very gentle."

"Did he—"

"God, Nick, no. Where's your sense of humor? That's not to say he didn't try. When his charm failed, he said he would rebate part of my fare for one night of ecstasy."

He smiled forlornly.

"What is it, Nick?"

"I'm frightened for you, Hilary. You should not have come back. I don't think we can be lucky a second time."

"I'll take care of myself."

"If you do something they don't like, they won't blunder like the former crowd. They'll get rid of you straightaway."

"That's a chance I'll have to take."

When he thought about it later, he thought it must have been at this moment that he realized he could no longer help Hilary, that she was rushing ineluctably toward the darkness. And he had no intention of going along for the ride.

13

By the end of the third week after the coup, the world community had decided that the junta led by General Ujimbu was firmly in control and therefore recognized his government. The Manhattan Banking jumbo for Maraka reached seven hundred twenty-five million dollars and the lead managers decided that they had taken it as far as they could, having contacted over three hundred banks. Tony Gould decided that Howe could no longer be trusted to do what Tony Gould wanted him to do.

In a guerrilla camp in the Northwest Province of Maraka, Arthur Ekaba met his classmate from the London School of Economics James Nijima for the first time in twenty years.

They had taken widely divergent paths after LSE. Ekaba had gone to study in Moscow, and Nijima had taken a Ph.D. in Economics at Berkeley, and had returned to Maraka to teach at the University.

Ekaba was declared persona non grata by reason of his venue and some of his radical writings that surfaced in Bolivia in the late sixties. Nijima was forced underground because his teaching in the Politics and Economics faculty of the University was considered subversive by Tena Maraka personally. He taught for a while in Britain and the United States, but, burning with the zeal of a missionary after he watched the rape of his homeland by its leaders, he returned clandestinely to Maraka.

Both eventually organized guerrilla units. Ekaba's was well supplied by the Soviets and now had Cuban advisers. Nijima's group, which was financed by the French and the Chinese, was not well organized, and tended to arm itself with whatever it could get at inflated prices on the world arms market, and a number of merchants grew rich dealing with Nijima's agents, who grew rich themselves.

The CIA had recommended support for Tena Maraka and his ministers, as a result of which the American taxpayer received no return on his investment.

Until Ujimbu's coup, neither Nijima nor Ekaba was strong enough to make much headway against the regime, which was conservative like most of the population. After the coup, and particularly after the measures that Ujimbu had taken to deal with the opposition and to consolidate his position, both realized that the General had created a situation of instability that could be exploited. Each independently arrived at the judgment that they would be far more effective working together than separately.

Nijima knew who was supporting Ekaba and why, but knew also that Ekaba was essentially a political conspirator—and a brilliant one at that—who had no loyalties except to himself. He was, *en effet*, taking the Russians for a ride. Nijima believed that his recognition of Ekaba's character could be used as the ultimate weapon against him, after the General had been removed—to neutralize if not to eliminate him.

Ekaba valued Nijima's intelligence, but valued more the large numbers he controlled, albeit loosely. He knew Nijima to be an idealist, and he knew that in the final analysis the word "ruth-less" was not in Nijima's vocabulary.

So it was, shortly after the coup, that the two men met in an atmosphere of great cordiality and forged an agreement to coop-erate for the benefit of Maraka. They planned a meeting of their chiefs of staff with the object to design a swift offensive whose purpose was to destroy Ujimbu and take control of the country. It was thought that the population, if not actually supportive of their efforts, would do nothing to impede them either. One thing was absolute: they had to strike during the height of the rainy season, when the tanks and armored cars and personnel carriers supplied by the Americans would not be able to use the roads, which by then would be quagmires, while their own units would travel with relative ease through the surrounding jungle, demoralizing the already demoralized government troops, whose resistance would simply melt away.

For a couple of weeks, Miles Vanderpane had awakened feel-ing as if he had not slept at all, and this morning was no excep-tion. He struggled to get out of bed, and showered and shaved and dressed wearily.

Sam was, as usual, reading the newspapers when he got to the breakfast table. He kissed her cheek and sat down, wondering if she felt as well as she looked. She had recently taken on a glow, and become a good deal more relaxed than he had sensed in a long time, and while he had reluctantly come to the conclusion that she had taken a new lover, nonetheless she was looking smashing and was extremely pleasant to be around. She even occasionally made love to him, in rather a languid way; which it had to have been in any event, because by the end of the work-ing day he was hardly able to move.

"You don't look at all well, Miles," she said, with the greatest solicitude as he addressed his egg.

He cracked the egg carefully and removed the top. It was perfectly cooked.

"Just feeling my age at last, my dear." He sprinkled a little salt, ground some pepper.

"Nonetheless, I wish you'd see Dr. Farley."

The egg tasted of nothing. The toast tasted of nothing. The coffee was hot nothing.

"Perhaps you're right, Sam. I'll see him as soon as I can." He ate and drank everything in front of him, although it was difficult. He hoped she hadn't noticed.

"Anything of note in the papers this morning, Sam?" he asked with a heartiness he did not feel.

"Not much. There's a small article about the Maraka syndication, unkindly pointing out that it hasn't reached the billion that was projected."

"Yes, well, the coup didn't help much there, Sam."

She wanted to ask him why, despite the ample warning, the bank had found itself trying to syndicate a loan while the government was being overthrown; but she did not, could not, because he looked so awful. She was going to call Farley as soon as Miles left for work.

They heard the familiar crunch of the car on the gravel outside. Sam touched his hand. "Miles, why don't you stay home today and rest?"

He simply smiled and rose and kissed her on the cheek. He picked up his attaché case in the front hall and walked outside.

It was a beautiful summer morning with a promise of heat later in the day, but still refreshingly cool. Miles hardly noticed. Tommy handed him the *Daily News*, put the attaché case on the front seat, and they started off.

Before they had even reached the Bear Mountain Bridge, Miles was asleep, the newspaper slipping from his knees onto the floor. Sometime later, although he could not have told how long, something woke him with a start. The black man who had visited with Okubu and Kalama, and whom he had seen in the car on the parkway the other morning, was sitting beside him, but it did not startle or frighten him, because he suddenly understood it all with a greater clarity than he had ever understood anything in his life. He was sad about Sam, because he had truly liked her so much, and because she had been such a good friend, and he felt sad about leaving his comfortable house and his pleasant life; but after all, he was tired and perhaps it was time that he should rest.

He looked at the black man, who smiled warmly and patted his wrist.

It was not unusual for Miles Vanderpane to slump so low in the back seat while he was napping that Tommy couldn't see him in the rearview mirror; but it was unusual for him not to be sitting up straight by the time they had reached Manhattan. One quick glance while they were going down the East River Drive at the gray-faced thing behind him told Tommy that he had driven a dead man from Garrison.

"Holy shit," he said, but made three signs of the cross and headed for the emergency room at New York Hospital.

The messages of condolence poured into Manhattan Banking from banks, governments, and corporations around the world, from the International Monetary Fund and the World Bank, from the Fed and the Bank for International Settlements, for Chairman Miles Vanderpane, who had died still in his prime, at the pinnacle of his career, and almost at his desk; he had, in any event, been working, according to his chauffeur, who had managed to retrieve his *Daily News* folded open, as it usually was, to Jumble. It had been, of course, a heart attack, and it was thought that death had been instantaneous.

Samantha was given a strong sedative and put to bed by Dr. Farley. Maureen Gould spent part of the day sitting by her bedside. Indeed, Maureen was the only person other than the doctor and her two children whom Samantha allowed into her bedroom that day.

An extraordinary meeting of the board of directors was called for the afternoon of the funeral. Tony Gould wondered what the board would do; he felt certain, but he didn't know. He was astonished by the relationship that had developed between Samantha Vanderpane and Maureen, but realized that it couldn't possibly hurt his career prospects. Ben Kincaid shed a tear for old

Miles, and thought he knew pretty much what the board was going to do, especially since it had been he who had personally phoned every director with the sad news. Max Fougere simply waited.

"I think I'm reaching the end of the tether," Webb said.

"If you're talking about Manhattan Banking, that's super," Catherine said. "More beer."

They were sitting in a booth at Teddy's. Chris poured from the pitcher.

"You know what's happened?"

"Not until you tell me. I don't even know what you're talking about yet."

"Rumored to happen. The board meeting was this afternoon. Nothing official yet. They've made Tony Gould president."

"Good for him," Catherine said. "Just what he wanted."

"Now he can practice his advanced management techniques on the entire bank, instead of only on International Banking."

"What are you going to do?"

"Dust off my résumé."

"You want to continue in banking?"

"I'm not ready to try something else, Cath."

"Chicken."

"I'm not ready to give up Brookfield yet."

"Materialist."

"I'm not ready to have you support me."

"Chauvinist."

"I love you."

"I love you too."

At the same meeting at which Tony Gould was made president of Manhattan Banking, despite strong opposition from several of the directors, who were ultimately reconciled because of the need to act quickly, Ben Kincaid was made chairman and chief executive officer and Max Fougere was promoted to head of international banking. And in a gesture of superlative magnanimity, and as a fitting memorial to Miles, Samantha Vanderpane was elected to the board to fill Miles's unexpired term, which ran out in ten months. It was Charles Houston who proposed the move, and it was to Charles that Samantha had suggested that he might make such a proposal, vaguely letting him infer that he wouldn't regret it, and Houston had gone along. He knew Samantha because he had slept with her.

Little by little, things in Maraka began to change. The change was slow, and it was only with an accumulation of experiences that Nick began to notice.

There were the power failures, for example. They had always had power failures, of shorter or longer duration, and owing to a variety of causes, but now there seemed to be a few more of them per week. The streets had always been filthy, but now they were filthier still. Shortages, which were a way of life for the bulk of the Marakan population, began to occur as well in shops where the rest went, what was left of the Marakan elite, and the middle class, and the large expatriate community. The crime rate— always very high—was increasing, and there was a new element that arrived with what was officially being called the Revolution, and that was incidents of assaults by troops on civilians, especially robbery, usually at gunpoint, and rape.

Nick observed all of this with a jaded eye and duly reported it all in his memos to Max Fougere, who maintained his interest in the Africa area, and to Waldo Carter, the new division head. Stewart did not regard the deterioration as permanent, but judged that it would take some time for the country to settle down. He continued to consider Maraka as having the potential to be economically sound, and felt that someday the country would be decently managed and the potential would be realized.

Stewart was called to another meeting with Colonel Ngoa to discuss the first draft of the loan agreement, and afterward was given rather a good dinner at the Officers' Club. They discussed various provisions of the agreement in a desultory way—someone had obviously given Ngoa a crash course in Eurocurrency agreements—but the Colonel had no real problems with the document, and it was obvious to Nick that they would like to sign, and draw the money, as quickly as possible. The negotiations were therefore pressed ahead, the final draft agreed among the lenders and between the lenders and the borrower and their respective counsel, and the signing was subsequently scheduled for the first week in July in London. It was hinted that General Ujimbu himself might attend.

George Maguire ignored the knock on the door. He sipped bourbon and watched John Wayne and Dean Martin and Ricky Nelson in *Rio Bravo* for the twentieth time, or the fiftieth time, on his video recorder. The knocking continued.

"Who is it?"

"Mr. Maguire?" said a Marakan voice.

"Yes."

"I have an envelope for you, sir."

"Just put it under the door."

"It is too bulky to go under the door, sir."

"Then leave it in my mailbox downstairs."

"I was told to hand it to you personally, sir."

"Shit," Maguire said. He put the chain on the door and opened it wide enough to see who was outside. The barrel of a revolver was shoved at his face.

"Take the chain off, Mr. Maguire, if you please."

Not your usual goon, Maguire thought slowly. Sounds educated, for a monkey, that is.

"The chain, Mr. Maguire. No funny business. We can shoot it off and it will go hard for you."

"Who the hell are you?"

"Police."

"Let me see your identification."

"The chain, Mr. Maguire."

Fuck it, Maguire thought. I didn't like Maraka much, anyway. He slipped off the chain and two men pushed quickly into the room and shut the door. They both had guns. One motioned to him to sit down, while the other looked into the bathroom. He came out and stood behind George. The other stood in front of him.

194

"Why did you tell Stewart that his car was blown up by government agents?"

"I don't know what the hell you're talking about." His head was clearing fast and he was frightened.

"For whom do you work?"

"Childs Construction."

"That is your cover. For whom do you work?"

"You boys have got the wrong man. I don't work for nobody but Childs."

"You will come with us, Mr. Maguire."

"No, sir. I ain't going nowhere."

The man behind pushed the gun barrel against the back of his head.

"Goddammit, that hurt," he said. He started to get out of the chair and kicked as hard as he could and caught the man in front of him squarely in the balls. The man folded like an accordion, dropped his gun, and collapsed whimpering to the floor. If it had even occurred to Maguire to go for the gun, he was too old and slow and out of shape to have reached it in time. The man behind hit him across the back of the head with his revolver and he fell to his hands and knees.

Through the haze in front of his eyes he could see the man he kicked getting slowly to his feet. The guy was really hurt and really pissed. The two were shouting Marakan at each other. The argument ended when one of them kicked Maguire in the side and he fell over.

They dragged and carried him out onto the balcony. The guy he'd kicked was bawling and George thought that was funny until he realized what they were going to do. He started to scream but no one came. They draped him over the balustrade head first and, using the momentum, continued by tipping his legs after, and he fell five stories to the ground below.

It was the third time she had called and he knew he had to take it.

"You're avoiding me, Nick."

"I'm awfully busy right now, Hilary, with the jumbo. I'm going

195

to have to go to London in three weeks' time to sign the agreement."

"Can we have a drink at the Intercontie? I'll buy."

"Sure," he said.

"Sixish?"

He could not believe that Hilary had come back to Maraka, or that she had begun to write articles that were almost as waspish as the ones she had written about the previous regime, and now she was writing for syndication. Hilary was accident-prone, and he didn't want that quality rubbing off on himself.

When he arrived at the Intercontinental, there was a crowd milling around the side, which parted just as he reached it. A military ambulance, olive drab with large red crosses on the sides and the bonnet, emerged and drove off.

"What's up, Ralph," he said to the Bank of Illinois representative who was standing on the steps. The crowd had become individuals, most of whom were heading into the hotel.

"Seems like someone jumped or fell out of a window. I wasn't close enough to see the end product. Thank God."

"Suicide?"

"They haven't said. Suicide or accident."

"Who is 'they,' Ralph?"

"Who indeed? Buy you a drink to celebrate the successful termination of this year's, or this quarter's, Marakan jumbo?"

"Thanks very much. I have a previous engagement."

"Ah yes. Hilary's back, isn't she?"

Nick simply winked and went inside. He scanned the bar, but did not see her. He took a table from which he could watch the entrance to the bar and ordered a whisky and soda.

She saw him before he saw her, and waved.

"I'm sorry I'm late, Nick," she said, and leaned over and kissed him. "There was a story." She was slightly flushed, and her hair was awry. She looked lovely. Stop it, he said to himself. She asked for whisky.

"I know. I saw the fag end of it."

"Man out of the window?"

"Yes. Do you know who it was?"

"No, not yet. Caucasian."

"Ah. Suicide or accident?"

"The police said it was an accident, no doubt. No supporting evidence. It was an accident because they say it was."

"Quite right. You'd better believe them, my dear."

"I bloody well won't."

"You bloody well are going to get into trouble if you don't. Goddammit, Hilary, you're pushing your luck. And for what?"

She looked away from him across the room, and then at the table and back at him. Her eyes were shiny and there was a catch in her voice.

"We're scrapping again, Nick, and there's no reason for it."

"I'm sorry. But you haven't answered my question," he said, more gently. "Why this relentless search for truth and justice?"

"It ought to be obvious."

"I come from the school of every man for himself. To me it's not obvious."

"Am I talking to the same man who smuggled me out of Maraka when my life was in danger?"

"Yes. And I'm talking to the woman who's chucked all that effort away by coming back."

"Goodness, Nick, is that what's bothering you? I've done the unexpected?"

"You've done the stupid. Drink up and let's get out of here."

She stared for a long time into her drink, which she'd hardly touched.

"I didn't hear you," he said, raising his voice, sounding harsh even to himself.

"I said," she said looking into his eyes, "'you don't care any longer.'"

"I do care."

"Then you don't love me any longer."

He couldn't look at her. He looked instead toward the bar. Derek Houndswell was propping it up as usual. "I never said I did love you, you know."

He dragged his eyes from the bar and looked across the table. Tears were running down her cheeks and she was nodding.

197

"Technically you're correct," she said with difficulty. "You never said you loved me." She searched through her bag and threw some notes on the table.

"I'll take care—" he began.

"Fuck you," she said and stood up. "Fuck you, you selfish, self-absorbed bastard. Good-bye, Nick." She turned and walked away without waiting for a response. He watched her weave her way through the tables and out the door. Still the finest ass in Maraka. He rubbed his hand across his eyes. Good-bye, old girl, he thought to himself.

He called for another whisky and soda and drank Hilary's while he was waiting. The money she had thrown on the table mocked him. Houndswell came to the table with a gin and tonic and sat down.

"Shame about George Maguire," he said.

"Who gives a damn about George Maguire?" Nick responded.

"No need to bite my head off, old man. Just a horrible way to die is what I mean."

Nick felt as if he had been in a deep cave, well below the surface, and was being summoned back up top.

"You mean that was George?"

Houndswell nodded.

Nick shook his head. "That poor son of a bitch. Probably got so drunk he didn't know where the hell he was and just fell off his balcony."

"He was really hitting the stuff, was he?"

Nick grunted in the affirmative. "Seemed all he did after work was watch a video recorder and get pissed."

"Not much of a life. Well, I've got to get on home. Good night, Nick."

"Good night, Derek. Look, the next time I see you, I hope you have some good news for a change, or else I'm going to hide under the table when I see you coming."

Houndswell chuckled and slapped him on the back and with a little wave walked off. Nick thought, I bet he thought I was kidding.

When he went to the front of the hotel to pick up a taxi, he saw Colin Mackintosh, to whom he waved as he walked past. These people, Houndswell and Mackintosh, kept turning up, like bad pennies.

The taxi bumped on broken springs toward Stewart's compound, the warm, fetid air blowing in the open windows. Nick began to think about Maguire. How likely was it that George had fallen off his own balcony? Nick visualized Maguire slumped in a chair with his bottle of bourbon and his ciggies and his video recorder, the air-conditioner going flat out, and *all the windows closed.*

Suicide? No. He wasn't the type. George's despair was only skin deep, just like George.

But if he hadn't jumped, and he hadn't fallen, then he was pushed. I'll be damned. Wonder who had it in for old George besides me? Or is it just getting insalubrious for expats in Maraka? And if that's so, shouldn't I be getting out?

He had the feeling that his association with the Manhattan Banking Corporation might be coming to an end.

Hilary. What about Hilary? He paid off the driver, nodded to the guards at the gate, and walked through the courtyard toward his front door.

She knows what she wants, he decided. She wants the darkness. I can't afford the pain.

The July board meeting of the Manhattan Banking Corporation took place on the second Monday of the month, as did all the bank's board meetings, and was a double meeting, as were all July meetings, there being no meeting in August. It was the first meeting in which Ben Kincaid took the chair, and in which Tony Gould and Samantha Vanderpane participated as new directors.

Samantha was the only woman director, and was the center of attention as a result, dressed in black, with a strand of pearls, and pearl earrings, her hair pulled back tightly into a bun, tall, slim, and very attractive; this was not to mention the sympathy that flowed her way from people who had been fond of Miles, and the sexual interest she generated.

199

The board discussed the minutes of the previous ordinary meeting and the results for the second quarter, which, at seventy-three cents a share, were no better or worse than anyone had any right to expect. Samantha Vanderpane did question the wisdom of eliminating the quarterly provision for loan losses in order to show a four percent gain on the comparable period for the preceding year, instead of a one percent downturn, but the question seemed rhetorical more than anything else, and hence, while the question was noted, it was not answered. The board then voted routinely on two months' worth of promotions, and turned to the last matter of substance on the agenda.

Ben Kincaid was sitting at the head of the table in the softly lit board room, trying to look less pleased with himself than he felt. At his right hand was a glass of Dr. Pepper on ice, and behind it was an unopened can of Dr. Pepper. It was a picture of Ben that all the old members of the board knew intimately and were amused by when he was president. But now he was chairman of the board and chief executive officer, and he was sitting in a room full of directors who had gone to the best Eastern boarding schools, and the Ivy League universities, and who had little tolerance for idiosyncrasy in their chairman. Miles Vanderpane hadn't been odd, and he was Hotchkiss and Princeton (and Ivy as well!). Ben, the directors were thinking, jointly and severally, ought to have known better. And not knowing better, Kincaid was starting badly.

He proposed the creation of the office of vice-chairman, and the selection of two vice-chairmen, one to manage the commercial banking departments, the other to take care of the fiduciary departments. Ben further proposed the creation of an asset and liability committee, of which he would be chairman, and of which the new vice-chairmen and Tony Gould would be members.

Kincaid's proposals came as a complete surprise to Gould, and he was horrified. If the vice-chairmen were to have real power, Kincaid was putting another layer between the president and the chairman, and squeezing Gould between the vice-chairmen and the department heads. Tony began to chew the inside of his lower lip furiously, trying to develop arguments to counter Kincaid.

When Ben asked for discussion, Samantha raised her hand. Instantly, all eyes turned her way. She had met them all on many occasions with Miles. They knew her and mostly liked her, and some had been impressed with the comments she had made about the provision for loan losses. She knew them pretty well also, and knew them to be the usual collection of fools, lackwits, mountebanks, and reasonably intelligent people that any group of men would be. A few would need to be persuaded; most could simply be led. She had known also that sooner or later Ben Kincaid would make a serious error, but she had not foreseen that it would have been quite as soon as the first meeting.

"Excuse me, Ben," she began in a deliberately modulated voice. The room became absolutely still. "I think I understand what you are trying to do. You are attempting to address the organizational problems of a large, complex, modern corporation, and perforce the answers are going to be complex."

Samantha was addressing Ben, but she made eye contact with each of the directors, and especially with Tony Gould and Charles Houston.

"I applaud your efforts. What I'm not sure I understand is how a chief executive officer can remain an effective chief executive officer by putting more layers of bureaucracy between himself and the department heads through whom he manages the corporation."

The directors were hushed. In her first meeting, Samantha Vanderpane had spoken with more authority than Miles—God rest his soul—had in twelve years. And she was Miss Porter's and Vassar. Nothing idiosyncratic about Samantha.

Kincaid did not dare pick up his glass of Dr. Pepper for fear that the distraction of his arm motion or the clink of the ice in his glass would provoke hostility toward himself.

"What I'm suggesting, Ben," Samantha continued, "is not that your ideas be dismissed—far from it, and far be it from me to presume such a thing—but that they be studied. Perhaps two vice-chairmen and a new committee or so are what should be done, and perhaps not. All I'm saying is, it is probably time that we all rethought what ought to be the form of our corporation to meet the challenges that lie ahead.

"But this isn't a thing to be undertaken lightly. So let us, yes, create a committee today—one only—drawn from among the directors and the senior banking and trust heads that will discuss the alternatives and make recommendations to the full board, let us say, at the November meeting."

Charles Houston roundly praised Samantha's suggestion, and was echoed by a number of others. Ernest Pelletier suggested that Samantha herself be made chairman of the future study committee. Nearly everyone concurred, and those who didn't kept silent. Samantha was instructed by the board to form a committee from among the directors, no more than four, including herself as chairman, and from the senior banking and trust department heads, and to come up with a recommendation for a plan of organization that would take the Manhattan Banking Corporation through the eighties. By the end of the meeting, very few of the directors remembered that Ben had said anything at all.

At the lunch that followed the board meeting there was some confusion about who was going to be able to sit to Samantha's right and left—and it was obvious that there had been some tampering with the place cards—which Kincaid solved by having Samantha sit on his left, across from Tony Gould, and next to Erskine Walker, who was nearing eighty and couldn't hear very well, and lunched mostly on mineral water.

In his new office after lunch, Ben Kincaid sat in Miles Vanderpane's old wing chair and stared out the window. Sweet Jesus, he thought, and resolved never to take Samantha Vanderpane for granted again. There was no question in his mind that her first term on the board would have to be her last as well.

Tony Gould was delighted at the outcome of the board meeting. It remained only for him to persuade the board that it ought to be he, not Ben, who ought to hold the executive reins. Ben could be a superb representative of Manhattan Banking, but he did not have the mind for the organizational complexity that

Tony Gould and Samantha Vanderpane foresaw would be necessary in the future.

That evening Maureen made an omelette for him and then, to his great surprise, sat with him while he began to eat it.

"Samantha Vanderpane has invited us to spend some time in August with her on Martha's Vineyard, Tony."

He deliberately suppressed his excitement. What could that possibly mean but that Samantha was taking an interest in his career, and, as he had learned today, she was a director with clout?

"But how about Bridgehampton?" he asked, feigning indifference to the Vineyard proposal.

"Bridgehampton can do without us this summer. You know we can rent the house in a flash. Since you get out only on the weekends anyway, I thought you wouldn't mind. In fact, I suspect that it would be no more difficult for you to get to Martha's Vineyard on the weekend than it is for you to get out to the Island."

"Perhaps," he said. He looked at Maureen more closely. She looked better than it seemed to him that she had looked in a long time. She seemed more self-confident, somehow, and at the same time calmer, almost serene. Well, if that's what having Samantha Vanderpane for a friend did for Maureen, what might it not do for him? "I don't know, Maureen. My responsibilities are greater now."

"I know. Poor Tony. I can't imagine how they could be any greater than they have been. But I obviously don't understand."

With Maureen and the kids out of his hair in August, and able to depend on someone other than himself for entertainment, he could really get down to work; perhaps go up to the Vineyard for the last few days of the month and have some real heart-to-hearts with Samantha about the bank.

"Let me think about it, Maureen. It's not a bad idea. I'm a little tired of Long Island anyway. How nice of Samantha. You seem to have hit it off with her."

"We do get along very well."

"She's fairly bright. I saw her at the board meeting today."

"She's very bright, actually."

"Not a bad sort at all."

"I'm so glad you think so."

A few days before Stewart was scheduled to fly to London for the loan signing, Colin Mackintosh invited him home for dinner. Nick was astonished by the invitation, since it had always seemed to him that Mackintosh had no social life to speak of, and certainly not at home, particularly as he was something of an outcast in both the Marakan and the expat communities. It was therefore with some misgivings, and a great deal of curiosity, that he accepted.

Mackintosh lived in a modest bungalow in a middle-class Marakan road. The white Mercedes that Nick drove there and parked in front of the house looked clearly out of place. The house itself was buried in a thick stand of tall shrubs, and from the front it looked as if no one was at home. When he reached the front door, however, he could see through the screen that there was a dim orange light in the hall, and the silhouette of a woman came out of the gloom to unlatch the door.

"Mr. Stewart?" she asked in the lilting Marakan accent.

"Yes. You are . . ."

She said nothing and turned. He followed her through the dark hallway and out onto a screened veranda at the back of the house overlooking a scruffy back garden. The light had started to fail, and was going quickly, and the air was heavy with humidity.

"Hello, Nick." Mackintosh rose out of a rickety cane chair. He waved at a drinks tray on a low table. "What can I get you?"

Mackintosh poured two large whiskys. The woman had left them. "Soda? Good."

They sat in the unsteady cane chairs and contemplated the gloom in the garden. In a few minutes' time, it became night.

"It's been a gray day," Stewart ventured.

"Yes. Rain's about to let loose at any moment."

"Night seems much darker now."

Mackintosh sighed in a way that startled Nick.

"Night is coming to Maraka, I fear."

"What do you mean?"

"So bankerly, Nick," Mackintosh smiled dismally. "I don't mean economic problems. I mean political and social ones. This regime can't be good for the country. Only going to precipitate more problems. But the banks will always be repaid, no matter who's in power. Even a Marxist." He sipped the whisky. "Did you know that the Ministry of State Security has survived the coup almost intact? Shall we eat?"

They moved to a table on one side of the veranda and Mackintosh lit the candle and put a storm chimney over it. The cacophony of night insects grew around them.

Mackintosh opened bottles of Cheetah and filled the glasses at their places. They were silent while the woman who had met Stewart at the door brought them food.

"There's a storm coming," Mackintosh said.

"Well, it is the rainy season."

"I wasn't referring to the weather."

Stewart watched the candlelight flicker on Mackintosh's face.

"We choose all the time. So much of life is making choices and most of the time we're so ill equipped to do it."

Stewart wondered if Colin was going to prattle on like this for the rest of the evening.

"Did you know George Maguire?" Mackintosh said.

"Yes," Nick said. "Can't say I cared for him much."

"No more did I."

The woman came to remove their plates and returned with sliced melon.

"He was murdered by State Security."

Mackintosh's eyes were hidden in shadow.

"Why are you telling me these things? And how do you know them?"

"Because I want someone else to know. That's not entirely it either. The truth is I'm tired of all of it. Because it's a time when one makes choices." He had not answered the other question and Nick knew he wasn't going to.

When he was leaving, Mackintosh said, "Be careful of your friends, Nick."

Friends? Whom did he mean? Hilary? Derek Houndswell? Ralph Smith? Fraeser? Mackintosh himself? They weren't friends; they were encounters.

He saw Hilary once more before he left for London. She was sitting at a table in the Sundial Lounge on top of the Meridien Hotel with a scruffy-looking, overweight type in a rumpled tropical suit; probably a fellow journalist. Nick waved. She looked away.

Stewart continued to be troubled by what Mackintosh had said, and perhaps more by what he had not said. He knew a lot of people in Maraka who might, with a certain looseness about the use of the word, be called friends. About whom must he be cautious? What the hell had he meant about "making choices"? Who the hell was Colin Mackintosh, come to that? A friend.

The world would not come to an end because he was absent from the office a little. The staff knew that any problem could be referred either to the Africa desk in London or directly to himself. After Ahmed had helped him put the attaché case into the Mercedes, they shook hands.

"We shall miss you, sah," he said.

"It will only be a week, Ahmed. But thank you."

"Yes, sah, of course, Mr. Stewart." But he was not smiling.

It began to rain while he was driving to the airport, tentatively at first, fat drops splattering down, rattling dully on the body of the car, stopping then starting again. By the time he had checked in and got rid of the car at the airport car hire, it was raining steadily, falling straight and fast, but it had not reached the intensity it would later in the month.

Just before he went through immigration, he looked casually at the black and white faces of those who had collected around the barrier and thought he saw Derek Houndswell; but the man turned just as Nick noticed him and walked off. Either he was mistaken, or Houndswell was seeing someone off. He went into the international departure lounge—the duty-free shop, which wasn't much anyway, was shuttered and the lounge had not been cleaned in some time—and thought no more about it.

The British Airways 747 sat on the runway for half an hour while the rain fell steadily. Then the captain came on the speaker system.

"We apologize for the delay, ladies and gentlemen, but we've been given no explanation by the tower. I trust we'll be away shortly."

And when at last the plane had accelerated down the runway and lifted heavily into the air, Stewart felt an enormous sense of relief, so much so that when the stewardess—a small trim blonde with large blue eyes and round firm little tits—asked him what he wanted to drink before lunch, he had champagne by way of celebration. He let his seat recline a little and stretched his legs out beneath the seat in front. He sipped the champagne and stared at the empty space between the top of the seat back and the overhead compartment and let his mind go blank. He could still hear the last conversation he'd had with Colin Mackintosh. And for no reason, he began to imagine himself sitting at a table in the Intercontinental with Derek Houndswell. And he heard the alarm bells going off again. Who told you it was State Security that bombed your car, Nick? Why George Maguire. The bells continued. Someone was calling a stewardess.

After Maraka City, London—poor dowdy old London, looking more and more rundown every year—seemed spotless and crisp. Stewart checked into the Savoy at four o'clock on Saturday afternoon, and, the little blonde stewardess having promised a good deal more than she delivered, which was nothing, he spent the next hour ringing women he knew in London. He ended up with the last on his list, a not-so-gay divorcée whom he had to buy an expensive dinner in order to get her into bed. She wanted him to spend the night, but after one mechanical rutting, he lost interest, disappeared with a wave down the stairwell, and took a cab back to the hotel, where he spent most of the night trying to get to sleep. But he was unable to come to terms with the pointlessness of the evening.

The signing of the loan agreement was held in a large room in the Dorchester at eleven o'clock on Monday morning. Each of the twenty-four banks participating in the loan was represented by at least two officers, and many by three, although only one would be a signatory on all copies of the agreement. It is a common practice to have those who had a major role in putting together a loan at the signing. Max Fougere, John Howe, and Nick Stewart represented Manhattan Banking. Contrary to expectations, General Ujimbu was not able to attend; the Republic of Maraka was represented therefore by Colonel Ngoa and three of his aides. Fougere gave a pleasant, meaningless little speech, rather more heavily accented than normal, noting how delighted they all were to be able to assist in the development of the vast potential of Maraka, and Colonel Ngoa answered that Maraka was delighted as well.

No one mentioned Okubu or Jimmy Moshu or Robert Kalama.

The lawyers for the banks then started copies of the agreement circulating clockwise around the vast hollow square formed by four tables. The opinions of counsel for the banks and counsel for the borrower with respect to the enforceability of the agreement in accordance with its terms were bound into the agreement as appendices, and the statement from Colonel Ngoa as Minister of Finance that all things that ought to have been done and seen to prior to the signing of the agreement had in fact been done or seen to was given as a separate document by counsel for the borrower to counsel for the banks.

Much as he would have liked to, Fougere could not, as head of international banking, avoid signing the agreement without insulting the Finance Minister and making the other banks angry, although he had suggested that Nick sign. Howe took the suggestion seriously. "Just kidding, John," Fougere told him. Stewart wondered.

Counsel for the banks collected all the signed agreements, looked at all of them to ensure that they had all been signed and in the right places, and asked that if anyone had not yet supplied a copy of his signing authority, could he please do so as soon as possible. And with great relief, everyone adjourned to the neighboring room for drinks before lunch.

"We are extremely pleased with the way the facility has developed, Colonel Ngoa," Fougere said, and raised his small sherry. Ngoa raised his orange juice and said, "Cheers."

"Reasonably satisfactory, I should say, Mr. Fougere. But this is, after all, just a beginning, both for you and for us. Within the next twelve to eighteen months, my staff assures me, we shall really be testing your mettle."

Meaning, Stewart thought, a longer tenor, lower rates, and conceivably greater risk: a deal, say, that depends on the world price for a single commodity being maintained.

Just before they went in to lunch, Ngoa took Nick by the elbow. "Let's make sure we have dinner together again as soon as we return to Maraka City, Mr. Stewart."

"Absolutely, Colonel Ngoa. I'll ring your office as soon as I'm back. I'm going to take a spot of holiday first."

In the taxi returning to Moorgate after lunch, Fougere said, "I expect this effort to be exploited to its full advantage, Nick. We want better balances from Maraka and I expect you to get them. You should also be pushing ancillary products. And I want to expand our share of the export business from the multinationals, so you'll have to get a lot closer to them than you have so far. You also have to follow up on the hint that Ngoa dropped just before lunch."

"Those are good ideas, Max," Stewart said, almost dreamily, looking out of the cab window at the south bank of the Thames. "But I'm not going back."

The silence in the back of the taxi became palpable.

"Would you like to explain?" Fougere asked brittlely.

"I don't know that I can. I didn't think of it until now. But I'm not returning to Maraka."

Howe was ashen. He had never before heard anyone defy authority in such a manner at Manhattan Banking.

Fougere was enraged and trying not to show it because it didn't fit the image of sangfroid that he had developed so carefully over many years. He was enraged for two reasons: he was furious at Stewart for wanting to leave Maraka at the very moment that they had gained an advantage that could be exploited, but one that would not last long; and he was enraged at what he perceived might be an early symptom of the house of cards that Tony Gould had built. And that Tony was probably beyond getting blamed for.

"Nothing personal, you understand, Max," Stewart continued. "We've always gotten along fine. Delighted that you've been made head of IB. It's simply that . . . let's say I've been warned away. Things accumulate. And a man I know advised that it was time to make a choice. I suddenly understood what he meant."

The cab left the Embankment at Puddle Dock and turned into Queen Victoria Street.

"Your position is entirely unacceptable," Fougere said, quietly and firmly.

"With respect, old chum, your car has not been bombed and your driver killed, you have not been followed, your phones have not been tapped, you have not been told to be cautious about your friends. Maraka is not healthy at the moment."

"What the hell do you mean?" Fougere's patience broke. "We've just signed away almost three-quarters of a billion dollars to these people. And I've got the notice of drawdown next Monday in my pocket. Has there been a material adverse change?"

"Nothing's happened that you don't know about, Max. But I'm talking only about myself. I think Maraka is unhealthy for me, so I'm not going back."

The rest of the ride to Manhattan Banking House took place without further conversation.

The Republic of Maraka, through the agency of the Ministry of Finance, drew down the loan on the following Monday and placed the proceeds, less the management fee that was shared equally among the lead managers after payment of smaller participating fees to the participants, and less fifty-three million dollars left on current account with Manhattan Banking in London, in time deposits in the name of the Central Bank of Maraka in Swiss banks in various locations. On Tuesday, the fifty-three million dollars was transferred to the Cayman Islands branch of the Norddeutsche Handelsbank for the account of the Maraka Mining and Engineering Company S.A., Vaduz, Liechtenstein. From this account over the following ten days, payments in odd amounts were made for advising and consulting services, or mining equipment, to eighteen bank accounts in seven different banks in Geneva, Basel, Zurich, Lucerne, and Lugano. By the end of the ten days, there were only two thousand dollars left in the Cayman Island account of the Maraka Mining and Engineering Company S.A., sufficient to pay cable charges and other expenses. The account was closed. In Vaduz, Liechtenstein, the name of Maraka Mining and Engineering was striken from the Commercial Register by Dr. Jacobs, a lawyer acting for the principals, who at the same time registered a new company called Oil Exploration Company of Maraka S.A.

The rains came to Maraka, heavy and sustained; roads flooded, sewers and riverbanks overflowed. There was an outbreak of cholera, which the health services and the World Health Organization managed to confine to the eastern provinces. Whenever it stopped raining, the skies remained dull and gray, and the humidity hung with a great, drooping weight on everything. Mold grew overnight on anything that was damp— shoes, clothing, walls, food—and the smell of decay filled the air.

At the end of the first month of the rainy season, the combined forces of James Nijima and Arthur Ekaba, under the command of Ekaba's most trusted general, and with the help of a thousand Cuban troops, began their campaign to capture Maraka City and seize power from the usurpers. The possible tactical objectives, such as the rich ore deposits in the mining district, were bypassed as being pointless to waste time and resources on, because they were so easily isolated by disruption of the flimsy distribution system. Being pragmatists, each in his own way, Ekaba and Nijima ordered only disruption, not destruction, of the distribution system.

Without the world's noticing, civil war had begun in Maraka.

The first battles were fought with loudspeakers. Government outposts in the middle of the jungle—ten or a dozen men huddled in a tin hut smoking and listening to the rain and drinking palm wine—heard the calls crackling from the surrounding forest.

"We are the forces of free Maraka, brothers. Come join us and eliminate the bloodsuckers who are destroying our lives, our families, our country."

In the rain forest of the Northwest Province, far from the influence of Maraka City, or even of the district commander, this tactic was effective. Most of the men disappeared immediately into the jungle, leaving their equipment, including their weapons, behind; a few joined the rebels, taking their weapons and those of their departed colleagues with them; fewer still headed for Marakan Army units closer to the capital with the story of the ghostly voices moving through the jungle and of what had happened, which had a demoralizing effect on the units they joined. The only shots that were fired in the first part of the campaign were at the officer or NCO in charge who tried to prevent the dissolution of his unit, and these were fired by his own men.

As predicted, resistance to the advance of the rebel army simply melted away.

Tony Gould spent much of July thinking about the organization of the bank and how he might manipulate Samantha Vanderpane's committee, although he had not been made a member of it.

In truth, he was not happy with his new job. Even though Ben's scheme for creating two vice-chairmen had been balked, Kincaid was working effectively to isolate Gould from the real center of power, which was the commercial banking division. For the moment Gould could only continue his practice of cultivating directors, particularly Samantha, who was far more influential than any of them could possibly have known; Maureen had inadvertently given him a leg up there. His normal expectation would have been that his job as president of Manhattan Banking was simply a way station on his way to the top; but Samantha Vanderpane made him a little uncertain, and he recognized that he would have to massage her a little.

He had also not forgotten—because it was not in Tony Gould's nature to forget—that he had a few scores to settle. John Howe he had taken care of. Howe had managed nearly to screw up a deal that practically sold itself. Almost the last thing Gould had done before he left international banking was to set into motion a transfer for Howe to Hong Kong; not a bad post, but clearly a demotion: the normal career path was from Hong Kong to London.

He was going to put maximum pressure on Nick Stewart to return to Maraka.

Webb. Chris Webb continued to be a thorn in his side. He often appeared to report on various loans to the Credit Committee, a committee of the board of which Gould was deputy head, and continued his waspish sniping remarks and generally negative attitude. His performance on the Maraka loan had been execrable, and he had nearly scuttled it. Tony had not yet decided where Webb might best learn how things were going to be done in the future at Manhattan Banking, but he intended to make a decision by Labor Day.

Such were Tony Gould's end-of-July thoughts. Gould understood well the uses of innuendo and therefore trusted nothing that anyone told him unless it was someone who was or could be useful.

•   •   •

Samantha was napping. Maureen turned onto her side to watch her. Samantha's hair was loose and a little damp from the heat in the room and from the heat of their lovemaking. Her profile was strong and her body was well cared for. Her chest rose and fell with the regular rhythm of untroubled breathing. With the blinds drawn against the afternoon light, they were lying together in Samantha's bedroom in her house in Chilmark. The children were at the beach with their nanny. Samantha had shared the simple white room with Miles and now, whenever they could, she shared it with Maureen.

This woman—this wonderful woman, so strong in some ways, so gentle in others—had led her to think about herself in ways she never had before, or if she ever had, had forgotten during her marriage to Tony Gould. She knew herself now—it would have been incorrect to say "better" because that implied that she had known something of herself before, which was not true. So she knew herself now: knew that she was a person, a human being, desirable physically and intellectually, and realizing it, becoming more desirable still.

The last ten days had been nearly perfect. The weather had been a flawless rapture of blue skies and fleecy clouds and hot sun. Mornings and late afternoons they had usually spent on the beach. During the middle part of the day, Samantha took them on excursions around the island she knew very well and loved. She was very good at organizing things for John and Sally. They went to the old-fashioned carousel in Oak Bluffs and to see the ox draws at the Agricultural Fair in West Tisbury and to watch the ducks and geese at Felix Neck Wildlife Sanctuary. She had the children feeling very grown-up and self-sufficient putting on their own insect repellent to keep off the mosquitoes when they went walking in the woods.

And with the leisure and the serenity that she gained on the Vineyard, Maureen began to think about her life and her relationships. Even John and Sally seemed to sense that she was engaged in important things and left her alone; but it could have been too that they were having such a good time with tennis lessons and swimming lessons and sailing lessons. She loved

215

them very much and had a residual affection—or perhaps, she thought, she ought to have called it historical—for the father that had been necessary to produce them. Beyond that she felt nothing for Tony. She and Samantha had been to five cocktail or dinner parties since she had been on the Vineyard, at none of which had Maureen encountered anyone as driven as her husband, who began to seem as remote from her as a creature who lived on the moon. Maureen was enjoying herself for the first time in a long time. She no longer felt that she had to perform, and there was no performance review from Tony after each social encounter because Tony was not there.

She had nothing in common with him, she did not care about his ambition, she was not impressed by his achievements (youngest bank president in New York!), he had no sense of humor, he was not gentle, she saw no evidence that he cared either for the children or herself. And he was impotent. She could not understand what had made her accept him fourteen years before, when he proposed. And she knew further that reviewing the past was of no use. She must not waste any more of her life being married to Tony; or waste any more of it than was necessary to get a divorce.

And there was Samantha, dear, lovely Samantha, who had led her to love again, so gentle, so passionate. There was a tiny cloud in the clear sky of their relationship. Samantha had awakened her sexually from a long sleep; and recognizing herself now as a sexual being, Maureen wanted to find a man. The idea frightened her because she had had nothing but abuse—although she was sure he didn't realize it—from the only man she had ever known; certainly none of the ecstasy that she had experienced with Samantha. But there was the lingering question to which she needed the answer. She knew she was vulnerable. She was in danger of making a mistake, of falling in love easily with the wrong man. But at the moment, it was difficult to believe she could care for any adult as much as she cared for Samantha.

Two evenings later, Samantha and Maureen went to a cocktail party at a modern house that looked across Vineyard Sound toward Woods Hole. They talked with the other guests on a screened deck and watched the sea grow dark.

Maureen was talking with her hostess when a man moved to their sides.

"This is Michael Shepard, Mrs. Gould. He's been teaching at Yale the past year."

Maureen nodded. The man was her height in flat shoes; he wore a neatly trimmed beard that was growing gray. His brown tweed jacket was obviously an old but well-loved friend. The other woman was drawn away by another guest.

"Do you come to the Vineyard every summer, Mrs. Gould?" He spoke with an English accent.

"It's my first time," she said.

"Oh dear," he responded.

His tone made her laugh. "But why 'oh dear,' Mr. Shepard?"

"I'm rather in need of someone to show me round the island. May I get you more wine?"

"No, thank you. But surely your hosts have shown you the island already?"

"In truth, that is the case, but I can't imagine anything more pleasant than another such excursion, nor more pleasant company on it than yours."

"Really, Mr. Shepard, you don't know me at all."

"Precisely the point, Mrs. Gould. I should very much like to know you a good deal better. Is there a Mr. Gould?"

"There is."

"Is he here?"

"No, he's working in New York. He'll be coming up on the weekend."

Michael Shepard nodded and looked into his drink.

"With whom are you staying?" he said.

Maureen nodded towards Samantha, who was not far away, standing with three men.

"Ah. So sad about Miles. Samantha is another jewel in the crown of Martha's Vineyard."

Maureen felt her cheeks flush with pleasure for her lover, and hoped her reaction was not as obvious as she sensed it might be.

"Mrs. Gould, I am quite overcome," he said, holding out his hand. "It has been a great pleasure, and I hope we shall meet again soon." Michael Shepard moved away, disappearing into the crush of guests on the deck.

They returned in time to kiss the children goodnight. Samantha heated a casserole, and they had a bottle of wine with dinner. Maureen described her encounter.

"Michael is quite an attractive man. We met him last summer when he was staying here with the Olsens before he started on his year at Yale."

"So he knows the Vineyard."

"I should think so." Samantha laughed when she realized the conclusion Maureen had drawn.

"Really, Samantha, how brazen." But she was smiling.

"Absolutely, darling."

"He's English."

"Yes. He teaches literature at Cambridge and was here on a visiting professorship. He's also something of a poet."

"And most forward. Not unpleasantly so, but he was forward."

"But, darling, he was obviously quite taken with you. And who can blame him?"

"Samantha, I'm not interested in having him interested in me." She reached across the table and took Samantha's hand.

"Even so," Samantha said, smiling, "I wouldn't be surprised if you found yourself growing quite fond of him after you've gotten to know him better."

"But doesn't he have to return to Cambridge?" Maureen said, trying not to sound interested, which Samantha noted with some amusement.

"Not, I believe, until the end of the year."

On Friday morning, when they returned from an expedition to Menemsha for fresh fish, Maureen found a brown paper parcel addressed to "Mrs. Gould" on the porch. Inside was a book called *Pictures from Languedoc, Poems by Michael Shepard.* The flyleaf was signed "With best wishes from Michael Shepard" and dated August twentieth, which was the date of the cocktail party at which they had met.

"The inscription is harmless enough, Maureen," Samantha said, but there was a sparkle in her eyes.

Maureen left the book on the table in the living room. She told herself that she had no interest in Michael Shepard and she resented Samantha's pushing him on her. In fact, if there was anything about which she could have found fault with Samantha, it was this quality of knowing what was best for everyone. Samantha wanted to be in control all the time.

That evening, Samantha and Maureen, with John and Sally, drove to the airport to meet Tony's Air New England flight from LaGuardia. How out of place he looked, Maureen thought, walking across the tarmac in his dark suit and with a stuffed briefcase. He was even more pale than usual—pasty in fact—as if he had just emerged from a dark cave where he'd been for a long time without fresh air, and he was looking around, blinking in the sunlight. He seemed ill at ease, and she knew he felt guilty because he'd have had to have left the bank shortly after four to catch the plane.

Gould kissed Maureen briefly on the lips, kissed Sally on the cheek, ran his hands through John's hair, and shook hands with Samantha.

Although she knew it would probably happen, Maureen was amazed still to observe how her family all reverted to type shortly after his arrival. She herself felt somewhat cowed in Tony's presence, and the children, after an initial excitement, when they thought that because they had had new experiences, perhaps everything else would change as well, grew quarrelsome when they found it hadn't. She hoped that they could not put a name to their father's unbending and unaffectionate nature, but knew as soon as she wished it that it was a vain hope; children knew when they were not wanted. They stood awkwardly about the arrival gate waiting for the luggage to be unloaded from the aircraft and trundled over on a handcart, Samantha talking pleasantly away about nothing of consequence ("Nice flight, Tony?" "How was the weather in New York? Ours has been glorious." "The children have been loves. They're so well be-haved."). When Tony got his bag at last, Samantha drove them back to the house in her station wagon.

Maureen had given the nanny, whom Tony did not approve of in any event, the night off, so that they all had dinner together. Gould hardly noticed the lovely bluefish and new potatoes, so interested was he in discussing the bank with Samantha, and the table was divided in two, Maureen left to talk with the children. When they were helping to clear the table, Sally said to her mother quietly, "Mummy, doesn't Daddy ever talk about any-thing else?"

Maureen could almost have predicted the change in the weather that happened overnight. When they rose the next morning, it was cold and gray and dark, and the wind was whip-ping the rain against the glass doors that led out onto the deck. After failing to persuade Samantha that he had matters of sub-stance to discuss with her, Tony settled after breakfast into a chair in the living room with his fat briefcase while the rest of them went to Edgartown to tour the shops, have lunch, and see the matinee at the Town Hall.

Tony spent the remainder of the weekend, whenever an op-portunity came, in pursuit of Samantha's support for his ideas about the future of the bank and, Maureen guessed, for his qualifications for the top job. On her part, Samantha spent the weekend gracefully refusing to be drawn on any subject that concerned the bank. She gave a dinner party on Saturday night to introduce the Goulds, at which Tony practiced his newly acquired social skill of chuckling and nodding at almost every-thing that anyone said to him. The only time he didn't was when someone asked him about the bank's view of the economy, to which he responded at great length, and, Maureen was pained to observe, failed to notice that his interlocutor lost interest and wandered to another part of the room.

On Sunday afternoon they all went with Tony, in his dark suit, back to the airport, and stood waving while the plane taxied away from the gate, although Maureen was certain that he never once looked out of the window and must already have had his briefcase opened before the engines had been started.

Later that evening, well after John and Sally had gone to bed, Samantha and Maureen sat on the deck listening to the night sounds. They were both wearing heavy sweaters against the cool air that hinted at the coming fall, although the sky had cleared and was full of stars.

"Can he really not notice, Samantha?" Maureen asked quietly and without emotion. "Isn't it all pretense? Isn't it deliberate?"

Samantha's hand found her own. "I think—I truly think, darling—that he doesn't notice. I hadn't noticed until this weekend how mechanical he is, how unable he is to respond to others, as if such a thing might be taken as an admission of weakness and be taken advantage of. Somehow, his development as a person has been stunted. I'm sorry, Maureen, but I think Tony is only partly human."

"Yes," she said. "It's a cross we—the kids and I—have to bear, but only for a little longer."

"Would you like some more wine, dear? No?" Samantha poured the remainder into her own glass. "What was there about Tony that made you want to marry him? What was the quality that he had, but has no longer?"

Maureen was quiet for so long that Samantha began to think that she had offended her. Instead, Maureen held her hand more tightly and at last she spoke.

"I married him because he wouldn't take no for an answer. He was persistent. And I was very young and didn't know any better. It is so awful that we make these decisions when we have so little experience to go on."

They were silent for a while.

"Have you read any of Michael Shepard's book, Maureen?"

"No. Well, no, that's not quite right. I've glanced through it."

"You ought to, you know. Some of the poems are quite lovely."

"I've never really gotten along with poetry."

"Such a shame for someone as poetically beautiful as you."

"You've made me blush, Samantha."

"Nonsense, darling. But do read Michael's book. It suggests a sensitive person as well as an intelligent one."

Perhaps, Maureen thought. But I must make my own decisions about such things. Long afterward, when she thought about that summer on Martha's Vineyard, she recognized that it had been during this conversation that she began to distance herself from Samantha.

The first serious resistance the Marakan rebels encountered was at a country town called Imo, which straddled the rail line leading to the iron mines in the north. The large government force in the town was too big to be left at the rebel rear while the rebels moved toward Maraka City.

By this time, the world community knew that something very big was going on in one of the richest nations in black Africa, but it had yet to put a name to it. The Marakan UN Ambassador in New York accused the Soviet Union of initiating and supporting armed aggression by its surrogates, the Cubans. The Soviet Union accused the United States of trying to stifle the legitimate aspirations of the Marakan people for freedom and self-determination through CIA support of the reactionary puppet regime of Ujimbu. China blamed both superpowers for preying on Third World nations. Mrs. Gandhi blamed everyone.

Max Fougere tried not to think much about the hundred twenty-five million dollar exposure of the Manhattan Banking Corporation to a country that looked as if it was slipping into civil war. The official word that the bank put about to journalists and participating banks alike was that it had no reason to believe that Maraka would not honor her commitments. Privately, Fougere realized that he would have to wait to see which way the wind was blowing before he blamed someone for the fact that his signature was on the Marakan jumbo.

The battle at Imo lasted four hours, although after the first half hour, the outcome was never in doubt. The rebels advanced on the town in three separate columns through the jungle to the north and west. At first light on a gloomy and windswept day,

they tried the loudspeaker tack, which was answered with machine-gun fire. At that point, the rebel mortars and rockets
opened up against the government positions. By the time
Ujimbu's troops fell back in disorder, most of Imo was burning
and there were dead and wounded, the majority of them civilians, everywhere. Army lorries, two tanks, and an armored car
were abandoned in the mud.

The casualties on the rebel side were relatively light, and the
rebels had been fighting the troops of a colonel who owed a great
deal to General Ujimbu. Had Ekaba and Nijima known how
weak was the glue that bound the government army together,
and had it been the dry season, the rebels could have struck off
down the road straight to Maraka City two hundred miles to the
southeast, and taken the country in two weeks. But they didn't
know, and progress through the dripping jungle, while almost
irresistible, was very slow. The government troops had time to
regroup, and while they seldom had heart for a fight, they acquit-
ted themselves decently, particularly when supported by helicopter gunships, which early on had made mincemeat of a rebel
battalion caught in the open. That mistake was not repeated,
and as the war ground on, the small force of gunships was wasted
by Czech-made SAMs.

James Nijima was surprised at the discipline of Arthur Ekaba's
troops and by the sophistication of their equipment, in contrast
with those of his own soldiers. He was surprised and less con-
fident, and realized that he was going to have to change his
tactics to prevent Ekaba from taking power in his stead.

Journalists began to pour into Maraka City. It was a new war
to write about, in a more exotic place than Nicaragua or El
Salvador, which, for the Americans at least, were too close to
home to be interesting. There was much sharing of rooms at the
Intercontinental, except for some of the television journalists,
who were more famous than any Marakan, and commanded their
own rooms.

Hilary Ashton-Brooke was much prized and sought after, as
much for her knowledge of the country as for her looks, which,

223

however, were not ignored. When the government at first re-fused to allow any reporter to go anywhere near the fighting, Hilary found herself being interviewed for nationwide news pro-grams in the United States, where she was admired by the men who watched, and resented by the women, for her pretty face, her excellent figure set off in the khaki shirts and tailored fatigue trousers she wore, and her British accent. She seemed a creature of incalculable glamour.

For two weeks Hilary became known in those parts of the world that paid attention to the disintegration of Maraka. A well-known photograph showed her helping a black soldier who was limping along a road with a bandaged foot. That the picture was posed by a photojournalist with one Pulitzer Prize already to his credit did not detract from the fact that Hilary had actually helped the man walk about thirty feet, from the point at which the jeep dropped him off to where it picked him up again.

But General Ujimbu realized that he was getting nowhere in his campaign for world condemnation of the invaders, as he called them, by restricting journalists to Maraka City and giving briefings that none of them believed. And he continued to have faith in the power of the world press to produce the kind of support he needed from their respective governments to stop the invaders.

The press reported that the U.S. Secretary of State was warn-ing of the direst consequences if Cuba continued to support the invasion of a sovereign state, but when the Ambassador of Ma-raka went to call on the Secretary to ask for more aid and equip-ment, he found that the Secretary was not available, and that the Undersecretary whom he saw could give no undertakings. The CIA recommended too late that the United States support the Ujimbu government as being the lesser of the two evils in the Marakan civil war. But even if the Agency had been more timely with its recommendations, it may not have been listened to. The CIA no longer gave off the odor of sanctity, and an American administration would have to have had much more at stake than one overpopulated, albeit rich, West African nation—and Maraka a much stronger lobby in Washington—before the President could make a commitment of any real substance.

Thus the world press was allowed to go toward the fighting front, which was another mistake on Ujimbu's part. Their first-hand observations, and contacts with the rebels themselves through the porous front, confirmed what the journalists already suspected, which was that the rebels had popular support and that the government troops were seriously demoralized. Hilary's fame fell away as quickly as it had come, and she became merely another war correspondent.

They waited, without speaking, at a table in a corner of the Intercontinental bar. Hilary remembered that it was the same table at which she met Jimmy Moshu. Bob Parker finished the bowl of groundnuts and signaled to the waiter for another, and another round.

The bar was less crowded than usual because permission had finally begun to come through for journalists to visit the front, although getting the proper papers involved having to deal with incredible bureaucratic muddle. Neither Hilary nor Bob Parker had applied yet, because they had gotten a lead on another story that they preferred to keep to themselves.

A Marakan whom Parker called No Name, because he had never learned it, claimed that one of the expatriate community, perhaps more than one, was in the pay of the Ministry of State Security and had been for a long time. His job was to spy on expats and to arrange for them to be inconvenienced if they were found to be causing difficulties. The bombing of the car of an American bank representative was thought to have been one example of his work; and the death of the Childs Construction managing director was no longer thought to have been suicide or an accident.

Hilary had mentally reviewed the catalog of expats whom she had met on her first tour in Maraka and admitted to herself that at first blush the story seemed fairly unlikely. Most of them were a dull bunch: businessmen making a lot of money because of the hardship location, doing the same things that at home wouldn't make them nearly as much. Nick Stewart had been by far the most interesting of the lot, and she knew that he, at least in this regard, was beyond reproach. It had been after all his car that had been blown up and his driver who had been killed. And ultimately Hilary could not imagine what interest an expat would have in working for monsters like State Security, except perhaps someone such as Colin Mackintosh, the little bank manager with the Marakan wife, whom they might have threatened into doing some dirty work. It couldn't be just the money. Or could it?

Nonetheless, it was a lead that she and Parker felt ought to be followed up, and they were beginning by talking to people Hilary had seen often with Nick.

Derek Houndswell of United Aluminium appeared at the door of the bar. Hilary waved to him.

"Hello, Derek."

He nodded and smiled and shook hands with Parker.

"G and T if that's okay," he said in response to the question. When the waiter had gone, he said, "I've been making some discreet—Good God, I hope so—inquiries about the matter you put to me the other day, Hilary, and I regret to say there seems to be some truth to the story."

Parker paused a beat before popping a fresh palmful of groundnuts into his mouth. Hilary leaned forward, no longer feeling tired.

The waiter arrived with Houndswell's drink. He lifted it. "To your very good health," he said, and took a long draught.

"I have no details," he continued, "but I've been promised some."

"When?"

"Tomorrow night. At some dreadful place just outside town. I know where it is and I don't think it's the least bit healthy. But the three of us will be together."

"In fact, Derek," Hilary said, "is there any need for you to go at all?"

"I wish there weren't, to be perfectly candid. But it was to me that these confidences were given; and besides, I should never forgive myself if I sent you two off alone and you came to harm."

"Would it be impossible for you to arrange for us to see this person without you?"

"Not impossible. But—"

"Then please so arrange it. Derek, you're really being the most tremendous help. There's no need for you to come with us. You're not paid to take chances; we are."

"It shall be done, my dear." He leaned toward them. "The man who will meet us—sorry, you—is a black called Carvalho. Eight o'clock. I am now going to call for the bill. When it comes I will pay it, and I will leave a few notes on the table. Under the notes will be the sketch map that I was given of the place. Just pick it up as if it were the receipt. I was told that Carvalho will ask for the map as proof of your bona fides. Surrender it immediately."

How Hilary-Ashton Brooke disappeared—hence briefly regaining some of the fame she lost when the war became more important than secondhand opinions about it—was never fully uncovered. The story put out by the Ministry of Information at the time—that the light plane in which she and a photographer were flying over the battle zone had been destroyed by a surface-to-air missile fired from the rebel side—was dismissed as a total fabrication by the new Minister of Information after the war. He went on to say that at the time of her disappearance Miss Ashton-Brooke had been following a lead that a British business executive in Maraka was in the pay of the Ministry of State Security and had been since the days of Tena Maraka, himself a victim of maltreatment by the Ujimbu regime.

Derek Houndswell knew from the telegraph office that Hilary had sent a Telex to her wire service saying only that they were following a lead. There were no other details. They did not want to risk giving away what might be a scoop. *Tant pis.*

To assure himself that they had not indulged in greater foolishness, Houndswell visited the office of the assistant manager

227

shortly after Parker and Ashton-Brooke had left the hotel for their meeting the following evening. With the passkey, he let himself into their rooms and searched them. The only item of any interest was a hastily written note that Hilary had left in a paperback book on her night table stating where they had gone and why. Houndswell flushed the toilet to see if it was operating properly, burned the note, then waited an agonizingly long time for the tank to fill before he could flush the toilet again.

Without being seen in the corridor or the lift, he returned to the bar and ordered a gin and tonic. Looking at himself over the stockade of bottles reflected in the smoky mirror behind the bar and sipping his gin, Houndswell decided that it was time to think of severing his associations. He had just gone through a close-run thing; it had been easy but it had been pure chance, and the sort of thing with which he enriched and occasionally amused himself was best not left to chance. And besides, the Ujimbu government's days were numbered. The Reds were coming, and they would be putting together their own secret police without any outside help, thank you all the same. In the event, the Ministry of State Security had been too compromised by its role during the coup to continue in operation beyond the inevitable collapse of Ujimbu.

Derek Houndswell suspected that very shortly he was going to have to return to London for a conference.

The black man and the white man sat on the screened veranda in the darkness. Mackintosh could sense his wife listening to them just inside the doorway.

"As soon as they got out of the car, a man approached and asked for the map, which they gave him."

"The only bit of evidence," Mackintosh said. "Go on."

"They were then surrounded by armed men. No uniforms. About a dozen."

"All of them black?"

"Yes, sah. The two white people were forced back into their car. The man drove and the woman was made to go into the backseat and two men got in with them. They followed one car and were followed by another."

"But you couldn't follow on your bicycle."

"No, sah. But I knew where they were going. I went through the forest."

Mackintosh nodded; he felt old and sick.

"By the time I reached the place, the man was already dead. And they were raping the woman." He put his hand over his eyes as if to block out the sight. "But I think she was unconscious, sah, at least by the time I reached the edge of the clearing. Then they shot her in the head and pushed both bodies into the mangrove swamp."

"Did you recognize any of the men?"

"Some of them, sah. They were MSS, Mr. Mackintosh."

At one of the low periods of his life, living in a tiny flat the bank owned at the bottom of the Royal Hospital Road, Stewart had seen Hilary on the ten o'clock news on ITV. It brought him out of the alcoholic fog into which he had sunk himself, and he ached for her until his befuddled brain recalled how foolishly she was behaving. Having survived one round of Russian roulette, she had spun the cylinder again, and again put the barrel against her head and was squeezing the trigger.

Nick was assigned temporarily to the West African desk of the bank in London, while Manhattan Banking considered what to do with him and with the representative office in Maraka, and while he figured out what to do next. He was sorry—particularly when he'd had too much to drink and was feeling nostalgic— that his leaving the office and Ahmed had not been more decorous than a simple request for them to send his kit, but they continued to be paid in the normal way through remittances through the United Bank of Maraka; and besides, he had received ample indication that it was time for him to move on. Maybe it was that he was simply too old for a place like Maraka.

There was as well no doubt in his mind that he had reached the end of the road with Manhattan Banking. He was not going

229

to accept the exile they had forced on poor John Howe, who, after all, was being punished because he'd been so anxious to please his masters.

He could not, of course, avoid dealing with Maraka, because he was the bank's acknowledged expert thereon, and a lot of people were worried about the situation there. His opposite number in New York, where the accounts were kept, was constrained to monitor closely all activity in the Marakan accounts, to keep him informed with a daily Telex, and to allow no overdrafts—all payments out had to be covered by funds received. If something happened and Maraka for one reason or another defaulted on any of its obligations, the bank wanted to be in a position to exercise its right of setoff, and seize the deposits, which in fact would only partially cover the exposure. Since the monitoring had begun, however, there had been nothing irregular about the operation of any of the accounts.

One morning in late August, he was reading the *Times* at his desk when he saw the small article on the "Overseas News" page about the disappearance of Hilary Ashton-Brooke and Robert Parker, a photographer for the same wire service. He remembered then the scruffy fat man he had seen her with in the Sundial Lounge, and wondered if that had been Robert Parker and if Hilary had been sleeping with him. He decided not, because she could have done much better.

He was not surprised; but he was surprised by the pain it caused him. When the next day he read that their plane had been shot down by a missile, it was like a knife in the gut. Could he have done anything to counter the pursuit of darkness on which she had embarked? He doubted it: she would not have listened anyway, and he himself had been in trouble. But he had not known such agony since his first marriage broke up. He left work and did not return that day. He had half a dozen whiskies in a pub around the corner from the flat and went to bed at three in the afternoon with a headache.

At eight that night he awoke, still with a headache, to the sound of the phone ringing.

"Nick. I'm sorry to bother you at home. This is Waldo Carter. Tony Gould wants to see you in New York."

"When?" He still felt groggy, and his tongue was thick with sleep.

"ASAP."

"What does Max think?"

"Max isn't involved, Nick."

Max is never involved when things get sticky, he thought.

"Okay, Waldo. I'll book a flight and let you know when I'm coming. You'll fix a meeting with Gould?"

"Yes. It had better be soon, Nick."

"Understood, Waldo."

What the hell was the rush, he wondered, unless it was that Tough Tony was just back from his hols and ready to kick some ass. Rumors were flying around that the bank was going to be reorganized, that Ben Kincaid was about to be kicked out, that Gould was going to be made CEO and Kincaid was going to be left as a kind of figurehead chairman, that a number of directors were not amused to find the bank with an exposure in excess of a hundred million dollars to a country involved in a civil war, particularly as the auditors thought there was enough question about the value of the assets to classify them as substandard in quality.

The day before he went to New York, he had an interview with an American bank that was looking for a deputy manager of its Singapore branch who would succeed the manager when he retired in two years' time. Stewart was an experienced banker and manager, he had Far East experience, he was Australian, and he was ready to relocate. He appealed greatly to the bank, and the job appealed greatly to him. He had no doubt that they would make him an offer.

At ten o'clock on the morning of September 4, Nick appeared at Tony Gould's office. It had been a long time since he'd been in New York and a long time since he'd seen Tony Gould. He had forgotten how short he was. He remembered the abruptness, however. There were no pleasant preliminaries for someone who had just flown three thousand miles to see him.

"I want an explanation, Nick."

"I shouldn't have thought one was necessary, Tony. I made it clear to Max."

Gould waved away his explanations to Max.

"You cannot leave a rep office just like that. You're neglecting your duties."

"I don't consider it my duty to get blown up."

"As you know perfectly well, the Marakan situation is a mess right now. We need an experienced man in place there. That man is you. It's your job."

"No longer."

"You're trying my patience, Stewart. I'll give you one more chance."

"Tony, for God's sake, try to be a human being. I was in danger in Maraka. I had to get out and stay out. And that was before the place started to fall apart. It's even more dangerous now."

Gould made a short, chopping motion with his hand.

"The bank's interests must be protected."

Life is too short, Nick thought, to put up with such crap. "Perhaps you ought to have considered the bank's interests before you railroaded through the Marakan jumbo."

Gould gripped the armrests of his desk chair. His eyes, magnified by his glasses, protruded at Nick. "What did you say?"

"I have the feeling I have to keep repeating myself. I think you heard me."

"Do you know who you're talking to?"

Stewart laughed. Tony turned purple with anger.

"Get out," he said, controlling himself with difficulty. "You couldn't have the job now even if you crawled for it."

"I wouldn't hold my breath if I were you. Can I take it I'm officially sacked?"

"You can."

"It'll cost you rather a lot, old man."

"We'll see."

Stewart walked out of Gould's office and took the elevator to Max's floor.

"Can I see Mr. Fougere?" he asked his secretary.

"He's with someone right now, Mr. Stewart, and he's got meetings the rest of the day."

"Only for five minutes."

"Just a moment." She picked up the intercom and mumbled into it. "Can you wait about ten minutes?" she asked brightly.

He nodded and sat down to wait, leafing through a copy of the *Far Eastern Economic Review* on the low table next to the side chair outside Fougere's office. Twenty-five minutes later, the secretary told him he could go in.

"Hello, Nick," Fougere said with a distant cordiality. "How are you?" extending his hand. It was the greeting one might give some dimly remembered college classmate who was passing through town and mistakenly thought he might be welcome. Stewart realized that to Max Fougere, who possessed one of the finest sets of antennae in the bank, he was already a nonperson.

"I have just reached a mutual lack of understanding with Tony Gould," Nick said, "and he has fired me."

"Mm, so I've heard." His eyes became hooded and his accent thickened.

Heard? How the hell had he heard? The man must be able to hear through floors as well as walls.

"So I've just nipped in to say good-bye, Max. I'll be spending the rest of my stay in New York sorting things out with personnel."

"Mm, I expect so. Well, I'm sorry I didn't know you were coming over, Nick. We might have had lunch together." He stood and held out his hand. "Thanks for stopping by. Good luck."

There was no indication on Fougere's part that Stewart had ever worked for him, directly or indirectly.

Webb was on the phone when Stewart looked into his office. Chris motioned to him to enter and sit down.

"How are you, Nick?" Webb said as he replaced the hand set.

"Not bad."

"Here long?"

"Not very. Actually I'm on my way out."

"I saw your friend Hilary Ashton-Brooke on television one night."

"Ah, yes. You met her in London, didn't you? She was on British television as well."

"Is she dead, Nick?"

"So they say, old man."

"I'm sorry."

"Nothing to do with me, Chris," he said, which puzzled Webb. Almost the first thing Hilary Ashton-Brooke had said to him was to inquire about Stewart.

"Actually," Nick continued, "I'm here to say good-bye. Old Tony Ghoul has given me the boot."

"Why, for God's sake?"

"I decided not to go back to Maraka after the loan signing in London."

"Sounds like common sense to me."

"I guess he needs somebody else to shit on for his mistakes." Stewart looked sad. "Looks like you were right about Maraka all along. At least in the short run."

"It gives me no pleasure, Nick. There is a lot of misery on the end of those crummy statistics."

Nick smiled. "Sooner or later they'll come out of it. God help us all if they don't." He shrugged and extended his hand. "Ah, the hell with it. See you around, chum. I'm going back East where I belong."

And disappeared through the doorway of Webb's office.

15

The evening before Maureen returned to New York, Samantha gave a dinner party for ten, among whom was Michael Shepard. His manner towards Maureen when he approached her on the deck with a glass of white wine was diffident.

"How very nice to see you again, Mrs. Gould," he said taking her hand. His own was warm and gentle.

The evening was losing heat quickly and he helped Maureen slip a wool stole over her shoulders.

"Thank you," she said. "Thank you also for your book. I'm afraid I had difficulty understanding it."

He looked down at the field that ran away towards the sea.

"I teach English literature at Cambridge University. Occasionally I write poetry, of which you've seen some examples. Up to a point I enjoy my work and my life. But until recently something has been missing. That was true until the night of August twentieth."

His eyes were blue. His hair was gray and fine and blew softly in the slightest movement of air, and his beard was brown and streaked with gray. His mouth was gentle. His voice was gentle. And he was making her feel uncomfortable in the most pleasant way.

"And on the night of August twentieth, Mr. Shepard?"

"Michael."

"Michael then."

"You are truly *une belle dame sans merci*. I met you of course."

"Oh dear. I was so much enjoying this conversation, and now I'm afraid you're going to make it difficult for me."

"Nothing could be farther from my mind, dear lady. Is Mr. Gould here?"

"No. He's at work."

"That's what you said the night of August twentieth as well. What could be so important that he is somewhere else while you are here?"

"He's president of a bank."

"But that's a symptom, not a cause. I ask only what is so important that could keep him away from you?"

She found that she did not mind the impudence of his questions. "There is something that interests him more." He watched her closely. "The Manhattan Banking Corporation."

"I understand," he said, and she knew that he did. "But I know so little about you. Can we see each other again? May I take you to dinner when I'm next in New York?"

"Lunch would be easier," she responded, almost without hesitation.

She could not believe, when she thought about it later, how much pleasure she had derived from the attention that Michael Shepard had paid to her.

Later, when the guests had left and all the dishes were in the washer, and they were sitting on the deck, Samantha asked, "How did you get on with Michael?"

"Very well."

"I thought you might."

"He's very nice, just as you said."

"Mm. Are you going to see him again?"

Maureen started to answer and stopped herself. She and Samantha had been lovers for some months. What should she say?

"My dear Maureen," Samantha said without waiting for her to reply. She took her hand. "I have loved you more than I have ever loved anyone except my children. You have given me great satisfaction—more than I thought myself capable of, and I shall love you forever for it. But I would be foolish indeed to think that this white heat could, or should, last forever, or that either of us would want it to. I know that you are interested in men; at least, I have felt it since you've been on the Vineyard, and I'm not surprised because I am as well. You and I are similar, Maureen, which may have brought us together, along with all the delicious differences. But you are softer and warmer and younger than I, and ought to take the chance of being happy with a man. That would not be enough for me. I have other things I want to do, and I find you distracting me from my purpose. You exhaust me—in the nicest possible way—but it leaves me without the will or the strength to do what I must. I can't be everything to you, but you are dangerously close to being everything to me. But there's still a small gnawing hunger in me, and I must see if I can assuage it."

Maureen understood only part of what Samantha was saying to her, but she understood that if she wanted to take up with Michael Shepard or any other man, it would be with Samantha's understanding and blessing, and not otherwise.

Late the following afternoon, after one last morning visit to the beach, and a last lunch in Vineyard Haven, a last browse through the Bunch of Grapes bookshop, and a last tour to some of the children's favorite places around the island, Samantha drove Maureen and John and Sally to the airport. She was efficient and helpful and affectionate—the children by now called her Aunt Samantha—but there was something different about her. There was still warmth in their relationship, but the quality of it had changed. Samantha's hands were firm on her shoulders when they kissed each other's cheeks in farewell, but Maureen knew that a phase of her life was definitely over.

237

Samantha drove home to the empty house. It was time that she closed up the house and got back to New York. In a week's time she had her first meeting with the working members of the Reorganization Study Committee to review their preliminary recommendations, and two days after that the September board meeting. The shape of the bank in the years to come was already formed in her mind, and was down on paper, and needed only the filling in of details.

The house seemed to echo without Maureen and the kids in it. Samantha poured three fingers of Scotch and threw in one cube of ice and went out onto the deck. She sat in the chair in which she sat habitually next to that used by Maureen when they sat so late so often during the past three and a half weeks. Had it been that long? Except for the weekend that Tony had visited, it had gone by in a flash.

Michael Shepard would be helpful, but she couldn't tell whether ultimately he would satisfy Maureen. From what she knew of him, Samantha thought he might be a bit of an adventurer, a bit unwilling to make commitments. These were things she could not tell Maureen, because they would be meaningless to her. She would have to learn them herself. Oh yes, Michael would probably hurt her unless she was quick enough to perceive his limitations, but he was also a decent sort, and would teach her that men were capable of love as well as women, and that they were not all like the plastic man she was married to.

The sun was nearly out of sight away to the right, the sea was dark, and it had gotten cold, but still Samantha sat on staring sightless into the growing obscurity. The tears began quietly at first, but irresistibly, and soon she was shaken by sobs that came from deep within. She gave them rein, because there was no one to hear but the birds wheeling overhead. She cried for everything that was gone and would never return; but she cried too to purge herself of the detritus of the past.

Tony was not at home when they arrived, nor had Maureen expected him to be. And she was grateful that he wasn't. The children had become by turns querulous and sullen the closer they had gotten to home. She did not want to have to cope with their depression had their father been there.

They all had peanut butter and jelly sandwiches on toast shortly after they came back. John and Sally each had a bath and went to bed after a half hour of television. Maureen spent the rest of the time waiting for Tony, sorting clothing for Mrs. Parks to put through the washer or take to the dry cleaners.

Tony arrived at a quarter to ten, looking gray-faced with exhaustion, and came into the kitchen.

"I thought you were coming back on Friday," he said, sounding almost petulant.

"No, Tony, it was always supposed to be today. Have you eaten?"

"Of course. And now I'm going to bed. I'm beat."

"You're not going until I tell you something."

Something in the tone of her voice arrested him as he was passing through the doorway of the kitchen. He turned to look at her.

"I'm seeing a lawyer tomorrow, Tony. I want a divorce."

He had heard the words but appeared not to be able to sort out the meaning.

"What?"

"I said I want a divorce."

"You can't do that to me. What about my career?"

"I can do it, and I will do it, and the reason has been illustrated by your reaction."

"Who is the man?"

"There is no man. You and you alone are the reason that I want a divorce. I don't love you, I don't even like you. You pay no attention to me or the children—"

"Keep your voice down."

"I'll talk the way I please, Tony, and I won't be deflected by your little irrelevancies. Your only interest is yourself and your progress to the top of Manhattan Banking. That's fine with me. But it's going to have to be a solitary pursuit as far as I'm concerned. I'm not going to be around for you to overlook and take for granted anymore." She paused and waited for him to respond,

239

but all he did was stare out of his gray face. "For God's sake, don't you have anything to say?"

"What do you want me to say?"

She walked past him out of the kitchen and down the hall to her bedroom, listening to see if they had awakened the children. She heard nothing. She walked into her bedroom, quietly closed the door behind her, and locked it.

Tony was still standing in the middle of the kitchen beneath the harsh fluorescent light. He was furious with Maureen for causing him a problem; he had problems enough without her giving him more at home. And divorce was out of the question. It would look very bad to the board. God, what would Samantha Vanderpane think? Or what might Samantha not be thinking already? Maureen had probably been poisoning her against him for weeks; no wonder she had avoided his approaches on the Vineyard. He would have to have a chat with Samantha, and he would have to talk Maureen out of a divorce.

Toward the end of September and the end of the rainy season, government resistance collapsed. Ujimbu fled Maraka through Nigeria, which granted him the minimum courtesies due a former head of state before he was escorted to the airport at Ikeja and put on a plane for Tripoli. An unseemly *sauve qui peut* aspect developed among the General's followers. The way to Maraka City was open to the rebels, who entered it in mid-October in triumph, Ekaba and Nijima riding at the head of the column side by side in a captured jeep.

Violent crime trebled in the capital. There were assaults and rape and armed robberies throughout the day of shops and pedestrians and of automobiles held motionless in heavy traffic. At night there were lootings and gunfights between groups of drunken soldiers. Almost all of the problem was caused by Nijima's troops, of which he had lost control, in addition to his being preoccupied elsewhere. Arthur Ekaba kept his people in check (anyone caught looting was summarily executed) and waited.

James Nijima was too busy negotiating with representatives of the United States and other Western powers to bother much about what was going on in the capital. He was discussing his terms and conditions for mounting a campaign to drive Arthur Ekaba into exile and to establish a pro-Western regime. The representatives of the West were intrigued by Nijima's well-formulated, albeit expensive, plans, and not least by his smooth articulation of the economic problems besetting the industrial democracies and the possible role Maraka could play in alleviating some of them with her vast resources that wanted only capital for development.

During the period that these extended discussions were taking place, a group of soldiers burst into the lobby of the Intercontinental Hotel early one evening, automatic weapons blazing, killing a desk clerk and a correspondent from *France-Soir*, and wounding seventeen others. They charged up the stairs into the bar, while everyone else scattered through the fire exits, but by the time they emerged onto the front steps again, weapons slung and half-full bottles in their arms, they were met by two platoons of Ekaba's most trusted troops. Two or three of the looters were chosen at random and immediately shot. The others threw down their arms and dropped their bottles. They were loaded into trucks, driven out of town, executed, and buried in a mass grave.

Acting on his own, while Nijima's advisers tried to find James Nijima, Ekaba ordered all troops, except certain designated units, into camp, and ordered them to give up their weapons; what had happened to the Intercontinental group was a demonstration of what would happen if they did not comply. Very few held out, and these were either arrested and shot, or else disappeared into the jungle.

Shortly after the troops had given up their weapons, the units Ekaba had held secretly in reserve well outside Maraka City swept in, rearmed the rest of his troops, and took over the capital. By the time Nijima had found out what was happening, his troops were disarmed and Ekaba was master of Maraka.

The negotiators from the Western powers disappeared from the negotiating table and Nijima was left to discuss his requirements with the silence. He had been completely outmaneu-

241

vered. Ekaba called him to the Presidential Palace and offered
him the choice of either internal or external exile, and suggested
he take the latter. The leftist press trumpeted this action
throughout the world as magnanimity from Ekaba to Nijima,
who could henceforth be only the sworn enemy of the new ruler
of Maraka. Privately, many shook their heads at what they
regarded as weakness on Ekaba's part. Indeed, Ekaba had disregarded his own Cuban advisers, who had suggested elimina-
tion. He knew that James Nijima, his late brother-in-arms, was
toothless and without any support whatever.

The thousand-man force of Cuban regulars who had helped
Ekaba for years, and who were the conduit through which Soviet
arms and finance reached him, were publicly thanked profusely
and often by Ekaba for their contribution to the Marakan people's fight for freedom and self-determination.

At the ceremony in the house high on the hill above the city
at which he officially assumed the title of President of the Republic of Maraka, Arthur Ekaba gave a major speech, witnessed
by important journalists from the world press. It was during this
speech that the new President said that the heartfelt thanks and
good wishes of the Marakan people would accompany their
Cuban friends as they flew back to their homes. It was the first
time that the Cuban force had learned that it was going home.
And with the entire world watching, not to mention that they
were seriously outnumbered by Ekaba's troops, the Cubans could
hardly refuse to leave.

The government that Ekaba established was neutral, which
meant that he had decided that playing both ends against the
middle was the best way, at least for the time being, to run
Maraka. The Soviet bloc had supplied the technical wherewithal
for him to take over the country, but its role was now ended.
Weapons and tactical expertise were one thing; for development
of roads, railways, forestry, oil exploration, agriculture, mining,
manufacturing, construction, one turned to the West, and to
Japan and Korea.

Private enterprise was invited to come, or to return to, or to
stay in, Maraka, to help the process of rebuilding after the war

and after years of neglect and looting by the claques of self-centered, rapacious monsters who had nearly ruined the country and broken the heart of the great Marakan people.

Expropriation—nowhere on paper, but only in the mind of Arthur Ekaba—was left to the future.

And because of the great strain placed on the economy and the resources, both material and human, by years of disruption (including Ekaba's own) and by six months of war, the international banks were asked to reschedule over the following seven years all interest and principal coming due on their loans within the next two.

The autumn leaves were gone. The trees were bare and the bark was gray against a gray sky. On a cold morning in early November, just after Election Day, a meeting took place in Max Fougere's office. The subject of the meeting was the request from Maraka for a rescheduling of its debt. For the moment, the rescheduling of principal did not bother senior management as much as the capitalizing of interest, because that meant removing revenue already accrued from the income statement (and still having to pay for the deposits that had been lent), whereas there was no principal due for a couple of years anyway. It had not been a particularly good year for Manhattan Banking. The loan-loss reserve needed a healthy increase, and the bank was scraping around for pennies to report to the shareholders.

In addition to Fougere, Ted Cutler and Chris Webb were at the meeting, and Waldo Carter, head of the Africa Division, George Klein from the New York Economics Department, and Clarence Powell, a brand new assistant treasurer who was the desk officer for Maraka and Cameroon; he said nothing during the entire meeting and looked frightened. A cold drizzle fell steadily onto the balcony outside Fougere's windows.

"I remind you all," Max began, "that the President retains a strong interest in developments concerning Maraka, and will be very interested in our decision here," as if, Webb thought, Fougere's interest was purely academic, as if he had been in a monastery in Tibet when the loans to Maraka were made. Poor

243

Powell looked as if he were going to faint. "It hasn't helped that one of the people most intimately concerned with our exposure in Maraka has left the bank." Everyone knew he was talking about Nick Stewart.

"We understand that a developing country like Maraka should have a current account deficit. But that large? How about the overall payments deficit? And some of the jumbo was supposed to be available for debt service. How has this situation come about?" He looked at Waldo Carter.

Carter was new to the Africa division, having been transferred in haste in July from Latin America, and although he had devoted much of his time since to studying the Marakan situation, he had not fully mastered it yet, just as he had not yet been able to understand Fougere's personnel policies when he was running the Africa division. The cynical might conclude that they weren't policies at all, but Carter thought that it was probably simply that he didn't comprehend the big picture.

He did not understand either why the last loan had been made to Maraka, and thought that, for no doubt good reasons, the manifest gaps and anomalies in the economic data had been consciously disregarded. And whenever he talked with Gould or Fougere he assumed they knew more about Maraka than he did, and so was surprised by Max's question. And stuttered.

"Imports are now ahead of exports, Max. And invisibles, of course."

"What's wrong with the export picture?" Max said, looking toward George Klein, who was lighting a pipe.

"The country has been mismanaged for years," Webb said. "The infrastructure isn't there to carry to market the stuff they need to sell to get the economy back in balance. The prices of some of their commodities have fallen flat on their ass, and the price of energy is killing them. And the country has been looted by its leaders. Of course we have to reschedule. They don't have the money to pay their bills."

"We ought to have known all this before we went into the deal."

If he had not seen it all before, Chris would not have believed his ears. But he knew they were present at the rewriting of history, and he understood the process all too well.

"I said all this a number of times, Max. I even put it into a memo."

"Perhaps you should have said it to John Howe and Nick Stewart," Fougere said steadily. "All I recall is your waffling on about corruption. What do you think, George?"

Klein puffed at his pipe in deep thought. He had achieved some eminence as a bank economist and was often quoted in the business press. As a result, he weighed his words carefully to ensure that he couldn't be misquoted. "I'm of two minds about Maraka," he began. Cutler asked him for a match, which he handed over. "I think Chris could well be right. On the other hand, there's a possibility that he's misread the numbers."

"What position do we adopt for the bank committee meeting?"

"I recommend we agree to reschedule," Carter said, "along the lines that they've proposed. We're pretty certain the banks with significant exposure in Maraka are going along. Which means everybody will have to go along."

"Ben is not going to be pleased. Tony is going to be more than not pleased. He thinks we ought to be hard-nosed. He thinks they're playing chicken."

Once again, Chris thought, Tony Gould was stating gut feelings as facts and then insisting on them as truth.

"On what does he base that feeling?" Cutler asked.

"On the absurdity of their going from a successful syndication to rescheduling in less than six months."

"The numbers show the country is badly off, Max," Carter said. "Worse than we thought."

Only after he had said it did Waldo Carter realize that the economic information he had was no different from the kind of information that the bank had had when the loan was made, and wondered at the greater perspective of his superiors.

"Tony thinks the numbers might be questionable," Fougere said.

"Just like they were before," Webb said, "only different."

"I don't get your meaning," Max said. His eyes were opaque.

"I gather," Fougere went on, sighing, as if he were reluctantly relinquishing a position to which he had, up until now, held steadfastly, "that it's the opinion of the Africa division and the Central Credit Group that we go along with the request for rescheduling."

Cutler and Carter nodded assent.

"George?"

"I don't disagree," Klein said.

"Waldo, you'll represent us on the committee? Right. Thank you, gentlemen," Max said without warmth. They all stood. "Ted, could you wait a moment?"

Twenty minutes later, Cutler walked into Webb's office and sat in the chair next to his desk. Chris had been staring out of his window at the rain. Cutler took out a crumpled package of cigarettes and chose one of the straighter cigarettes and lit it. He looked weary, and his appearance belied the jolly tone of his words.

"You are being offered the chance to make your fame and fortune, my boy."

"That sounds awfully ominous, Ted."

"Tony and Max want you to become our representative in Maraka."

"Horseshit."

"They think you're the man best qualified to stay on top of the situation and to help Waldo with the rescheduling. Think of it as a vote of confidence, young man."

"I think of it as punishment for being right."

"I've gotten the distinct impression that this is something they badly want you to do."

"I don't doubt it, Ted. Does it make any sense to you?"

Cutler stubbed out the half inch of cigarette he had left in the wastebasket next to the chair and brushed the ash from his waistcoat.

"I no longer look for things to make sense, Chris. Things are not decided because they make sense."

"I'll think it over, Ted."

•   •   •

The second Monday in November was the day on which Samantha Vanderpane's committee was to present its report to the board on the reorganization of the bank.

At ten, before the meeting of the full board, the credit committee met to discuss the bank's exposure in Maraka. In a monotone, Waldo Carter gave a clear description of the situation and of the reasons, and of what the bank was going to do in the face of what appeared to be overwhelming acquiescence to the Republic's request for a rescheduling of debt. A lot of multinationals, Waldo added, as the directors shifted uneasily in their chairs, had added their weight to the request. They still saw the pot of gold at the end of the rainbow, Webb thought, although the end of the rainbow was a little farther away than they had estimated.

"Can you tell me, Mr. Carter," Charles Houston said, "how almost the richest country in black Africa could have gotten itself into such a pickle? Surely it didn't happen overnight?"

"No, it didn't, Mr. Houston. It took years to develop. Years of economic mismanagement. And the coup and the civil war just exacerbated the situation."

"But we knew what was going on?"

"I'm sure we did, sir, but we didn't recognize the extent to which it was."

"Some of you did, Mr. Carter. Some of you did. Are we going to have to write off any of this one hundred and twenty-five million dollar exposure?"

"No, Mr. Houston."

"You're quite sure?"

Waldo Carter chose to treat the last as a rhetorical question and simply grinned at Charles Houston.

As they were walking out of the conference room after the meeting, Webb overheard Houston say to Gould, "They don't make bankers like they used to, Tony . . . Carter . . ." at which Chris passed beyond earshot. He watched Gould's face, particularly as he knitted his brow slightly and nodded gravely at what Houston was saying; no doubt agreeing that Carter had blotted his copybook by misunderstanding the situation in Maraka.

When the directors gathered in the board room at eleven o'clock, each found at his place a slim spiral bound report. Attached to the cover was a two-page summary of the contents, the fruit of two months work by the reorganization study committee headed by Samantha Vanderpane. With the help of two members of the committee, Samantha in a clear, clipped yet attractive voice, and occasionally resorting to slides on an overhead projector, described their conclusions. The committee's recommendations went to every area of the bank and to the development of services and of managers. Recognizing the need for productivity and for cost control, they proposed eliminating much of the burgeoning bureaucracy of the bank to lessen the increasing burden of the line people in the banking and trust and money-trading departments, who had to work harder and harder to achieve the same results year after year, supporting an ever-expanding staff that sold nothing for revenue and produced nothing of value.

The presentation was detailed, but concise. The objectives were clear, and obtainable, the methods to achieve the objectives were already within the ken of the bank, and needed only to be organized and directed. There wasn't a single intimation of the need for an outside consultant. It was a staggering performance.

As the lights were turned on at the end of the hour-and-a-half presentation, the board sat in total silence. Then someone—it was probably Ernest Pelletier—said, "Hear, hear," followed by several others; and finally everyone rapped on the table and said, "Hear, hear," and everyone—almost everyone—thought how fine Samantha looked at the head of the board-room table. No one dreamed of sullying the perfection of the presentation with a question.

Then the directors adjourned for lunch and to discuss the reorganization group's recommendations informally. When they returned to the board room, Charles Houston moved that the group's plan be adopted and that the reorganization study committee be reconstituted as the reorganization committee, charged

CHAPTER 15

with working with senior management to bring the recommendations into reality. The motion was carried unanimously.

A conviction was growing among a number of directors, not as
yet expressed, nor as yet universally felt, that the bank might
well be better served if Samantha Vanderpane were tapped to
become Chairman and Chief Executive Officer, particularly in
the period of reorganization that was about to begin. But the
directors who felt this way kept their opinion for the time being
to themselves; not least among the reasons for which was, of
course, what to do about old Ben.

Chris Webb sat in the booth with his back to the wall and one
knee propped on the seat. They were drinking a pitcher of Bud
and waiting for George to bring the hamburgers. Someone that
Chris thought looked like one of his college classmates was playing "Stella by Starlight" on the piano.

"The question is," Webb said, "do I say 'no,' or do I say, 'no, I
quit'?"

"I don't see any reason to say the latter," Catherine answered.
"Blame me. Tell them there's no way on earth that I'll go to
Maraka. Which is true."

"But isn't that begging the question?"

"The trouble with you, Chris, is that you're not comfortable
with ambiguity."

"Bang on, Cath."

"But when are you going to understand that most questions of
importance don't have answers. Part answers maybe. Whole
ones almost never."

"You're so wise, Cath."

"I'll take that as a compliment."

"It was meant that way."

The arrival of the hamburgers shattered the tenseness that had
been growing between them.

"You know, much as I like Teddy's hamburgers, you might
spring for a plate of spaghetti once in a while."

"Count on it when my ship comes in." He poured more beer for both of them.

"Chris, honey," she said, sitting very still, and he thought there were tears in her eyes, "I want you to do whatever it is you think is right. If it's right for you, it will be right for me, for us."

"Even if it means giving up the house in Brookfield?"

"Especially if it means giving up the house in Brookfield."

"What will William of Orange think?"

"He'll go along happily. He loves you too."

When the man on the piano started playing Schubert, Webb became convinced that he was his classmate Charlie Share, whom he had not seen since they'd graduated. He thought briefly of approaching him, but he remembered that Charlie had been a private person even in 1961. The man on the piano was wearing a thin tweed jacket, and his hair was sparse, and he was totally lost in the music. No, I won't—can't—disturb him, Webb thought. Charlie just wants to be left alone like the rest of us.

"Don't worry, sweetheart. I won't do anything precipitate. But I'm going to say no to Maraka and see what the reaction is. Fact is, though, I can't take the flimflam of Manhattan Banking much longer. Life is a constant round of innuendo, accusation, and cover your ass. I could never figure out what that all has to do with the business of banking. So I suspect the problem is me, not the system. 'I didn't raise my boy to be a banker.' But I'll give it another whirl. I'll sell my soul—what's left of it, that is—to some other swell financial institution. But as far as old Manhattan Banking is concerned, I don't like spending my time anymore with people who don't read and who don't think about anything but themselves and whom they should screw next to get ahead. Hollow men."

"Hollow *persons*," Catherine admonished, her eyes shining.

Webb laughed.

On the Monday after Thanksgiving, Ben Kincaid, following a period of soul searching and some fruitful discussions with friends in Houston, solved the directors' problem by resigning from the bank, effective December 31. At the December board meeting, Samantha Vanderpane was elected Chairman and Chief Executive Officer. The *Wall Street Journal* called it a board-room coup; which in a way it was. The reasons that the directors decided the way they had were various: because she was obviously capable, and because under her leadership a brilliant scheme of reorganization for the bank had been devised; because she was called Vanderpane; because she was class, which Ben Kincaid was not; and because she was one of the family, which Kincaid was most certainly not; because, at fifty-four, she was palpably sexual, which many of their wives of the same age were not; because she would be the first woman chairman and CEO of a money center bank, and that set Manhattan Banking apart; because some were less frightened of what Samantha might do than of what Tony Gould, who was the only other logical choice, would do.

On a bitterly cold day in January, Chris Webb was asked to come up to the Chairman's office. He had only exchanged words of greeting before with Samantha Vanderpane, and that only rarely. He hardly remembered what she looked like.

When he was shown into her office, he was greeted by a tall, very attractive woman with a warm, firm handshake.

"Sit down, Chris. Coffee?"

"No, thanks, Mrs. Vanderpane."

"Please call me Samantha."

Webb nodded.

"I wanted to tell you how sorry I was to learn that you are leaving. We can't afford to lose people like you."

"Thank you," Webb said. He was put off-balance by how straightforward she was being. It was not a normal encounter at Manhattan Banking.

"Do you feel you can tell me why you're leaving?"

"An opportunity came up with a smaller bank that sounded interesting."

"More interesting than Manhattan Banking?"

"Perhaps more committed to the fundamentals. Less concerned with razzle-dazzle, high-visibility, high-risk deals. High-button shoe kind of banking. Sound, sensible returns for sound, sensible risks. I think I've become too conservative for Manhattan Banking. And the opportunity to go to Maraka wasn't really on the top of my list."

"Speaking of which, you know the rescheduling agreement was signed in London last week?"

"Yes I did. I don't know what choice the banks had."

"You opposed the last Maraka loan, didn't you?"

"Yes."

"And did anyone listen to you?"

In spite of the fact that he was leaving the bank, Webb remained so sensitive that he wondered what Samantha's game was. He was also alternately attracted by her sensuality and repelled by her power.

"Not anyone who mattered," he said finally.

Samantha nodded. "Well, Chris, I wish you the best of luck. If you change your mind after you've tried the other bank, let me know."

When he thought about their conversation later, Webb felt that he had found in Samantha Vanderpane someone in senior management who would have seen easily through Tony Gould's confidence game, who would have heard the objections that Chris and others like Henry Perkins in London were raising to the Marakan jumbo, and that the loan would probably not have been made, at least by Manhattan Banking. He wondered how long she and Tony would be able to work together; and he wondered how long it would be before she changed, before she grew weary of the internecine strife, the backstabbing and incompetence and petty-mindedness, and saw the advantage of the quick profit over the longer-term considerations.

No matter. Webb's fourteen years at Manhattan Banking were coming to an end. Their paths had diverged, and he knew he would not return. And just as she had wished for him, he wished her well.

Since Maureen and the children had moved out of their apartment in October, Tony Gould had taken to going home later and later, and some nights he didn't go home at all, but stayed in the bank apartment in a residential hotel on Lexington Avenue. He hardly ever used the car to which he was entitled as president, because it got him home to the empty, echoing rooms too quickly. The apartment was on the market, but there had been little interest shown in it, and he had to consider lowering his asking price, which he was not interested in doing.

One night in mid-January, he left the bank at ten o'clock and decided to walk home slowly up Madison Avenue with the lighted shop windows as his companions.

Tony was depressed. Life had gone stale and flat. His career was at a standstill. The bank's services had deteriorated and consequently customer complaints were growing geometrically. Turnover at all levels had increased, particularly among experienced managers, and people he had put in charge had betrayed him by not working out. Furthermore, he felt increasingly isolated from the people with whom he had grown up in the bank. In normal circumstances—had Ben still been chairman—Gould would have made a move to recapture some of the responsibility for the banking division. But Samantha Vanderpane had proved intractable. She had the full support of the board and had proved to be, even he had to admit, remarkably astute politically. Her primary interest was in commercial banking, and he found himself, no matter what he did, heading off in directions he had not chosen.

And he knew, had come to realize and finally admit, although only to himself and to no one else, that he was never going to get the top job at Manhattan Banking.

When he paused at a corner for a traffic light, he suddenly realized he had walked too far north. He turned west on Ninety-fifth Street. Partway along the block toward Fifth Avenue, Tony thought he saw movement in a dark doorway. The movement materialized into a human being, a skinny figure in a field jacket and a baseball cap with the visor turned around toward the rear, who stepped in front of him.

"Gimme your coat, motherfucker." He was just a kid, with a high, squeaky voice.

Tony looked at the hunting knife in his hand.

"You say one fuckin' thing, motherfucker, and I cut you bad."

Tony took off his coat.

"Drop it."

Gould let it fall to the ground.

"Wallet."

Tony handed it over.

"You go ahead, cocksucker, and don't you look back or I cut off your balls and shove 'em up your nose."

Tony did as he was told, the adrenaline pumping hard and keeping him warm despite the loss of his coat. When he reached the corner of Fifth Avenue, he looked around, but the kid was gone. He looked up Fifth to see if he could see a cab; but he saw a patrol car instead.

He waved to the police and the car drew up to the curb. The patrolman on the passenger side got out. The driver stared at him without expression through the side window.

"Problem, mister?" He looked, Tony thought, ten years old, despite the moustache and the hair over his ears.

"I've just been robbed."

"When and where?"

"Just now. On Ninety-fifth Street. Right down there."

The policeman got out a notebook and a pencil with what Tony thought was agonizing slowness.

"Aren't you going to try to catch the guy?"

"Sure. But he ain't walking along the street exactly shouting 'I just robbed a guy on Ninety-fifth Street.' He's halfway to the moon by now. I need some particulars. Name, please."

"I'm the president of the Manhattan Banking Corporation," Tony said.

"Congratulations. But I mean, can you tell me your name?"

For a moment Tony stared at him wildly as if the cop had just asked him to solve a complex mathematical problem in his head.

"But my wallet is gone," Gould said, and started to shiver.

"Let me have your name anyway. I'll take your word for it," the policeman said.

The bank had been like a man dying of thirst to whom they had managed at last to bring water; and the reorganization had begun to take hold. But Samantha had been astounded at the condition of Manhattan Banking—the lack of information systems, the lack of leadership, the managerial incompetence, the incoherence of personnel policies, where there were any, the guerrilla warfare that went on among department heads and within departments. It was incumbent upon her and the team she was assembling to clean up the mess that had been left, by Miles, God rest his soul, and by the likes of Tony Gould.

Tony was a major problem that she would have to address shortly. His single greatest qualification for the job he held, it seemed to her, was his ambition, his drive for power, and now that that had been thwarted by herself, he seemed to be falling apart. The divisions of which he was in charge were not functioning well under his stewardship and the senior managers he had chosen were remarkably inept. She also could not understand how anyone who spent such long hours at his desk accomplished so little, and that so badly.

Tony would have to go; but she didn't worry for him. Gould was like one of those toys with weighted bottoms—no matter how far over one knocked them, they always bounced upright again.

She thought of Maureen. She had had a short fling with Michael Shepard—predictably short, she supposed. Maureen was *au fond* a nest builder, and she wouldn't—couldn't—spend much time with a man who was not similarly inclined. She had come to the apartment once, and they had made love, but she talked afterward only about her relationship with Michael.

"He was so nice, Samantha; but we really didn't have much in common."

"Yes," was all Samantha could say. And although she had been beside her then, in bed, and they had just had a physical encounter, she knew that Maureen was lost to her forever.

Now Maureen had found someone else, a museum curator, a good man it seemed, a man the children were mad about, and she seemed happy.

I have some good years ahead, Samantha thought, some full ones, and all in all they will probably be satisfying ones. But perhaps that hunger will never be satisfied. God knows Miles never could satisfy it, nor any of the others, and Manhattan Banking has its limitations as a lover. Maureen Gould had been the closest.

She thought, maybe Charlie Houston isn't so bad after all. One thing is certain: he'll have to resign from the board if he wants to sleep with the chairman.

Envoi

On fine mornings, Derek Houndswell walked from Charing Cross to his office in Knightsbridge along the Mall by St. James's Park and up Constitution Hill.

On a morning in mid-April a year later, he followed his usual route, feeling very good and especially satisfied with himself, the feeling of a man with a comfortable house, good health, a decent job, and a fat Swiss bank account. The trees were light, feathery green and the air was soft, just a touch of warmth in the sunlight. He thought that London must be the only livable city left in the world.

"Lovely day," said a man who was walking next to him on the right.

"I should say," said a man who appeared suddenly at his left.

Houndswell's heart started pumping rapidly. Why should they want to kidnap a minor executive of a medium-size aluminium company?

"Don't you think it's a lovely day, Mr. Houndswell?"

"What the hell is this?"

A hand touched his left arm. "Shall we go into the park?"

Houndswell stopped. "I demand to know what this is about."

"We'd like to have a chat, Mr. Houndswell, on behalf of Her Majesty."

A different anxiety, from another level of Derek Houndswell's psyche, began to emerge.

"Shall we go into the park, Mr. Houndswell? Perhaps watch the ducks?"

He followed, dumbly. Thoughts of the comfortable house and the decent job and the fat bank account were fading.

They were walking along the lake. "May I see your identification?" Houndswell asked.

"Of course," they replied in unison, and showed it to him.

"We've received a request from the Republic of Maraka," said the man on his right, "for your extradition."

"Whatever for?" Unconvincingly.

"They say, 'for crimes against the Marakan people.'"

"Preposterous."

"Precisely what we should like to discuss, old man."

"I shall want my solicitor."

"Oh, indeed, Mr. Houndswell," said the man on his left. "But perhaps you wish to discuss your former relationship with the Ministry of State Security with us first, before you start asserting your rights."

"Ridiculous allegation."

"Our information has it otherwise, Mr. Houndswell."

"What is the source of your information?"

The man on his right smiled.

"Chap called Mackintosh," said the man on his left.

"Mackintosh? The little bank manager?"

"Just so."

"And you believe him?"

"Absolutely, Mr. Houndswell. Only his name is not Mackintosh. That was only his cover, you see."

Banking Terms

Euromarket: Short for Eurocurrency market, which is any financial market for a currency outside its country of origin. While Eurocurrencies (such as Eurodollars, Eurosterling, Euromarks, etc.) are bid for and offered in many money centers (e.g., Paris, Zurich, Singapore, Hong Kong, New York), the most important place for this activity is London.

Grace period: The period of time during which contractually no principal is repaid. Only interest is paid during this period.

Lead manager(s): The banks to whom the borrower is closest, who put the conditions of borrowing together, underwrite the loan, and share the loan with participants. The lead managers get the largest fees because they do the greatest amount of work and take the largest risk.

Loan syndication: A loan made by a group of banks to a single

259

borrower. The group is required because the amount of the loan is too large for any one bank to lend on its own, either for policy reasons or because of capital constraints. General syndication means offering up participations in the loan to other banks after the managers have underwritten it.

London interbank offered rate (known also as LIBOR): The rate offered for Eurocurrency deposits in London by first class banks to depositors, usually other first class banks or large corporations. LIBOR is assumed to be the cost of money to the institution that is quoting for the deposit; to this base rate is added a "spread" or "margin" (in effect a markup), the total of which a borrower must pay for a loan. The margin ostensibly represents the profit on the transaction to the lenders. In reality, the profit is almost always greater, because banks borrow the money they lend for a variety of maturities and hence a variety of rates, the average of which is the true cost of funding. This cost is normally lower than the six-month LIBOR that is often used as a reference base rate for loans.

Offering memo: This is the memorandum that is sent to banks interested in participating in a syndicated loan. It is usually composed of a term sheet, listing all the conditions (amount, tenor, repayment schedule) and rates and fees, and information, in greater or lesser detail, about the borrower. An offer is usually made by the lead banks by telex to potential participants, and the information memorandum is sent separately to those expressing interest. There is always an exculpatory paragraph in the information memo.

Opportunity cost: Any cost imputed to funds being used in one instance (a loan, say) while they might be more profitably, and perhaps more safely, employed elsewhere. There is thus an opportunity cost to a rescheduled loan.

Participation fee: A fee received for participating in the loan. The fee is based on the amount of the participation. Higher participations are quite often remunerated at higher percentages.

Selldown, final take: A selldown is the amount of the syndicated loan a lead manager wishes to participate (sell) to other banks. The final take is what the bank keeps on its own books (e.g., underwriting $50 million, selldown $15 million, final take $35 million).

Skim: What the lead manager or managers of a syndicated loan take off the top of the underwriting and management fees before sharing them with the other participants in the loan. The skim is an accepted method of compensating the major lenders in a syndicated credit.

Tenor: The amount of time a loan will be outstanding, in whole or in part, until its contractual maturity.

Underwrite: To commit to provide the funds in the first instance. If a bank underwrites $50 million, that means the borrower is certain he will receive the $50 million.

Underwriting fee; management fee: Fees received for underwriting and managing the syndication. Quite often they are synonymous; sometimes they are not. The fees are calculated on the total amount of the loan.